INTRODUCTION

With This Ring by Joyce Livi...
Sacramento, California, 1850-... ...om
the small town of Nicolaus, Ca... ...d, he meets
Aggie Wells, daughter of the to... ...hough he is penniless
by the world's standards, he is rich in faith, but Aggie, who may
have all she needs and wants, lacks the most important thing—
salvation. When her world is turned upside down, where will she
place her hope? Will Jeb return home without gold before she finds
her answers?

Band of Angel's by Cathy Marie Hake
Colorado, 1893—The first time Jarrod McLeod dips his pan in the
river, he strikes gold—a wedding ring! Sure the woman who lost
it must be beside herself, he goes upriver to return it. He meets
laundress Angel Taylor. She did lose the ring; however, she refuses
to take the ring back. Jarrod's first impressions of Angel are scan-
dalous, but he soon discovers the truth, bringing her a Christmas
gift to span the perimeters of time.

A Token of Promise by Rebecca Germany
Dyea, Alaska, 1897—Promised in marriage to a man she has never
met in exchange for a place to call home, Charlotte Vance is headed
to the Klondike and struggling not to fall in love with the wrong
man. Gabe Monroe has found a bride perfect for his widowed
brother. A wife will help his brother run his supply business and
raise his daughter, and Gabe will be freed to seek riches in the
Yukon rivers after the spring thaw. But what will become of
Charlotte when both brothers refuse to marry her—even though
one loves her?

Love's Far Country by Colleen Coble
Dyea, Alaska, 1898—Philip Monroe leases the *Dawson Belle*,
bringing supplies upriver to Dyea for gold miners. When her father
dies, Alexandria Peters travels from Michigan to the Yukon to claim
her father's portion of the *Dawson Belle*. She is determined to make
money and immediately clashes with Philip. Both are independent,
but Philip has a daughter Alexandria bonds with. When fire rushes
through Dyea on a frigid winter day, will it steal another woman
from Philip's life and leave him eternally distrustful of God?

Gold Rush Christmas

*Gold Fever Runs Through
Four Romantic Novellas*

Colleen Coble
Rebecca Germany
Cathy Marie Hake
Joyce Livingston

BARBOUR
PUBLISHING

With This Ring © 2003 by Joyce Livingston
Band of Angel's © 2003 by Cathy Marie Hake
A Token of Promise © 2003 by Rebecca Germany
Love's Far Country © 2003 by Colleen Coble

ISBN 1-58660-777-4

Cover image © Corbis

Published by Barbour Publishing, Inc., P.O. Box 719, Uhrichsville, Ohio 44683, www.barbourbooks.com

Our mission is to publish and distribute inspirational products offering exceptional value and biblical encouragement to the masses.

Member of the
Evangelical Christian
Publishers Association

Printed in the United States of America.
5 4 3 2

Gold Rush Christmas

With This Ring

by Joyce Livingston

Chapter 1

Outside Sacramento, California—1850

"Ouch!" Jeb sat down, tugged off his well-worn boot, and wiggled his toes. Everything, from his sunburnt face to his weary, blistered feet, hurt. He'd only come from Nicolaus and couldn't even begin to imagine how whole families had made it to California from as far away as St. Joseph.

He adjusted his sock, twisting it to make sure the hole was to the side of his foot where a toe wouldn't slip through as he walked, and pulled his boot back on. Although the sun was shining brightly, a few clouds were beginning to gather. Jeb knew he'd best be finding a place to spend the night. After taking a sip of water from his canteen, he gathered up his few belongings and lit off down the road.

He'd finally reached Sacramento. But the joy and excitement he'd expected to experience once he'd made it to the area weren't there. All he felt was loneliness and fear. What if he didn't find gold? How would he exist? He was strong and didn't mind hard labor—surely, he'd be able to find work. *God, Thou hast brought me here safely. I know Thou wilt provide my needs.*

"Hey, you!"

Jeb looked around. He hadn't noticed anyone near him.

"Over here."

He stuffed his hat onto his head and turned toward the voice. Seated on the ground beside a scruffy-looking old mule sat a man who looked to be about the age of Jeb's grandfather. He hurried over to the man with concern. "Are you sick?"

"No, I'm not sick! I'm resting." The man let out a slight chuckle as he separated the long, wispy hairs of his mustache from his disheveled beard. "My bones are old, and sometimes I need to sit for a spell, but I am thirsty. Ya got any water?"

Jeb couldn't help but laugh to himself. It was hard to tell where the man's mass of long gray hair and his tangled beard separated. Maybe they didn't! Other than two piercing dark eyes, a long bony nose, and a nearly covered mouth, the man's face was nothing but hair. Without hesitation, Jeb held out his canteen with its last few precious drops of water, then stood back and watched while the man drank. "You're sure you're all right?"

"Course, I'm sure." The stranger handed the canteen back to him, then with great effort, pulled himself to his feet, leaning on a makeshift cane and wiping his mouth on his tattered sleeve. "Thanks, Boy. Where ya headed?"

Jeb tugged his hat off and scratched his head. Where was he headed? "Don't rightly know."

The man gave a snort, bent, and spat upon the ground. "Lookin' to find gold?"

Jeb nodded. "Yes, Sir. I reckon I am."

The little man turned from right to left, then looked over his shoulder before leaning close to Jeb and cupping a weathered hand about his mouth. "I know where it is."

Jeb's eyes widened with sudden interest. "You do?"

"Yep," he answered, checking the area once more. He crooked his finger and Jeb moved closer. "But I need help gettin' it. My body is givin' out, and I don't see so good. You interested?"

Jeb nodded. "Maybe."

"Name's Blackie." The man stuck out a gnarled hand, then motioned proudly toward his mule. "This here's Hortense."

"I'm Jeb. Jeb Monroe." Jeb smiled and shook Blackie's hand vigorously, surprised at the man's strength when he'd looked so feeble. "Nice to meet both you and Hortense."

"You know the Lord, Jeb?"

He smiled. "Sure do. How about you?"

" 'My help cometh from the Lord, which made heaven and earth.' "

Blackie reached into a worn leather bag tied across his mule's back and pulled out a big, black Bible. Its cover was nearly torn off. "This here book has it all, Son. God's Word." He hugged it to his bosom as he lifted his eyes toward the sky. " 'Let every thing that hath breath praise the Lord. Praise ye the Lord.' "

Jeb allowed a grin to spread across his face. "Yes, praise God." *The first person I've met and he's a fellow believer!* He laid a hand on the old man's shoulder. "Sir, if you meant what you said about helping you, I'd be proud to do it."

Blackie smiled up into his face, his tired eyes now shining.

11

"You're a godsend, Son. I've been praying for someone with a strong back and a good heart. Praise God. You're the answer to my prayer."

"I–I don't know much about huntin' for gold."

"Don't matter, but all I can offer you is a place to sleep, a few vittles for your stomach, and hard, back-breaking days that may yield nothin' but pain."

Jeb pulled up his six-foot frame and extended a hand to his new friend. "That's more than I had before I met you, Blackie. Now where do we go, and how do we get started?"

Aggie stood outside the livery stable, waiting for her brother. He was talking to a couple other fellows his age, men she'd never seen before. But that wasn't unusual. In just a few months, Sacramento had more than doubled in size. It seemed everyone was rushing to California to seek gold.

She twisted the bodice on her dress, then smoothed her hair. She'd go on home without him, but her father had cautioned her that very day that some of the men coming into their area had their minds on things other than gold, and he didn't want her to be one of those things. She'd laughed and told him not to worry. She could take care of herself. But now, seeing these strange men talking to her brother and the way they looked at her, her father's words didn't seem quite so foolish. She had to admit, however, she was more than a little disenchanted with the boys with whom she'd grown up. They were so immature, so. . .so. . . She tried to think of a good word to describe them, but gave up. All she knew was that there wasn't one of them in the whole lot she was attracted to, and certainly none of them were husband material.

Especially not Wilford Stokes, the man her father had picked out for her. She was sure her sweet mother, if she'd lived, would never have approved of a man like Wilford Stokes for her. He was far too old and too stuffy. She'd die of boredom before their first anniversary!

She turned at a sudden noise behind her as two men approached leading an old mule. The older man she recognized immediately. It was Blackie, the Bible-spouting character who wandered around town yelling out Scriptures to anyone who would listen. She would have turned away, eager to avoid him, but the second man kept her eyes fixed on the pair. His clothing was nearly as worn as Blackie's, but his body was lean and lank, and he was the most handsome man she had ever seen. Just looking at his clear blue eyes made her heart sing.

" 'For the Lord seeth not as man seeth; for man looketh on the outward appearance, but the Lord looketh on the heart,' " Blackie called out loudly as the pair moved toward her.

She lifted her head haughtily but, not wanting his companion to think she was snooty, quickly donned a smile.

"Stay here with Hortense, Boy." Blackie handed the rope to the young man and headed toward the livery stable. "I won't be long."

Who is he? And why is he with that dreadful old man? Aggie smiled at him and was pleased when he smiled back. She sauntered across the few steps separating them, her head tipped coyly to one side. "Are you new around here?"

The young man quickly pulled his hat from his head and began moving the brim in a circle in his hands. "Yes, Ma'am. Just arrived today."

The sight of his chiseled good looks made her gasp. "Wh–what," she asked, pointing toward the stable, "are you doing with that crazy old man?"

Jeb frowned. "Beggin' your pardon, Ma'am, but he's more sane than I'll ever be."

She sashayed up to him. "All my friends call me Aggie. What's your name?"

The man appeared tongue-tied. "Uh. . .uh. . .Jeb. Jeb Mo–Monroe."

"Well, Jeb Monroe," Aggie said, making her voice sound as sweet as possible, "welcome to Sacramento."

"Thank you, Ma'am—Miss Aggie."

She smiled at his shyness as he avoided her eyes by lowering his gaze to the ground. "Where are you staying, Jeb?"

"With Blackie. He has a shack up near Farnes River. I aim to help him with his claim."

Oh, no! He can't be staying with that old man! "Isn't that a bit uncomfortable?" she asked, wanting to learn more about this handsome stranger. "I mean, I've heard others talk about the horrible living conditions in some of those mining camps."

Jeb backed away a step and laid a hand on Hortense's back. "I–I don't know. I haven't been there yet."

Her jaw dropped. "You haven't been there yet?"

"No, Miss Aggie. I just met Blackie. God led me to him."

Not another Bible preacher! Although she felt repelled by

his words, she couldn't keep her eyes off his face. There was something appealing about him. An honesty that was uplifting. No pretense. No big stories to impress her. Just a forthrightness that pleased her and challenged her to get to know him better.

She circled him slowly, her eyelashes fluttering shamefully. "How long are you planning to stay in the Sacramento area, Jeb Monroe?"

He stood still, eyeing her every move. "Not sure, Miss Aggie. Until I get enough gold to take home to my mama and my daddy, I reckon. Enough to make a better life for our family."

"And you? What about you?" She smiled coyly. "I mean, how much gold do you want for yourself?"

He gave her a puzzled look. "Don't necessarily want no gold for myself, but I would like to buy me a small piece of land someday, where I can plant me some good crops."

"You're an unusual man, Jeb Monroe. Most men are seeking a fortune for their own good. They want to be rich beyond their wildest dreams. Powerful."

He stared at her, as if thinking over what she'd said. "I don't reckon that type of man would be happy even if he were rich. Happiness doesn't lie in wealth or power. It comes from deep inside. It can't be bought or mined for."

She reared back and laughed. "I'll remind my father to tell that to those miners when they bring their gold to his bank!"

He dug the toe of his boot into the dust surrounding the stable. "Are you making fun of me, Miss Aggie?"

She lightly touched his wrist. "No! I'm only saying most men are not like you. It's refreshing to meet a man whose only interest in life isn't himself."

Jeb didn't answer, just continued to make little circles in the dust with his boot.

"My birthday is next week."

He forsook his drawing in the dust and lifted his eyes to meet hers. "Your birthday? Congratulations."

With a few blinks of her long lashes, she smiled up at him. "I want you to come to my party! I want you to meet my friends."

Jeb shook his head briskly and tried to pull away. "Oh, no, Ma'am. I couldn't!"

Aggie let her lower lip droop. "Why? I want you there."

"I–I have to help Blackie."

No one told Aggie Wells no. She was used to having her way. She stomped her foot playfully. "If you don't come, I'll cry!"

He patted Hortense's back, and she knew he was only doing it to avoid looking at her.

"I don't want you to cry, Ma'am—"

"Aggie. Call me Aggie, and not Miss Aggie either."

"Aggie," he began again. "I appreciate your invitation, but I can't come. You don't understand. Blackie's body is weak and his eyesight is failing him. I need to be there to help him, and—"

"He's gotten along without you so far," she pointed out, her lower lip still pouting. "It'd just be for one day. Surely he could make it on his own for that long."

"Even if he could, I still couldn't come."

She took on the saddest look she could muster, still determined to have her way. "I really want you there, Jeb."

"I–I. . ."

She watched as he fumbled for words, wondering if he simply didn't want to be around her, or if his excuses were honest.

"I–I don't have no fancy clothes to wear to a party, and I wouldn't want to embarrass you," he finally blurted out.

"That's no problem." She lifted her skirts slightly and moved as close to him as she dared. "I have a cousin who is just about your size. I'll borrow some from him."

"I–I can't buy you a gift, and I wouldn't fit in with your friends. I'm just a poor, uneducated boy from Nicolaus."

His honesty twanged at a string on her heart.

"Let's git goin', Boy," Blackie said, taking hold of Hortense's rope. "We got a mighty long way to go before dark."

Jeb backed away from Aggie, nearly tripping over his feet.

"You will come, won't you, Jeb?" she asked, lowering her lip again, still hoping he'd come despite his refusals. "My birthday won't be the same without you."

"Boy, are you ready or not?" Blackie asked impatiently as he began to lead Hortense away.

"Please, Jeb?" Aggie leaned toward him, her hand extended, palm upward. "For me?"

"Well, all right," he said, backing away, then hurrying after Blackie. "I'll try to make it."

"I'll get my cousin to ask the livery stable man where Blackie's shack is. He'll bring the clothing to you," she called after him as he disappeared behind the stable.

"Who was that?" her brother asked as he finally joined her.

"Someone very special" was all Aggie would say as they turned and headed for home.

Her father was waiting for them in the parlor and pulled out his pocket watch when they came in. "Where have you two been?"

"Nowhere," Richard said, with a glance toward his sister. "Just talking to friends."

Martin Wells frowned at his only son. "I was expecting you at the bank. Don't you think it's about time you settled down and started showing some responsibility?"

Richard glared at his father. "I hate working at that bank."

"You're my only son, Richard. Who'll take my place when I'm gone? If your sister ever comes to her senses and marries Wilford Stokes, she'll be taken care of in style. It's you I'm worried about." He turned to his daughter with a smile. "And how did you spend your day, Aggie? Was it fruitful?"

Aggie could hardly contain herself as her enthusiasm bubbled over and she clapped her hands with glee. "Oh, yes, Father. Very fruitful! More fruitful than I'd ever imagined it could be!"

He cupped a hand to her cheek and smiled into her eyes. "Oh? And what did you do to make you this happy?"

Aggie let her eyelashes flutter as she gazed into her beloved father's face. "I met the man I'm going to marry!"

Aggie's father gagged and sputtered at her words. "You what?"

Richard grabbed onto her arm, spinning her toward him. "Not that old miner's friend I saw at the stable, I hope!"

"What old miner?" her father asked, grabbing her shoulder and spinning her back to face him before looking her eye to eye. "Tell me, Girl. What man? Is it someone I know?"

Aggie continued to smile despite their negative reaction to her words, her joy as high as ever. "No, Father, you don't know him. But you will. He's coming to my birthday party next week."

"I hope he has a change of clothing," her brother said sarcastically, holding his nose. "I'll bet the guy smelled. He didn't look like he'd bathed for a month."

Aggie pointed a warning finger at him. "You hush up, Richard. At least the man is willing to work. That's more than I can say for you!"

"Here, here, you two." Her father stepped between them, holding up his hands. "I won't have my children arguing." He turned to Richard. "You. Go wash up for supper."

Richard walked away, mumbling something about not being appreciated as his father turned to Aggie and motioned her toward the sofa. "Now, tell me about this man you've met."

Aggie was all smiles as she sat down beside him. "Oh, Father, he's nothing like the boys here in Sacramento. He's kind and considerate, and he's a real worker. He's—"

Her father frowned. "You just met this man today and you know that much about him? Who is he, Aggie, and where did he come from?"

"He just arrived in town today from Nicolaus. And he's going to live and work with that old miner we see around town."

"Blackie? That lunatic who waves that big Bible in everyone's face? What kind of a man would want to subject himself to that kind of punishment? Can you imagine living with that demented old man?"

"He's doing it because Blackie needs him," she said proudly, remembering Jeb's explanation. "He said that old miner's body is giving out on him and he's nearly blind. Jeb is going to help him. He's the most unselfish man I've ever met."

His father huffed. "I've heard many a tale about that old man. Most folks think he's hit a rich vein and he's not telling so everyone will leave him alone. That boy is probably going to get old Blackie to trust him, take his gold, and leave him to die."

Aggie gasped and, standing quickly, planted a hand on her hip as she glared at her father. "How can you say such dreadful things about Jeb? You don't even know him!"

He stood beside her and placed his hands on her shoulders. "And you do? You told me yourself you just met the man today. How can you be so sure I'm not right?"

Aggie lifted her chin and held her ground. "Because. . . because he's a Christian! He wouldn't do anything like that."

Her father reared back and let out a belly laugh. "A Christian, eh? Like that deranged old man? Perhaps they deserve each other. Perhaps they're both daffy."

Aggie felt the fire in her eyes as her anger boiled over. "I'm going to marry him, Father. You just wait and see!" She spun around, picked up her skirts, and fled toward her room.

"You'll soon get tired of him. You always do."

Aggie slammed the door and threw herself across the bed.

It was dark by the time Blackie and Jeb reached Blackie's shack, but even in the darkness Jeb could see it wasn't much more than a lean-to, barely enough to keep them dry on a wet day. But at least it was a place to call home. That's more than he'd had when he'd entered town that morning. And even better, he had a new friend and a place to work.

"Welcome to Utopia, Boy. I ain't got much, but what I got is yours." Blackie lit the lamp and sat down on a broken chair.

"Utopia, Sir?" Jeb quickly knelt beside him and pulled the boots from the old man's feet.

"Yep, that's what I call my claim. Utopia. Didn't ya ever hear of Sir Thomas More's book *Utopia?* He described Utopia as an imaginary island. This is my imaginary island, Son. My imagination can take me anywhere I want to go." Blackie's hand went to the small of his back, and he arched it with a groan. "Too much walking in one day." He motioned Jeb toward a pile of blankets in a box in the corner of the room where the roof sloped low. "Sorry I ain't got no fancy bed for ya," he said, motioning to the floor. "If'n you spread out a couple of those, it ain't so bad."

Jeb grinned. "It'll be fine, but what about you? Surely you haven't been sleeping on the ground. Where's your bed?" In the flickering light of the lamp, Jeb could see the makings of a smile under the heavy mustache.

"Ain't got no bed. Sleep on the floor like you, and when it ain't too cold, I sleep out under the stars. Amazing how comfortable it is lookin' up at God's handiwork before you go to sleep. 'And [God] said, Look now toward heaven, and tell the stars, if thou be able to number them!' "

Jeb smiled. " 'The heavens declare the glory of God; and the firmament sheweth his handywork,' " he quoted in response.

"You do know your Scripture, don't you, Boy?" Blackie nodded. "God sent you to me, Jeb."

"I know that, Sir."

Blackie rested his head against the wobbly chair back. "Been a long time since someone called me Sir."

"My parents taught me to respect my elders, Sir."

The old man leaned forward and rested his hand on Jeb's arm. "Call me Blackie."

Jeb nodded. "Whatever you say, Sir."

"Hungry?"

Again, Jeb nodded. He'd only had a hunk of bread all day.

From somewhere in the darkness, Blackie pulled out two biscuits, handing one to Jeb, then filled two tin mugs with water from a bucket on the floor. "Here you go."

Jeb took a drink of the water, then stared at the biscuit. He'd hoped for more. His stomach was so hungry, it was paining him, but he thanked the man, then bowed his head and thanked the Lord.

❧

Jeb opened one eye, surprised that morning had come so quickly. He bounced to his feet and surveyed his surroundings. In the dim light of the lantern when he'd arrived, Blackie's place had looked like nothing more than a heap of broken boards, tree branches, and discarded bits of broken furniture. But in the early morning light, with the bright rays of sun wiggling their way through cracks big enough to thrust an arm, the place looked even worse. This was Blackie's home?

" 'My voice shalt thou hear in the morning, O Lord; in the morning will I direct my prayer unto thee, and will look up.' "

Jeb moved to the doorway. Outside, Blackie stood, his arms

stretched toward the sky; and what little of his face showed was shining and bright, as if he'd just scoured it with a bar of soap.

" 'I will sing of thy power; yea, I will sing aloud of thy mercy in the morning: for thou hast been my defense and refuge in the day of my trouble,' " Jeb quoted, then he grinned at Blackie. "Beautiful day, isn't it?"

Blackie nodded, moved inside, placed a small pan on the table, and lifted the lid from a rusty can inside an old cupboard that looked as if it was about to tumble from the wall. "Have a biscuit. It's a might hard. I cooked it a few days ago." He pulled two more tin mugs from a shelf and blew into them, forcing a small cloud of dust to escape, before pouring a cup of coffee for each of them from the pan. "Tain't much, but we'll cook us some fresh biscuits for supper tonight."

Aggie's eyes popped open at the crack of dawn, her thoughts filled with Jeb's image. How strange. She'd thought of him before going to sleep, dreamed about him, and now she was thinking about him again. She smiled as she stretched first one arm and then the other, remembering the look on her father's face when she told him she'd met the man she was going to marry.

Jeb Monroe. What a nice name. A giggle escaped her lips as she pulled herself to a standing position and stared into the little mirror on her dressing table. *Mrs. Jeb Monroe. Aggie Monroe. Agatha Monroe.*

She turned to the lovely china doll on a shelf above the bed and tipped her head coyly. "Annabelle," she said in a falsetto voice that brought on another giggle, "I'd like you to meet my husband, Jeb Monroe." She raised her brows dramatically, turning slightly, as if Jeb were standing beside her. "Jeb, this is my dearest friend, Annabelle. I've told her all about you. How we met and how you came to my birthday party." She tilted her head shyly, her gaze still trained on the imaginary Jeb. "We love each other very much, and someday we're going to have children, aren't we, Dearest?" Her heart gave a flutter as she uttered the words. She'd never before thought of having children. Yet here she was talking about them to Annabelle.

"Oh, you want to dance with me, Jeb?" she asked, bowing slightly. "Of course, I'll dance with you." As she held out her hands, she imagined the room lined with envious women and rejected suitors, all eyeing her and Jeb as they twirled about.

"Aggie!"

Her daydream vanished as the sound of her father's voice drifted up the stairway. "Yes, Father?"

"I'm leaving for the bank. You're not planning on seeing that young man today, are you? The one you told me about last night."

"No, Father." But oh, how she wished she could. "Not today. I probably won't see him until my birthday party. Why do you ask?"

There was a pause. "I–I wish you wouldn't see him again. Your brother says he's not the sort of fellow you should be spending time with. I'm concerned about you."

Anger rose from within her, and she wanted to strangle her brother. "Richard doesn't even know Jeb. He's never met him.

How could he know what sort of fellow he is?"

"Isn't he living with that crazy old miner?"

"Yes," she said adamantly, feeling the need to defend her new acquaintance. "That old man needs help. Jeb says he's nearly blind. And, Father," she called out to him, "you should be more concerned about the new friends Richard is making. I don't like any of the boys I've seen him with, and I don't think you'd like them either."

"We'll talk about this later, Agatha, and no more of this talk about you marrying that young man."

She hated it when he called her by that name. It reminded her of the stuffy old aunt for whom she was named. "But I am going to marry him, Father. Just you wait and see."

Shaking his head, he raised a heavy brow and cleared his throat. "I only wish your mother were here. You, my darling daughter, are almost more than I can handle."

"I love you, Father," Aggie called out with a smile as she leaned over the railing and blew him a kiss.

Jeb hadn't had any idea how a person would go about looking for gold, and the way Blackie did it was nothing like he'd imagined. It was not only hard work; it was tedious and discouraging. He'd expected to chip away at a spot with his pickax, find slivers of gold embedded in the rock and dirt, and go after them. But that wasn't the way it was. He learned from Blackie that a miner could go for days on end without even seeing a speck of gold and that not everything that looked like gold was gold.

"Good thing ya got a strong back, Boy," Blackie told him as

he watched him from his place on the ground. The afternoon sun and a morning of digging had been taking their toll on the old man. After much persuasion, he'd agreed to sit a spell, rest, and watch.

Jeb grinned. " 'The glory of young men is their strength: and the beauty of old men is the gray head.' "

Blackie surveyed him, his eyes sparkling, and Jeb could see the Scripture had amused the old man. He liked Blackie. He liked helping him, and he liked being around him. Yes, even if they never found gold, he would be a richer man just from having known this man of God who was not ashamed to go about the streets of Sacramento shouting out God's Word.

It was late afternoon before Blackie signaled for Jeb to stop picking away at the rocky hillside. Jeb wiped the sweat from his brow and stood waiting for further instructions.

Blackie pulled a worn canvas bag from his shack. "Grab up a couple of those bucketfuls of dirt and follow me."

Jeb followed obediently, lugging two of the fuller buckets in his calloused hands, flinching as the handles pierced at two newly formed blisters. They walked across a rocky knoll, down a ragged slope, through a narrow opening in the rock, to a sliver of a stream nearly hidden behind a tall rock formation.

Blackie lowered his haunches onto a fairly flat rock and handed Jeb an old rusty pan. "Now we look for gold." He scooped a small handful of dirt from the bucket and carefully placed it in the pan. "Watch me, and do exactly what I do, and don't get too exuberant or you may lose some gold before you ever find it."

Jeb could see the excitement in Blackie's eyes, and he too began to anticipate what might happen. Would they actually find gold?

Taking care, Blackie lowered the pan into the stream. Slowly and methodically, he began to rotate it in his hand, making the water gently swirl over the edges. "If we got any gold, it'll be heavier than the dirt and fall to the bottom."

Jeb's heart raced. You could find gold with simply a pickax and a rusty pan? He watched Blackie, trying desperately to duplicate his rhythmic movements with the water and the pan, and soon he began to feel pretty adept at it.

They worked until sundown and found not one piece of gold. Jeb's back ached from bending over the stream, and he was hungry; but hearing no complaints from Blackie, he kept quiet about it.

The old man adjusted his position with a groan. "I got a feelin' in these old bones, there's gold in that last bucket."

Jeb arched his back and for a brief moment wished he was back home, sitting at his father's table and enjoying some of his mother's good bacon gravy.

Silently, the two worked side-by-side, filling, dipping, swirling, waiting.

"There she is!" Blackie finally said with a victorious shout. "Look, there in your pan. See!" He pointed to a tiny, shiny speck, so small Jeb had to look twice to make sure it was there.

"That's it? That tiny little thing?" Jeb asked incredulously.

Blackie's mustache wiggled. "Yep, Boy. Gold. Real gold."

Chapter 2

Jeb stared into the pan. "How much is it worth?"

"Not much, but that tells us there's more where ya been diggin'! Tomorrow, we'll probably find us some more!"

Blackie's enthusiasm was contagious, and Jeb found himself actually looking forward to tomorrow. "Have you found much gold up here, Blackie?"

The man eyed him suspiciously. "Did someone tell you I had?"

Jeb's eyes widened. "No! The only person I've talked to since I arrived yesterday morning, other than Miss Aggie, is you!"

With great effort, Blackie turned himself over onto his knees; then bracing himself against a stone, he groaned and stood up, one palm pressing against the flat of his back. "Some folks in town think I've hit a rich vein and I'm hidin' gold up here somewhere. 'Lay not up for yourselves treasures upon earth. . . , But lay up for yourselves treasures in heaven, where neither moth nor rust doth corrupt, and where thieves do not break through nor steal: For where your treasure is, there will your heart be also.'"

Jeb laughed. "Guess they haven't seen your old shack."

"There is gold in these parts, Boy. I'm convinced of it." Blackie put a trembling hand on Jeb's arm. "I'm an old man. An old man without a family. Stay with me, Jeb. Help me, and whatever gold we find will be ours, yours and mine. We will each keep half."

Jeb was touched by Blackie's generosity. The old man barely knew him, yet he was putting his trust and faith in him, and right there, Jeb vowed to help Blackie all he could, even if it delayed his quest for gold.

For the next two days, the two partners got up early, worked until late, and found only traces of the elusive gold. Their days were filled with laughter and good fellowship as they hurled Scripture at one another, with each enjoying the excitement of reciting God's Word aloud. Blackie fixed a new supply of biscuits, and Jeb had to admit, they weren't half bad; either that, or he was so hungry, he didn't realize how awful they tasted. On the morning of the third day, Jeb was able to catch two small birds, and that night they had a feast.

"Your name Jeb?"

Jeb turned and wiped the sweat from his brow as a young, well-dressed man approached him, leading a fine horse.

Jeb nodded. Who would know his name or where he was?

"I'm Tom, Aggie's cousin." He pulled a bag from his horse's back and held it toward Jeb. "Aggie asked me to bring you some of my clothes to wear to her birthday party."

Jeb backed away and shook his head. Never did he expect

the lovely young woman he'd met at the stable to follow through with her words. "I–I'm not going."

Tom reared back and let out a raucous laugh. "Haven't you heard, old boy, no one tells Miss Agatha Wells no."

"I–I can't make it. I have work to do here."

Tom brushed at his trousers with his hand, then climbed onto his horse. "Aggie is going to be very upset if you don't show up. She said to tell you there'd be all sorts of fancy food."

He gave Jeb an appraising glance that Jeb didn't like very much. The look was condescending and uncalled for, as far as he was concerned.

"I'd show up if I were you," Tom said. "The party will be at midday. Anyone in town can tell you where she lives." He tipped his hat and rode off, leaving Jeb leaning on the handle of his pickax, staring after him.

"You'd better go," Blackie said, looking as though he was trying to mask a grin. "We ain't got no food like that here on Utopia."

Jeb had to admit, his mouth had watered at the mention of the fancy food, but he had no business attending such a party. He hadn't wanted to tell Aggie, but he'd never been to a party before, unless you could call sitting around the table, singing to your siblings on their birthday, a party. Even if he went, he wouldn't know how to act, and he sure didn't want to embarrass Aggie after she'd been so nice to him. "No, I'm not going."

"Up to you, but I'm afraid if you don't go, that nice little girl might come looking for you herself."

Jeb stiffened. "I thought you didn't like her!"

"She's rebellious, and I don't like the way she dresses and goes around town showin' herself off, but she's got a soul, Jeb. She needs the Lord just like everyone else does. She's taken a liking to you. You may be the only one she'll listen to. I think you should go." The old man leaned against a rock and crossed his arms. "You wouldn't want to miss out on that food, would you?"

Jeb shrugged. "Don't folks usually take a gift to a birthday party? I have no gift to give her and nothing to buy one with."

Blackie gave him a wink. "Then make her one. I've seen you whittlin' with that knife of yours when the day is done."

Jeb gave his words some thought. He'd always liked to take a worthless piece of an old tree branch and turn it into something recognizable. His mother had loved the things he'd whittled for her. She kept each one on a shelf in her kitchen. Yes, maybe he could make a birthday present for Aggie—if he decided to go.

Jeb stood outside Aggie's house trying to get up the courage to rap on the door. *What if she doesn't remember me? Of course, she'll remember me. She sent her cousin to bring me these fine clothes. What if I embarrass her in front of all her friends?*

He could hear laughter and voices coming from inside the house, and his knees began to buckle. Maybe he'd better turn around and—

"Jeb! You've come!"

Aggie appeared in the doorway, all smiles, and Jeb felt his heart clench. He'd never had a feeling like that before, and it scared him. "He—hello, Miss Aggie. Happy birthday," he said shyly, getting his tongue all tangled as he spoke.

31

She quickly grabbed his hand and dragged him inside. "Look who's here! The handsome man I've told all of you about!"

At least a dozen girls Aggie's age crowded around him, each trying to tell him her name at the same time. Aggie pulled him away with a coy grin. "He's mine. You must all leave him alone."

She pulled him into a corner, sat down on a red velvet sofa, and pulled him down beside her. "I knew you'd come."

"I–I almost didn't." His glance fell to the borrowed jacket and pants he was wearing. "Th–thanks for the clothes," he said, his eyes pinned on his worn, dusty boots.

She put a finger to his lips. "Never you mind about that, Jeb Monroe. You're still the handsomest man here. I know I'm the envy of all the girls, and all the boys probably wish they looked just like you." Her slim fingers rose and touched his hair. "Your kind face makes you look like an angel."

Jeb gasped. An angel? Him? "I–I have a small present for you," he said, his hand flattening over his pocket.

She clapped her hands together excitedly, her eyes shining with expectation. "A present? Oh, Jeb. You didn't have to bring me a present." She leaped to her feet and dragged him to a large table in the corner of the magnificent room. "You can put it there with the other presents. I'm going to open them after we all have cake."

Jeb reached into his pocket and pulled out his gift, a tiny rose he'd carved out of a piece of oak he'd found on a hillside up near Farnes River. Since he hadn't had a box or any other way to wrap it for her, he'd taken his most prized possession—the only fine linen handkerchief his mother had ever owned, the one she'd given him to bring with him as a remembrance of her—and wrapped it around Aggie's rose, tying the four corners loosely together. He eyed the exquisitely wrapped presents covering the table. His gift paled to nothing beside them, and he wanted to slide it back into his pocket, making sure Aggie never saw it. But he'd carved it for her, and it was too late to do anything but place it on the table with the other packages. Aggie was so caught up in conversation with another partygoer, she never saw him do it. He quickly backed away, hoping she wouldn't realize the handkerchief present was from him.

Aggie treated him as if he were her special guest at the party. He'd never had anyone make so much over him, and he had to admit it felt good, although he did sense the stares of some of the boys as they pointed to his feet and laughed.

He was with her every second, and she barely ever let go of his hand. She smelled nice. Like flowers. And she looked pretty too, in her shiny blue dress with her long, black curls piled up on top of her head. He wished his mama could see her, but he knew that would never be possible.

There was wonderful food and music and dancing, and although many of the men at the party asked Aggie to dance with them, she refused, saying she preferred to stay with Jeb. She hadn't even seemed to mind it when he'd told her he didn't dance. The party was, by far, the most enjoyable afternoon he'd ever spent. But when it came time for Aggie to open her presents, Jeb froze. He'd gotten through the entire time without embarrassing her, but when she got to his gift. . .

He shuddered at the thought and suddenly felt out of place.

He had no business being here, pretending he was something he was not. What if all these people were to find out he was a penniless gold seeker, living in a rundown shack up in the hills and working with the man most of the town thought was a crazy old fool? He sat rigid on the chair as Aggie moved to the table and began opening the presents, reading off the giver's name each time with a flourish and pointing them out to the other guests.

Jeb forced himself to stay until nearly half of the presents had been unwrapped and everyone had oohhed and ahhed over each one, then stood and backed slowly toward the door, hoping since all eyes were on the birthday girl, his movements wouldn't be noticed. He carefully opened the door, slipped quietly through it, and onto the big wraparound porch. To his relief, no one had seemed to notice. Not even Aggie. Once he was outside, he took off in a run across the dusty street, between the houses, through the yard surrounding the blacksmith's shop, and across a field, before he stopped to catch his breath. He stood panting for air, wondering how Aggie would react when she got to his lowly gift. A hand-carved rose wrapped in a handkerchief.

❧

Aggie was having so much fun opening her presents, she nearly forgot about her special guest, and she was shocked when she spied the empty chair where he'd been sitting. Still keeping her smile, she glanced quickly around the room, but Jeb wasn't there. Hoping perhaps he'd just stepped out for a bit of air, she continued pulling the wrappings off her gifts and extolling their virtues to her guests, thanking them profusely for each one. She was finally down to three gifts, when she noticed the handkerchief with its four corners tied up into a knot. Wherever had that come from? She reached past the two other gifts and pulled the mysterious handkerchief toward her, lifting it high in her hands. "Did anyone leave this on the table?"

No one responded. She was about to set it aside, when she remembered Jeb's words. "I can't buy you a gift." Instantly she knew the handkerchief was from him, but what was inside? Her smile broadened as she carefully untied the handkerchief and pulled out the tiny, intricately carved rose. Jeb! She held both the hanky and the rose to her heart. It was the sweetest, most thoughtful gift she had received. A tear came to her eyes as she examined each tiny petal. A fine, hand-carved rose like that would be quite expensive if purchased in one of the shops in San Francisco. She'd been there with her father. This one was so delicate, so lifelike, she could almost smell its sweet fragrance.

"What is it?" one of her guests called out.

"Who is it from?" another asked.

"Yes?" her father asked as he came through the front door and walked up proudly beside her, slipping his arm about her waist and kissing her cheek. "Who gave you that beautiful gift?"

She proudly placed the rose on her palm and held it out for all to see. "It's from Jeb. I guess he had to leave. Isn't this the most beautiful thing you have ever seen?"

"Jeb?" her father repeated, pushing her away a bit and looking into her face.

She cupped her hand about her father's cheek and smiled

up at him. "Yes, Father. Jeb. The man I'm going to marry!"

※

Jeb trudged the last few steps up the hill toward Utopia and fell into a heap at Blackie's feet, panting for breath. He'd run most of the way, anxious to put as much distance between Aggie and himself as possible.

"So how was the party?" Blackie dipped him a cup of water from the bucket and handed it to him.

Jeb took the cup and drank nearly all of the water before answering, "Wonderful, and awful."

Blackie watched him from his place on the broken chair, finally saying, " 'But God hath chosen the foolish things of the world to confound the wise; and God hath chosen the weak things of the world to confound the things which are mighty.' "

"That's the way I felt, Blackie. Confused. I loved being there with Aggie, but I knew I didn't belong." Jeb pulled off his borrowed jacket and trousers and donned his work clothes. "I felt like a king being with Aggie, but I also felt like a deceiver. Not once did I mention my Lord to any of them."

"Did you do anything to bring shame upon the Lord's name?"

"No," Jeb exclaimed, "I'd never do that!"

" 'Wherefore by their fruits ye shall know them.' "

Jeb sat down on the dirt floor by the old man and crossed his legs. "But how can they know I'm a Christian if I don't tell them? You always tell people, Blackie, anyone who will listen. Why don't I do that? I love the Lord too."

The old man laid a hand on Jeb's shoulder. "I'm an old man,

Jeb. I live like a hermit up in these hills and have for years. Who would listen to me if I didn't go about town, shouting the good news of salvation? My time is short. I don't have as many years ahead of me as you do. You have time to live for Christ, to let your light shine before men. I don't. I'm trying desperately to reach everyone I can with God's Word before my time on earth is up. Don't you see? You'll probably reach more people for Him by your kind, gentle ways and by living a godly life before them than I have in my lifetime." He patted Jeb's shoulder. "Live Christ before them, Jeb. It's your calling from the Master."

Jeb savored Blackie's words carefully, mulling them over in his heart. Had he been a witness to Aggie and her friends simply by being himself? Or had he kept his light under a bushel?

❧

"I think you'd better go in to town and get some supplies," Blackie told Jeb the next morning over their coffee and biscuits. "My old body could use a day of rest. I won't do any digging or panning while you're gone."

Jeb nodded. "I'll need to return Aggie's cousin's clothes."

Not sure where he should leave them and not exactly wanting to go by Aggie's house, Jeb decided to make the general store his first stop. He took what little gold dust Blackie had given him and wandered about the store, his mind intent on his mission, trying to make the most reasonable purchases he could.

"Hello, Jeb."

His heart raced even before he looked up. He knew it was Aggie. He'd recognize that sweet voice anywhere. "Ah. . .Aggie. I have your cousin's clothes in a bag on Hortense's back. Ca–can you tell me where to take them?"

Aggie moved forward and linked her arm in his, smiling up into his face and causing his heart to skip a beat, her alabaster skin smooth against his arm. "I can do better than that. My cousin will be at our house this evening. When you're finished, you can walk me home. But first, you have to tell me why you left my party."

He stuttered and stammered, trying to find something witty to say, but being witty didn't come easy for him.

"Jeb, I do believe you're blushing." Aggie touched a finger-tip to his nose. He could feel her short little wisps of breath.

"Yo—you surprised me," he finally managed to say, swallowing hard. Though he'd never admit it to Blackie, she'd been on his mind constantly since the birthday party. "I—I didn't expect to see you here—at the store—this time of day." Was he making any sense at all? "Sorry I left early. Blackie wasn't feelin' so good."

"You could've told me. I was worried when I couldn't find you." She angled her head slightly and smiled, blinking her long lashes. "Your birthday present was the most wonderful present I received, Jeb. Far more special than any of the others. Wherever did you find such a lovely rose? I've never seen anything like it."

A lump caught in his throat. Was she mocking his gift? Why did he ever give her such a ridiculous thing? A flower carved with his old pocketknife from a piece of wood he'd found up in the hills. Not a very fitting gift for the banker's daughter. "I—I shouldn't have given it to you. I—I don't know what I was thinking." He jammed his hands into his pockets and turned away. "You must think I'm nothing but a fool."

She grabbed onto his arm, her dark brows lifted. "You? A fool? Why? It was a wonderful present!"

He pulled away and gazed down at her. "Wonderful? A piece of a tree carved with my pocketknife?"

Aggie's lower jaw dropped. "You? You carved it?"

He nodded, ashamed to admit he'd given her such a lowly gift.

"Oh, Jeb, I didn't know. You didn't buy it from some artist?"

Jeb's heart sank. Now she was mocking him. "I didn't. I didn't have any way to buy you a real gift, Aggie."

She stood on tiptoes and planted a gentle kiss on his cheek. "Oh, Jeb, no one has ever given me a sweeter gift. I'll cherish it always. The rose and the handkerchief." She reached into her little drawstring bag and pulled out the folded white hanky. "See, I carry the hanky with me. It's so beautiful."

Her unexpected praise left him nearly speechless. "It. . .that hanky was. . .it was. . .it was. . .my mother's. To re–remember her by."

Aggie's eyes misted over as she gazed up at him. "Oh, Jeb. You brought so little when you came to Sacramento. Remember that first time I saw you? All you had with you was your knapsack, and you gave me one of the most precious things you had. Your mother's handkerchief. As much as I love it, I can't keep it."

He brightened. Could she be telling the truth? Did she really like it that much? Enough to keep it always? Before he could stop himself, he took her hand in his and held it tight.

"No! Don't you see? I can't take it back. I want you to have it."

"I'm glad, because I wanted to keep it." She flashed him a smile, placed the handkerchief back in her bag, and drew the strings up tight. "Hurry, Jeb. Finish your shopping. I'll wait for you."

Twenty minutes later, Jeb was tying Hortense to the hitching post in front of the Wells family's home, with Aggie giggling at his side. She led him up the steps and to the porch swing, sitting down and patting the seat beside her. Jeb tried hard not to get his feet tangled as he slowly lowered himself next to her. She smelled so good. Like some kind of flower, though he didn't know what kind. He wondered if he smelled like Hortense, since he'd ridden the animal partway into town. He hoped not. He wouldn't want to offend her.

Aggie gave a little push with her foot, and the swing moved slowly back and forth. "Tell me about your family, Jeb."

He sat rigid as their elbows touched. *My family. She asked about my family.* Her closeness made his mind cloudy. "Besides my mama and my dad, I got me two brothers and three sisters. I'm the oldest." Her interest in him seemed genuine, so he went on. "We live in a little town called Nicolaus, up north of Sacramento."

They sat swinging for awhile, with no words between them. Living in Sacramento most of her life, the daughter of a wealthy banker, Jeb knew Aggie had no idea what it was like to be poor.

She scooted closer to him, watching him with rapt attention. "What's it like to be a miner, Jeb? How do you look for gold?"

Jeb shrugged. "I wish Blackie was here to answer that question. From what he tells me, he's been searchin' for gold ever since that James Marshall fellow first found it at Coloma in January of last year. I don't know much about it yet. Mostly, Blackie and I dig around with a pick and shovel in hills and in the dry creek beds on his claim, then take the bucketsful of dirt and rock down to the river and wash the dirt out."

"That sounds rather hopeless." In an almost whisper, Aggie asked, "Are you finding any gold?"

Although he'd heard most miners kept the results of their labors a secret to keep people from stealing from them, Jeb laughed. "Well, if you say finding several small slivers is finding gold, I guess we have!" His gaze lowered as her hand went to his arm again. Just sitting by Aggie made his heart tingle.

"I know it must have been hard to leave your family and come all the way here from—where did you say it was? Nicolaus?"

He nodded. "I wouldn't have come just for myself. I have hopes of finding enough gold to be able to take it back to my parents. I want my mama to have a nice house and the garden she's always talked about. I'm praying, if God wills it, I'll find that gold."

Jeb felt Aggie stiffen. "I know Blackie believes that God stuff he's always talking about, but you don't believe it, do you?"

Eyeing her, he worked to choose his words carefully. Hadn't he prayed God would let him be a witness to her? "Yes, Aggie, I do. I believe what my Bible says. I have no reason to believe otherwise. I've believed in God since I was a little child."

"Be—because your parents did?"

He shook his head. "No. Although they have encouraged me to read my Bible and pray. God's Word makes it very clear He loves us and created us to have fellowship with Him."

Aggie frowned thoughtfully, as if pondering his words. "If God did that, why doesn't everyone feel about Him the way you do?"

"Because He gave us a free will. He didn't make us love Him; He wanted us to want to love Him."

She shot Jeb a look of frustration. "If He loves us so much, why did He make hell? And why does He send good people there?"

She has to understand. Lord, put the words in my mouth. Jeb drew in a fresh breath. "God doesn't send anyone to hell. He—"

"Oh? I've heard that Bible of yours says He does!"

He took her hand and stroked the pad of his thumb gently over her knuckles. "Aggie, God has given us two choices. We can confess our sins and ask His forgiveness, let Him cleanse us from all unrighteousness, and spend eternity with Him in heaven, or. . ."

He paused, wanting to make sure she understood his words. "Or we can turn our backs on Him, pretend He doesn't exist, ignore His Word, and go about our merry way, doing what we want to do—even if it is against all the principles He has laid down in the Bible—and spend eternity in hell. He doesn't make that decision. We earthly folks do."

Her gaze fell to the floor, and Jeb was sure she was thinking over what he'd said. *Lord, let this seed fall on good ground.*

"I—I—" She paused and stared at him, her voice shaky. "My father is a good man. The best I know. He has never done anything to hurt anyone. He has taken good care of my brother and me since my mother died. He helps the poor and needy. Are you telling me God would send him to hell? I doubt there is any sin in his life! How could he ask forgiveness when he hasn't done anything wrong?"

Lord, I need Blackie here to explain it to her, but knowing the way she and the others feel about him, I doubt she'd listen. Is this what Blackie meant when he said I may be the only shining example to come into her life?

Jeb took a deep breath and tried to answer her question. "We've all sinned and come short of the glory of God, Aggie. Me, you, your father. No person who was ever born has lived without sinning. Except Jesus."

"Well," she conceded slowly, "I've never seen my father pray, and I've never really heard—" She paused. "He does swear sometimes, when something or someone is really bothering him."

"Using God's name in vain is a sin. And if your father is like the rest of us folks, he sins more than you know." *How can I say this delicately, Lord?* "You sin, Aggie."

She gasped. "Me? How do I sin? I've never done anything bad." Her hand went to her throat, and her eyes widened. "Not really bad."

"Just refusing God and His Word is sin." His answer was soft and nearly inaudible.

To his surprise, Aggie reached up and planted a gentle kiss on his cheek, much like she'd done when she'd told him how much she liked her birthday present; and he found himself every bit as speechless and even more in awe of her beauty than before.

"I don't want to talk about this anymore, Jeb. The entire subject is depressing. Let's talk about something more joyous. Like the dance my friend Rosalee Garcia is going to give at her house on Saturday night. Can you come?"

Her sudden change of subject caught him off guard and he blinked hard. "Ah, no. Blackie and I will be working all day."

She leaned back in the swing, her feet pushing quickly against the floor, sending the swing higher. Jeb grabbed onto the chains, afraid their sudden weight shift might throw them over backward.

"I don't know how you live with that crazy old man, Jeb," she said, leaning her shoulders into him as she gave another quick push with her foot. "You must be the only one around who can tolerate him. How do you do it?"

"I don't tolerate Blackie, Aggie. I love him and respect him. That man knows more Scripture by memory than any man I know, and no man has more love for God than he does."

Jeb slowed the swing's momentum and stood, extending his hand toward Aggie and helping her rise. "I'd better be going. I need to get those supplies up to our camp before dark." He gestured toward the hitching post. "I think Hortense is gettin' a bit impatient."

She held onto his hand tightly, refusing to let it go, smiling at him with that smile that made his heart do funny things in his chest. Things he'd never felt before meeting Aggie.

"I like you, Jeb." She cupped her free hand about his cheek, looking up into his eyes in a way that made his head spin.

He stared back at her, feeling caught up in her spell and not sure what to say. "I—I like you too."

"Do you know what I told my father? That first day I met you?"

He could feel the warmth of her touch; and although her smile seemed winsome, he could also detect a bit of mischief in her face. It made his heart crazy. "No, I reckon I don't."

Aggie's grin was unreadable. He could never tell when she was serious and when she was poking fun at him.

"I told him I'd met the man I was going to marry."

Jeb's mind raced. He had no idea what she was talking about.

"You, Jeb! You're the man I'm going to marry."

Chapter 3

I . . .you told your father. . .he. . ."

Aggie laughed at Jeb's look of bewilderment and his shuffling for words. He might think she was jesting, but she wasn't. "Don't look at me like that," she said, enjoying his awkwardness. "Aggie Wells gets what she wants, Jeb, and I want you to be my husband!"

Jeb stood motionless, staring at her as if she'd sprouted wings. "You can't. . . . We aren't. . . . It's. . ."

She tipped her head coyly to one side. "Why, Jeb Monroe, are you turning me down?"

"No, but we. . .the Bible. . ."

Giving his arm a pinch, she grinned up at him, batting her eyelashes with the hope that he wouldn't jump and run like a frightened rabbit. "I know you'll need time to get used to the idea. I don't mean to rush you, but I think we're destined to be together. I like being around you; and when I'm not, you're on my mind constantly. Don't you like being with me, Jeb?"

He nodded. "Yes, I like being around you—but I'm a poor

boy, Aggie, with nothing to offer you."

"Haven't you ever thought of marriage, Jeb?" She smiled as she watched him gulp, his Adam's apple rising and falling.

"Ah. . .yes, Ma'am. I'd be dishonest if I said I hadn't."

She moved a tad closer to him, still smiling up at him. "Have you ever thought of what it would be like to be married to me?"

"Ah. . .yes, Ma'am." He let out a long, low whistle. "I reckon I have. But that could never happen."

She raised her dark brows. "Why, Jeb? If we love one another, what could stop us?"

The look on his face warned her she was about to hear the answer to her question, and she wasn't going to like it one bit.

"Several things, Ma'am. A union between the two of us would be impossible. I'm poor, with nothing to offer you. You're from a rich family and able to have anything you'd ever want. It's obvious by your talk and your ways, you've had way more book-learning. If I don't find gold, I'd have no future to offer you."

She listened carefully to each word, confident she would be able to think of ways to refute each of his arguments. "All of those things either don't matter or they can be easily overcome."

"Your father would never allow it."

"I can talk my father into anything, Jeb. He wants me to be happy, and marrying you will make me happy. I just have to convince him. I'm sure he'll give you a job at the bank, and you can study books to get more book-learning."

"My Father won't allow it, Aggie."

His father? Why would any father deny his son marrying the woman he loved? Especially a woman from a fine family like mine?

"My heavenly Father," Jeb explained soberly. "He tells me in His Word I should never be united to someone who doesn't love Him and feel the same way about Him that I do. I could never be married to a woman who didn't love Him and put Him first in her life."

Aggie had never been rejected before. Just the opposite. She was always the one who did the rejecting. As her eyes filled with tears, she felt a feeling of melancholy come over her. Perhaps he didn't feel the same way about her as she felt about him, and this God thing of his was merely an easy way to let her down. She took his hand in hers and lifted it to her face, flattening his palm against her cheek, and gazed up at him. "I think I love you, Jeb. I've never had these feelings for any of the boys in Sacramento."

"Oh, Aggie, you don't love me. Maybe I'm just a new interest to fill up your life. Someone different than you're used to."

She detected a sadness in his gaze that made her want to throw her arms about his neck and hug him, but she knew doing something as spontaneous as that would more than likely frighten him and she'd never see him again, so she restrained herself.

"I've got to go, Aggie. Honest. I have to get back to our camp before it's too dark to find my way."

She sniffled as she brushed a tear from her cheek and forced a smile. "Promise me you'll think about what I've said?"

He nodded. "Only if you'll think about what I've said too."

"When will I see you again, Jeb?"

He backed away, shoving his hands into his worn pockets. "Don't rightly know. With Blackie not feelin' so good, it's gonna be up to me to carry the biggest share of work."

"Can you come to Rosalee's party with me? Please?"

He shook his head. "I can't, Aggie."

She felt her heart sink. Had she gone too far? Told him too soon about her plans to marry him?

"Wait, I have something for you," she said as she hurried from him and into the house.

When she returned, she was carrying three of the shiniest apples he had ever seen.

"Here, take these. You may get hungry on the way back."

"Ah, thanks." Jeb shoved two of the apples into his pockets and took a big bite of the third one, then moved away from her and backed off the porch, giving her a slight wave as he hurried to untie Hortense from the post.

Blackie was already stretched out on his blanket when Jeb got back to Utopia. Jeb pulled one of the apples from his pocket and handed it to him. "Betcha haven't had one of these in a long time."

The old man rose on one elbow and took a bite of the apple with a loud crunch. "You get them supplies I sent you for?"

Jeb nodded.

"You see that girl?"

He nodded again, unable to keep a smile off his face.

"Be careful, Jeb. Many a man has turned his back on God because of a woman and her enticing ways."

Jeb sat down beside him in the dim light that barely illuminated the area. "I thought you said I may be the only one to reach her."

Blackie took another bite of the apple. "I did. But you have to be careful, Jeb. Careful that you influence her for God, and she doesn't influence you for evil. 'Love not the world, neither the things that are in the world.' "

Jeb snorted. "I can't imagine anyone as nice and as lovely as Aggie doing anything evil."

A bony finger pointed Jeb's way. "See, Boy, that's what I mean. You're already coming to her defense."

"I'm not coming to her defense. I'm only trying to say it's harder to make someone see they have a need for God when their life is filled with good. She can't imagine any good person, such as the father she adores, being sent to hell. I've told her God doesn't send anyone to hell; they make that choice on their own. But I don't think I did a very good job of it."

"I'll be praying for you, Boy. As long as you keep your heart right and your guard up, you'll be fine."

Jeb pondered both Aggie's and Blackie's words long into the night, praying all the while for God's guidance. Finally he realized that if he was sure of anything, it was that his every waking moment was filled with thoughts of Aggie Wells, and he didn't know how to keep himself from thinking about her and wanting to be with her. Jeb had never been in love before; but remembering what his mother had told him about his parents' courtship, he thought maybe what he was feeling for Aggie was love. Perhaps that would explain the strange feelings in the pit of his stomach.

The next week both flew by and dragged for Jeb. With Blackie feeling down in the back, Jeb did most of the work. But his thoughts were of Aggie. Her tantalizing smile was ever before him, and her words of love worked continually at his heart.

It seemed each afternoon as Jeb carried the buckets of rock and dirt to the river, they found more tiny bits of gold than they'd found the day before. He'd give them to Blackie, who would carry them back up to Utopia, where he would hide them in a place unknown to Jeb in case someone tried to steal them. Jeb had been surprised to learn how many miners had lost all their findings to thieves.

Jeb stopped digging, put the shovel to one side, and wiped at the sweat on his brow. Blackie was feeling a bit better now and able to take over a part of the work. They both turned as they heard a horse whinny somewhere below them.

"You up there, Jeb?" a feminine voice called up, a voice Jeb recognized immediately.

"Wait, I'll come down to you," he called out as he leaped over a rock and slid down the hill, coming to a stop at a flat place. The sight of Aggie in her bright red dress made his breath catch in his throat, and he nearly choked as he hurried to take her horse's reins and tie them to a small sapling. "What're you doing here? How did you know where to find me?"

She grinned and motioned down the hill. "My cousin is down there, waiting for me. The one who brought you the clothes."

"But what—"

"What am I doing here?" She reached out and took his dusty, calloused hand in hers. "I've missed you, and I'd hoped you missed me too. Have you?"

Only every minute we've been apart. "I–I guess so."

His answer didn't seem to please her, but she went on.

"I know you don't come to town often, and I thought you might enjoy a nice meal." She pulled a large bag from the saddle and opened it, reaching inside and pulling out a baked hen. Jeb's mouth watered at the sight. "And I brought you some bacon, and eggs, and some fresh vegetables, and several apples, and—"

Jeb took the hen from her and savored the wonderful fragrance. How long had it been since he'd had such a delicacy?

"That's not all. I have some dried fruit, some nuts, a few potatoes, butter. Some bread our cook baked yesterday and some little cakes." She handed him the bag, then giggled. "Oh, yes. I brought you some soap."

"Oh, Aggie. Please don't come again. It's nearly half a day's journey, and it's not safe. You could fall, or your horse could stumble, or you might meet up with—"

She touched a finger to his lips. "It's nice to know you're concerned about me. Does that mean you've decided you love me?"

Her words took him aback. "I–I. . .we. . ."

She pointed a finger in his face. "Now, Jeb. Don't start that stuttering again. If you don't love me, just say so!"

He tried to say it, but he couldn't. He did love her. He hadn't fully realized it until she asked him to deny it.

"Well, do you or don't you?" Aggie asked, her face so close to his, he could make one swift, simple move and kiss her before she could get away.

"Aw, Aggie" was all he could force himself to say.

"Well," she said, planting a hand on her hip, "at least you didn't say you didn't love me, so I guess there's hope for us."

"Be ye not unequally yoked together with unbelievers: for what fellowship hath righteousness with unrighteousness? and what communion hath light with darkness?" a voice seemed to be saying in his head. Or was it his heart? He couldn't be sure. All he knew was he loved God, but he loved Aggie too. Jeb kept his silence.

"I won't leave you alone, Jeb," Aggie said, still looking at him with a smile that set his temperature rising and his heart pounding. "I'll be in your thoughts. In the wind you hear rustling through the oaks at night. In the midday sun as it beats down upon your body. I'll be in the singing of the birds, the rippling of the stream. Wherever you look, Jeb Monroe, I'll be there to remind you of my love. And hopefully, soon, you'll admit you love me too."

She didn't have to tell him that. Everything he saw, everything he heard, reminded him of Aggie.

"I'd better be going now. But you'll see me again soon, Jeb. If you won't come to me, I'll come to you." After pulling her horse's reins from the sapling, she reached up without warning and planted a kiss on Jeb's lips, then mounted and began her descent of the hill to where her cousin was waiting for her.

Jeb stood frozen to the spot, his jaw dropped, sure his face was drained of all color. Finally one hand rose and his fingers touched his dried lips. Aggie Wells had kissed him.

Despite Jeb's warning her against making the long journey

from Sacramento, she rode up to Utopia more times that week, each time bringing food—and once bringing fresh flowers from her garden. Jeb found himself listening for her horse's whinny, and when he heard it, he'd rush down to where the area flattened, tie her horse to the tree, and then help her up to Utopia, where the three of them would enjoy their dinnertime together. Each time Jeb and Blackie would bow their heads and one of them would thank God for their food, Aggie would playfully remind them that it was she who brought the food to them, not God.

In no time, Aggie had captivated Blackie as well, and the old man smiled more often than Jeb had ever seen him do, as he and Aggie would tease each other about silly things. He called her a spoiled baby girl, and she called him a silly old fossil, all in good fun. Jeb loved the sound of her voice as the three of them giggled at some ridiculous story she would relate to them. It seemed Blackie began to look forward to her visits as much as Jeb.

Each day, as Jeb would walk her down the hill to her horse, pleading with her not to come again, she would ask him the same question. "Do you love me yet, Jeb?"

And each day, he would tease her and put off a direct answer by saying, "You're too ugly to love," and they'd both have a good laugh. But when the laughter was over, she'd look into his eyes, kiss his lips, and tell him how much she loved him and that she would wait until he could tell her the same thing. Only now, Jeb participated in the kiss equally, wrapping his arms about her and holding her close as long as he dared. He was glad she had to leave her horse on the flattened area and walk up the rest of the way to Utopia. When he walked her back down, it gave him time to spend a few minutes alone with her, without Blackie's scrutiny.

"I can see why you love that girl," Blackie said one night as the two of them lay out under the stars on their blankets. "She's as sweet as sugar and not at all what I thought she was."

Jeb crossed his arms beneath his head and gazed up at the North Star. "I know."

"Whatcha gonna do about it, Jeb?"

The words drilled into Jeb, piercing his conscience. "Don't know, Blackie. I do love her. I tried not to, but I can't help it. I want nothing more than to spend my life with her, taking care of her, protecting her, loving her."

"Ya told her?"

Jeb flipped over on his side, folding his hands under his face. "I can't. Not yet. Not until she gets herself right with God. And besides, what kind of a life would she have with me? A poor boy from Nicolaus? She'd never leave her father and her fine home to live with the likes of me, and I could never stay in Sacramento. I promised my folks I'd come back home, with or without gold."

"You talked about her soul lately?"

"Yeah. Nearly every time I see her." The wind rustled through the trees, and it seemed Aggie was right there with them as she'd promised she'd be. "I don't know, Blackie. I was convinced God had sent me to witness to her, but I'm not sure she's any closer to getting right with Him now than she was the day I met her."

" 'Let all those that seek thee rejoice and be glad in thee: let such as love thy salvation say continually, The Lord be magnified,' " Blackie quoted, adjusting his blanket. "God knows your heart, Boy, and He loves that girl. Keep praying, and praising, and standing your ground, and trust the Lord."

Blackie's words brought a new peace to Jeb. He wasn't the only one who loved Aggie. Blackie loved her, and God loved her. Why hadn't he realized that before?

"What's on your mind, Girl?" Aggie's father asked her as they sat in the parlor one evening after an especially good dinner.

She sighed. "Jeb."

He frowned. "That boy who gave you that carved rose for your birthday?"

"Yes, the one I told you I was going to marry."

Her father shook his head and rolled his eyes. "Oh, Daughter, where do you get these ideas? That boy is not the kind of man I want for you. He has nothing to offer you. You should be thinking about some of the other boys here in Sacramento. Like Gordon or John, my dearest friend's sons. Those young men have a real future ahead of them. Why only yesterday their father purchased the Stanton place to put in a fine restaurant, and the way things are going here in Sacramento, they'll be wealthy men in no time at all."

Aggie sat down in her father's lap, wrapping her arms about his neck. "I told Jeb you could give him a job at the bank."

Her father snapped his fingers. "I knew it. That's probably what he was after all along. He thinks if he can worm his way into your life, he'll have access to all we have. I won't hear—"

Aggie pushed back and stood up quickly. "No! You have it all wrong. Jeb wouldn't even listen to me. He doesn't want to work in your bank. He isn't interested in whatever fortune you might have. All he wants is to dig for enough gold to help his parents buy a small house and some land. That's all. Nothing for himself."

"Then how does he expect to marry you, if he has nothing and wants nothing?" he barked at her.

"He doesn't expect to marry me. He won't even tell me he loves me." Aggie's eyes filled with tears, but she brushed them away with the lacy cuff of her sleeve.

Her father's brows lifted as he stared at her. "You mean this marriage thing has been all your idea?"

She nodded, her tears still flowing. "Yes, only mine."

"But why? I haven't met a man yet that wouldn't want to marry you. You're beautiful, far more beautiful than any of the single women I know. Most men would give up their fortunes to be able to call you their wife. What's the matter with that man?"

Aggie laughed through her tears. "First, you forbid me to marry him; now you're concerned because he isn't willing to marry me. Oh, Father. Help me! I've fallen in love with this man. He's like no man I've ever known. He's the first man I haven't been able to wrap around my little finger."

Her father used his hand to brush away her tears. "Perhaps that's his attraction. Perhaps you want him because you can't have him. Have you considered that, Daughter?"

"Oh, Father, this isn't a game I'm playing with him, like I've done with most of the boys I know. I sincerely love Jeb. But I know he won't acknowledge his love for me until I confess I'm a sinner and ask God's forgiveness."

Her father's eyes flashed with sudden anger at her words, and he cursed. "You? A sinner? Just who does he think he is? No one in the Wells family has ever been or ever will be a sinner. We come from fine, upstanding stock. I won't have anyone speak about my daughter in such a derogatory way!"

She tugged on his arm. "Oh, Father, don't be mad at Jeb. He means well. It's just that he's been raised differently than I have. He means no harm. He honestly believes everyone is a sinner and needs to repent." She smiled as her fingers gently stroked her father's arm. "He's a good man. I wish you could get to know him. He has the sweetest, gentlest spirit of any man I've ever met. And he's so unselfish—"

"He may be a good man, but I refuse to have him upsetting you with his talk about your being a sinner!"

Aggie lowered her head. "But what if I am a sinner?"

Martin Wells grabbed onto her arm tightly and spun her around. "Agatha! What have you done? Is there something you're not telling me? Why would you say such a thing?"

She jerked her arm away and rubbed at the spot where his hand had been. "Because the Bible says everyone is a sinner. Jeb says sin is anything we do or think that displeases God or separates us from Him. I think I've done that by not even reading the Bible, since it is God's Word. And I'm sure I've done other things to displease God too."

He shook his index finger at her. "Don't listen to him,

Aggie. He's only trying to confuse you."

She lifted her eyes to his and searched his face. "Can you honestly tell me, Father, that you have never sinned?"

He huffed loudly. "Don't ever ask me that foolish question again, Agatha. Of course, I haven't sinned."

"Not even once?"

His expression hardened. "Not even once."

Aggie stared at her father but kept silent, Jeb's words ringing in her ears about everyone being a sinner.

You sinned just now, Father, by telling a lie. I know you've sinned. I've heard you tell other lies too, and I've heard you use God's name in vain. I've seen you gambling with those other men, and once, I even saw you pull a card from your sleeve. But I can see arguing with you will do no good. You may not believe you're a sinner, but I'm not so convinced about myself.

Jeb stretched first his left arm, then his right, and arched his back. The sun was nearly straight up in the sky, and he was hungry. The biscuits and coffee they'd had for breakfast had done little to fill his stomach. It'd been two days since he'd seen Aggie; and although he hated to admit it, his every thought during that time had been of her. Even his dreams held visions of the lovely Aggie.

"Think that girl will come to see you today?" Blackie asked as he wiped the sweat from his brow and sat down on a rock beside Jeb. "Seems she's been a regular visitor up here, bringin' you fancy vittles and flowers."

Jeb sat down on the rock next to Blackie, wiping his forehead with his sleeve. "Oh, Blackie. I don't know what I'm going to do. I keep witnessing to Aggie and reading her God's Word, but I'm not sure I'm getting through to her."

"You're gettin' in pretty deep with that woman, Jeb. Ya got love written all over your face every time ya see her."

"I know, Blackie, but I can't help it." Jeb's shoulders slumped. "I'm so in love with Aggie it hurts. Maybe I should just head back to Nicolaus. Get myself clean away from her."

"Oh? You decided God can't answer prayer, have ya?"

"Of course not!"

"Then why not turn it all over to the Lord and let Him work out the answer? Did God not say, 'If ye abide in me, and my words abide in you, ye shall ask what ye will, and it shall be done unto you.' Is not that promise written in God's Word?"

"Jeb, I'm here!"

Both men turned at the sound of Aggie's voice as she called up to them from the landing below.

"I'm coming, Aggie," Jeb called out with a smile and a wink toward Blackie.

"Remember, Jeb. Pray, ask, and as long as it is in God's will, He'll give ya the desires of your heart," Blackie told him as Jeb started down the incline. "Just cling to His Word, Son."

Aggie's smile made Jeb's heart swell with love as he hurriedly slid down the embankment toward her. Each time he saw her, he thought her even lovelier than the time before. "Aw, Aggie, you didn't have to do that," he told her as she motioned toward the bag tied to her horse's saddle.

She giggled like a schoolgirl. "I like bringing your dinner to you, Jeb. Remember, you're the man I'm going to marry. A wife should take good care of her husband."

His face sobered. "Aw, Aggie, you know I love you. I can't hide it anymore, but we—"

Her face brightened, and a huge smile graced her face. "You said it, Jeb Monroe! You actually said you love me!" She clapped her hands with glee. "I knew you did! Why wouldn't you tell me?"

Although her enthusiasm was usually contagious and just looking at her always brought a smile to his face, his look waned. "I shouldn't have told you now. Can't you see, Aggie, there can be no future for the two of us? Even if you were to accept my God as your God, I still wouldn't have the means to marry you and take care of you like—"

"I'd be happy just being married to you, Jeb. I don't need fine things and parties to make me happy. Some of the happiest times of my life have been simply bringing your dinner up to you and spending time with you. Can't you see that?"

He took the bag in one hand and her hand in the other, and they started up the incline. "You say that now, Aggie, but what would you say when I couldn't offer you a roof over your head and food to eat? You'd no longer be able to wear those fine clothes or ride a fine horse." He gave her hand a squeeze. "I'm afraid you'd end up hating me."

"I could never hate you, Jeb, for anything. I love you too much. Admit it. Be honest with me. The main reason you'd never marry me is because I can't see myself as a sinner and haven't accepted your God, isn't that right?"

Jeb nodded. "Both of those things are what is keeping us from ever having a life together, Aggie. Can't you see that? No matter how much I love you and you say you love me, it's not enough to build a life on. I have to be true to my God."

Aggie placed her palms on his cheek, looking up at him with that mischievous smile he loved so much. "I have the solution to both our problems, Jeb!"

He stared into her eyes, waiting, hoping, and praying she was going to tell him she'd decided to make peace with God.

"You say your God can answer prayer?"

He nodded. "Yes, of course, I do."

"Then pray that you and Blackie will strike a vein of gold. If your God answers that prayer, you'll have enough to provide the kind of life I'm used to, and I'll confess I'm a sinner and ask His forgiveness because I know your God is real. Because He's answered your prayer!"

Chapter 4

Jeb lay on his back, staring up at the heavens. *God, would you do that? So Aggie will believe Thou canst answer prayer?*

Blackie's raspy voice cut through the darkness. "You asleep?"

"No, I have too many things on my mind."

"I heard what Aggie said, Son. You do know you can't bargain with God, don't you?"

Jeb considered his words. "I know, but if I pray for such a miracle, is that really bargaining with God? If finding gold would be the means to Aggie accepting my God?"

"Can't you trust God to draw her to Him, through you, without such a miracle? Do as God leads you, Jeb. If He wants the two of you together, He will make it happen."

"I do trust Him, Blackie. It's just that I love Aggie so much. I want us to spend our lives together. I want her to love Him too!"

"'I will go before thee, and make the crooked places straight: I will break in pieces the gates of brass, and cut in sunder the bars of iron: And I will give thee the treasures of darkness, and hidden riches of secret places, that thou mayest know that I, the LORD, which call thee by thy name, am the God of Israel.'"

"I know, Blackie. I love that Scripture, and I'm clinging to it with all my might. Sometimes, I even hope the 'hidden riches of secret places' means the gold we're seeking. But even as God didn't forsake His children in the wilderness, I know He won't forsake me. When I first met Aggie, I thought I was only attracted to her beauty. I'd never known a woman like her. But I now know I've fallen hopelessly in love with her, and I don't know how God would have me deal with it." He sighed and flipped over on his side, facing his friend and mentor. "I've given God my life to do as He sees fit, even though I may end up with a broken heart."

Jeb started for town early the next morning to purchase a few more supplies, including a new shovel to replace the rusty old one.

"Have you heard the news?" one of the miners asked him as he tied Hortense to the hitching post in front of the general store.

Jeb frowned, thinking the man was going to tell him about someone who had hit a rich vein. "Nope. Just got into town."

"The banker's been stealing our money! Seems he's been takin' a share for himself outta every deposit. The sheriff came for him this morning. They didn't even get him to the jail before one of the miners pulled a gun and shot him clean through the heart."

Jeb stared at the man, open-mouthed. "Ma—Martin Wells?"

"Yep, old Martin Wells, himself. Shot him dead right on the spot. I never liked that guy, but I feel sorry for that daughter of his. She's a right nice young lady. I got no use for his son."

Aggie! Jeb thought. *I've got to get to her as fast as I can. She must be devastated!*

Jeb left Hortense tied to the hitching post and rushed down the street to the Wellses' house and up to the front door, pounding on it as loudly as he dared, calling out her name. Without waiting to be invited in, Jeb burst right past Aggie's aunt as she opened the door. He tore down the hallway in search of his Aggie.

The young woman who came running to him with her arms open wide looked nothing like the Aggie he knew. Her eyes were swollen nearly shut from crying, and both her hair and dress were disheveled. She threw her arms about his neck and sobbed like a baby, her breath coming in short gasps. "Oh, Jeb, Fa–Father's dead! How could he do such a th–thing? I tr–trusted him. Everyone tr–trusted him, and he be–betrayed all of us."

"I don't know, Aggie." Jeb wrapped her in his arms and held her close. "Gold does strange things to men." Hadn't Aggie told him over and over what an honorable man her father was?

She lifted a tear-stained face, her sighs coming from deep within. He could feel them racking at her body. "Th–the sheriff came for him this mo–morning. I–I heard him tell Father they'd be–been watching him for months. Ma–many of the miners had complained th–they were being sh–shorted. O–one of them shot him!"

Jeb brushed the tears from her eyes. "I know. I heard. I'm glad your aunt and uncle live nearby. I'd hate for you to have been alone."

"Th—they came as soon as they he—heard." Aggie dabbed at her face and her swollen eyes with her handkerchief. "I have to fa—face it. My fa—father, the man who st—stood right in this ve—very room and to—told me he'd never si—sinned, is nothing but a th—thief and a liar. And no—now he's go—gone!"

Jeb cradled her head and pressed it to his chest, his chin softly grazing her hair. He ached for her. She'd loved and adored her father, holding him in the highest esteem. He remembered the look of horror on her face when he'd told her that her father, as good a man as she'd thought he was, was a sinner just like everyone else and how upset she'd gotten at his words. This was not the way he'd wanted her to accept that fact. Seeing her in such emotional pain was almost more than he could bear. *Lord, be with Aggie at this terrible time. She doesn't have Thee to turn to for comfort. Make her see her need of Thee. Make her see, though men will fail us, Thou never wilt.* "Where's your brother?"

"He—he and Father had a fi—fight. He ha—hasn't been home for da—days."

Jeb slipped a finger under her chin and drew her face up to his, kissing her damp eyelids, then letting his lips rest on hers. Finally as he held her, Aggie began to calm down a bit.

"Wh—why, Jeb? Why would my father do such a thing? He had so much, while others had so little."

Give me the right words, Lord. "Aggie, dear sweet Aggie, do you remember what I said about all men and women being sinners?"

She nodded as she gazed up into his eyes. "I remember."

"We were born with a sinful nature. Did you ever see a baby cry and throw a temper tantrum because they couldn't have their way? Or a child stand right before you and lie, telling you that they hadn't done something you knew they had done? Or see a youngster take something that belonged to someone else and deny it, when perhaps someone had witnessed their act of theft?"

"Yes," she said softly, closing her eyelids together tightly.

"That's the sinful nature I'm talking about. No one has taught them those things. Those tendencies come to them naturally. We were all born with it. Me, you, your father—even Blackie."

"Even Blackie?"

Jeb nodded. "You should hear some of the stories he's told me about when he was young, before he got himself right with God. It's tough for even those who have committed themselves to God to walk in the way we should. Life is a constant battle, but He's there for us to turn to. He's given us His written Word to use as a guide."

"Does this. . .mean it's too late. . .for my father?"

Jeb's words caught in his throat. "Unless he made his peace with God."

For a moment, Jeb felt her body go limp, and he thought she was going to faint. He swept her up in his arms and carried her to the sofa, where he gently laid her down. "I'm here, Aggie.

I'll stay as long as you need me."

Later that night, knowing her aunt and uncle would be there with her, Jeb left Aggie and made his way to the livery stable, with plans to spend the night in the field out back. Good thing he'd told Blackie he might stay in town that night or the old man might worry about him. "Oh, Lord," he prayed as he settled down for the night, his heart heavy, "comfort Aggie in her hour of grief. Use her loss to bring her to Yourself."

Although Aggie's face was still swollen the next morning from crying, to Jeb, it seemed she had finally faced the full realization of her father's crime and the fury that had caused the miner to take his life.

"I—I've thought a lot about what you said, Jeb," Aggie told him as she sat wrapped in his arms. "About sin. I can see why my father would be called a sinner, with what he did to those poor miners who trusted him with their gold. But I still can't see why God would call someone like you, who's never done anything wrong in his life, a sinner. It just doesn't make sense."

Jeb stroked her hair as he stared into her eyes. "God's Word says all men are sinners. We were born in sin. I have to constantly come to Him in prayer, confessing the wrong deeds and thoughts in my life. But I have the assurance He'll hear my confessions and forgive me and show me the way I should go."

With a deep sigh, she shrugged. "Oh, Jeb, what wrongs have you ever done in your life? You're about as perfect as a man can get."

He pressed his eyelids tightly shut and gave her question some serious thought. "Oh, Aggie girl, I am as far from perfect as a man can get. I haven't stolen anyone's goods or cheated any-one. But I've lied at times and complained when things didn't go my way. I've even questioned God's wisdom. But sometimes, what you've done isn't as bad as what you'd like to do. My mind has entertained thoughts you can't imagine."

Aggie frowned up at him. "Thoughts? What kind of thoughts?"

Should I tell her, Lord? "Ah. . .most of my thoughts were about you. I love you so much, at times I considered turning my back on God's will and whisking you away from Sacramento, your father, and everything you hold dear, just so I could be with you. I even considered never returning to my parents' home and asking your father for that job in his bank so I could be near you."

"Would that have been so bad?"

"If I had done those things, I would have sinned against God because I knew under those circumstances, it wouldn't be in His will. I would have sinned against you too, Aggie, because we would never have had a happy life together unless God willed it. And I could never have provided the things you're used to having, maybe not even the food for our table and the clothing for our backs. I would have sinned against my parents, breaking the promise I'd made to them to return. And I would have sinned against myself by forsaking God and going against His wishes, when I could stay in His will and have the life He wants me to have."

Her eyes misted over, and she sniffled. "A life without me?"

He hated to say it, but not saying it would be the same as

telling a lie. He swallowed hard. "If that is God's will." He kissed her again, then took her hands in his and kissed her fingertips. "I've got to get back to Blackie, but I'll be praying for you. I'll come back as soon as I can. Will you be all right?"

She backed away slightly, and he felt as though her eyes were pleading with him to stay. "Yes, I think so. Our cook is still here, and my aunt has said she will stay as long as I need her."

"I love you, Aggie, and so does God," he told her as he backed out the door.

By the time he'd purchased the new shovel and what few supplies they needed and gotten back up to Utopia, it was early evening. As Blackie leaned against a rock, seeming more tired than usual, Jeb explained why he'd stayed overnight in town and what had happened to Aggie's father. "I hated to leave her, but I didn't know what else to do," he told his friend.

"You did the right thing, Jeb. I've known Martin Wells for several years; and although I never really liked the man, I never thought him capable of doing such a deceitful thing. That girl has to be filled with doubts right now. The best thing you can do is pray for her and ask God to speak to her heart."

The next two days were miserable. Jeb wanted to go into town, hold Aggie in his arms, comfort her, and tell her everything would be all right. But he knew that would be a lie. After the terrible crime her father had committed against the community, Aggie's entire life would probably change. They might even take the Wellses' family home away from her and her brother. He shuddered at the thought.

By noon the third day, Jeb knew he had to go to her. He

was washing up by the river when he saw her coming up the trail on her horse, and he ran to meet her. She was crying, her dress was wrinkled and dirty, and she looked as though she hadn't slept a wink since he'd last seen her.

"Oh, Jeb, it's been awful! Everyone is treating me like a criminal too. No one will even speak to me when I go out onto the street. Even my aunt and uncle act differently toward me. I'm so alone! I had to see you. Please tell me you don't hate me too!"

He pulled her gently from her horse and hugged her to his chest. What could he say to comfort her? How could he help her?

She wrapped her arms about his waist and buried her head in his shirt, dampening it with her tears. "Now I understand, Jeb, about how we are all sinners. Do you think God can ever forgive me for being so blind and thinking I was without sin?"

Jeb's heart soared. "Of course, He can forgive you, Aggie, but you have to ask Him to. You have to admit to Him you are a sinner and tell Him that you want His forgiveness. Remember when I told you how God sent His only Son to die for mankind, that by faith, we could have eternal life with Him?"

She nodded. "I remember, but I never understood. Until now."

"Then tell Him, Aggie. No one else can do it for you."

Aggie blinked hard and lifted her face heavenward, pouring out her heart to God, confessing her sins and her need for His forgiveness, and asking Him to come into her life and be her Savior.

Jeb prayed along with her in his heart, praising God for letting him have the opportunity to explain His Word to her and being an influence on her life. When she finished, she gazed up at him, and to Jeb, it looked as though her face was shining. There was a glow and a purity about her that he was sure God alone could have placed there.

Jeb held her so tight, he was afraid she wouldn't be able to breathe. He never wanted to let her go, but if she was to get back home before dark, she'd have to leave soon. "I'll take you home." He took her hand and led her to where he'd tied her horse.

"But you'll never be able to get back to Utopia by nightfall!"

He kissed the tip of her nose. "Let me worry about that. Give me a minute to tell Blackie I'm leaving and get a blanket. I'll stay out behind the stable again. Don't you worry. I'll be right back."

Jeb could hardly contain his excitement as he told Blackie about Aggie and the decision she had made. "God answered my prayer, Blackie. I'm just sorry it had to be through her father's death."

Blackie smiled, then with a shake of his finger, offered a word of caution. "He only answered part of your prayer, Jeb."

Jeb sobered. "I know. I'm counting on Him for the rest."

He stayed with Aggie until nightfall. As he moved toward the door of her home, she caught him in her arms and held on tight. "Marry me, Jeb. Please! Take me away from all of this. I can't bear to stay here with the townspeople shunning me and whispering behind my back. I love you, Jeb, and I want to be with you. I'll live anywhere you say. At Utopia or Nicolaus—anywhere—just so I can be with you!"

Despite his desire to cling to her, he kissed her, then pushed her away. "I'd never do that to you, Aggie. In time, folks will settle down. Everyone knows you had nothing to do with your father's theft. They're still angry with him, and they're taking it out on you. You wouldn't last two days at Utopia, and Nicolaus is nothing like the Sacramento you're used to. If I had enough gold to take you there, and build you a fine house, and provide for your needs, I'd do it. But I don't. Your life would be nothing but poverty and hard work. You'd end up hating me. I can't let that happen. I love you too much. Although it will take a miracle, if we pray about it and God wants us to be together, it will happen."

"But—"

He put a finger to her lips, then slowly pulled it away and kissed her before bidding her good-bye. As he walked away, his fingers rubbed at his forehead wearily. *Lord, only Thou canst make it possible for me and Aggie to be together, and right now, I'm all out of suggestions. Our life together seems hopeless.*

❧

"I can't believe it's the middle of December already," Jeb told Blackie as he tightened his jacket about his neck.

Blackie handed him a cup of strong black coffee and lowered himself slowly onto a big rock. "Good thing you took time to shore up that shack of mine and cut all that firewood. I can't take the cold like I used to." He lifted the cup in salute. "Don't know how I'd have made it without you, Jeb. You've worked nearly a year with me now, and not one time have you demanded wages."

Jeb sat down beside him and took a careful sip as he watched Blackie out the corner of his eye. The old man's health was failing more each day, and he was growing weaker. Most of the time, he did little more than sit and watch as Jeb either dug away at the creek bed or used the water from the river to rinse the dirt from the few bits of gold they found. "Haven't needed any wages. You've taken care of all my needs. I trust you to keep my part until I'm ready."

"That girl loves you, Jeb. I see it in her eyes when she comes up here to be with you."

Jeb picked up a small, odd-shaped rock and idly threw it toward a tree. "I know. Not many women would have waited as patiently this many months for something that may never happen."

Blackie smoothed at his heavy beard, separating it with his fingers before taking another sip. "Take some of that gold we been savin' and get her a nice present for Christmas."

Jeb considered Blackie's words. He'd been thinking the same thing, but what? After paying back most of the miners, Aggie had been allowed to stay in the house. Her brother had gone to live in San Francisco with a distant cousin. Now, other than her aunt and uncle and their family, who lived nearby, she was pretty much alone. Disappointed by the sudden change in her since she'd turned her life over to God, most of her friends had turned away from her. Many of the townsfolk continued to shun her because of what her father had stolen from them. She hated what her father had done, but he had been a loving father to her, and she still mourned his death. There was only one thing Aggie really wanted, something Jeb knew would make her happy and cheer her heart, but he couldn't give it to her.

Not yet. Not until God provided a way.

"How about a nice gold pin for her to wear on them fancy dresses," Blackie suggested, jabbing his elbow into Jeb's side.

Or a ring! Jeb was immediately filled with enthusiasm. "I know God is going to answer our prayer and make it possible for us to marry someday, Blackie. He's filled my heart with peace about it. If you'll give me enough gold from my share, I'm going to have a wedding band made for Aggie. And I'll get her a fine gold chain so she can wear it around her neck until our miracle happens."

"Course, I'll give it to you, Jeb. You've earned it."

Two days later Jeb placed an order for Aggie's ring. "Don't know her size," he told the jeweler, "but her hands are small."

The man laughed. "You're in luck. Her daddy had me make a ring for her last year. I have her size written down." The man leaned on the counter and smiled at Jeb. "What kind of a ring shall it be? A basket weave? Or perhaps one with a little stone in it?"

"No, Sir, I want it to be a wedding band. A simple gold wedding band."

The man stared at him. "Yo—you're going to marry Aggie Wells?"

"Yes, Sir. As soon as God provides a way," Jeb said proudly.

The man muffled a chuckle with his hand. "Maybe you'd better wait until that happens. I'd hate to see you waste your money."

Jeb realized the man was making fun of him. "Sir, Aggie and I both trust in the Lord and are confident He wants us together."

The man looked him over skeptically. "You don't look like the kind of man Aggie Wells would marry. I mean, she's used to fine things. Can you give those to her?"

"If the Lord doesn't provide the means, I won't be able to and Aggie and I won't be married, but we're both hopeful."

"And you want a wedding band. Now."

"Yes, Sir, and I need it by Christmas. It's gonna be her Christmas present. I want AW–JM engraved inside, and I'll need a fine gold chain for her so she can wear the ring about her neck."

The man paused before writing down the information. "You can pay for this, can't you?"

Jeb placed his bag of gold on the counter. "Yes, Sir, I can, and I want to use my own gold for her ring."

The man's face brightened as he peered into the bag. "I'll get on it right away, and you shall have it in time for Christmas."

❧

Christmas Day finally arrived, and Aggie, despite the loss of her father and the drab mourning clothing she was still wearing, was so excited she could hardly contain herself. Jeb had promised to spend the entire day with her, and because Jeb and her cousin Tom had become such good friends, she'd arranged for Jeb to spend the night at her aunt and uncle's home. The two young men often joked about the way Tom had loaned Jeb his clothing for Aggie's party.

She was thankful for her aunt and uncle and their generosity. They'd always been good to her but had been especially so since her father's death. Later in the day, she and Jeb would be joining them at their house for Christmas dinner, but until then, the two of them would be alone. Her aunt had told them to invite Blackie to come too, but he'd said no. He'd asked Jeb to tell the nice lady he wasn't up for social functions, but knowing Blackie, they'd both suspected he wanted them to have the day together without an old man to entertain.

Aggie had hoped her brother would make it home for Christmas, but he'd decided to stay in San Francisco. He had sent a present to her with an acquaintance who would be passing through Sacramento, which had surprised her.

She fussed with the candlesticks, placing them first this way and that on top of the lovely lace tablecloth, then she moved to place the napkins just so, as if a king were coming instead of a lowly miner. When Jeb knocked at the door, she flung it open and leaped into his arms, smothering his face with kisses.

"Merry Christmas, Sweetheart," he told her as he whirled about the room with her locked in his arms. "I can't believe we have the whole day together. God is good, isn't He?"

She smiled up into his face, twisting her fingers around one of his dark curls. "Yes, Dearest, He is. I wish it hadn't taken me so long to discover His goodness."

"But you did, and that's the important part. Oh, Aggie, even if God never allows us to be together on this earth, at least we know we'll be able to spend eternity together."

The smile left her face. "I know that, Jeb, but I want us to be together now. Every time we have to part, I cry. I can't help it. I want to be your wife in every way."

He stroked her cheek with the back of his hand. "You know I want that too, but we have to be patient, my love. Leaving you is hard on me too. You're in my thoughts night and day. We have to trust our Lord. If our love is real, and we both know it is, He'll make a way. I know God led me to you."

They spent the morning with Aggie playing the pump organ and Jeb singing Christmas carols and the old hymns of the church. At noon, her cook served them a delicious meal of Jeb's favorite foods. Baked hen, mashed potatoes, dried apples, freshly baked bread, and a thick pudding for dessert.

Aggie watched him across the table as the light from the candles reflected in his eyes. He was so handsome, with his pale blue eyes and his dark curly hair. His smile captivated her and held her prisoner each time she saw it and made her heart overflow with thankfulness.

"What?"

His single word brought her out of her thoughts, and she realized he'd been watching her too. "Nothing. I was just thinking how much I love you."

He reached across the table and took her hand in his. "No more than I love you, Aggie. You're my light, my sunshine, the very air I breathe. I'll never forget that day I met you. I'd never seen anyone as lovely, and I fell in love with you at that very moment."

She thought her heart would burst with joy at his words. "And I with you, Jeb. One look into those sky blue eyes of yours and I knew I'd never love anyone but you."

"I have something for you." He rose, extending his hand.

"Come with me." He led her into the parlor and motioned for her to be seated on the red velvet sofa.

"Not until I get your present." She scurried off to her room. She was back in no time and rushed to sit by him. "Open it." She held out a small box tied up with a red ribbon.

He laughed and held up a palm between them. "Ladies first."

"I insist, and remember what I told you when we first met? That I always got my way?"

After giving her a teasing smile, he took the box from her hands and untied the ribbon. Aggie found herself filled with excitement. Until she'd met Jeb, Christmas had always been centered around the gifts people gave her, with little concern for what she would give them. Looking back now, she realized she'd given her father very few gifts during their years together. Now, her father was gone. There were no presents for him, and it broke her heart.

She watched with anticipation as Jeb lifted the lid and pulled out the gold pocket watch that had been her grandfather's.

"Oh, Aggie, I can't accept this," he told her as he peered at the inscription. "This is a family heirloom!" He closed the lid, slid the shiny gold watch back into the box, and tried to hand it to her; but she refused to take it from him.

She felt herself beaming at him as her love for him overflowed. "I want you to have it, Jeb. I love you. You're my family now, or at least you will be when God answers our prayers."

"Are you that sure that He will, Aggie?"

"Yes! I've been reading His Word every day. There are all

sorts of promises in there, and I'm claiming them as my own. He said if we but have faith as the grain of a mustard seed. . . My faith is far bigger than that!" She pulled the pocket watch from the box and pressed it into his hand. "Please, Jeb. Keep it, for my sake."

He took the fine gold watch and slipped it into the watch pocket of the new trousers he'd purchased to wear along with the new shirt and boots Blackie had insisted he buy for Christmas Day, then gently kissed her cheek. "If you ever want it back, it's yours." He reached into his pocket and pulled out a small satin bag. "This is for you."

She gave him a demure smile as she took his gift and began to tug on the string closure, then pulled out a fine gold chain. "Oh, Jeb, it's so beautiful. Would you put it on me, please?"

Instead of taking it, as she'd thought he would, he shook his head. "Not yet." He reached into his pocket and pulled out a second satin bag. "Not until you open this one."

She frowned as she took it. Could it be a matching bracelet? But as she reached into the tiny bag, what she felt wasn't a bracelet; it was a ring. Her heart pounding, she hurriedly pulled it from the bag, eager to see what kind of ring he had bought for her, yet hoping he hadn't spent too much of his hard-earned money to buy her a gift. The lovely chain would have been enough. "It—it looks like a wedding band!"

"It is." Jeb took the shiny, gold ring from her hand and rotated it slowly as he read the inscription. "AW–JM. Aggie Wells and Jeb Monroe. Someday I want to place this ring on your finger and say, 'With this ring, Agatha Wells, I thee wed.' "

"Oh, Jeb, I–I want that t–too." Aggie had never had anything affect her so emotionally, and she couldn't help breaking out in tears.

"Don't you like it?" Jeb asked, his face filled with concern.

Having great difficulty putting her words together between sobs, she finally blurted out, "I lo–love it, Jeb. I love it. It's the most be–beautiful ring I've ever seen."

He smiled, took the chain from her, and slid the ring onto it. "I can't put it on your finger now, but I hope you will wear it around your neck until God answers my prayer and we. can stand before the preacher. I want to place it on your finger, look into your eyes, and say, 'With this ring, I thee wed,' my dear, sweet Aggie. I love you and want to commit my life to you."

Sobbing, she turned her back toward him and lifted her hair. "I'd rather wear it on my finger, but wearing it around my neck will be fine until—" She turned slightly and let a kiss fall onto his hand as he struggled with the clasp. "Until we become husband and wife," she finished.

"I love you, Aggie," Jeb said as he was finally able to fasten the necklace's tiny clasp. He kissed her neck, then nuzzled his face in her hair. "Merry Christmas, my love."

Smiling through her tears, she slipped her hand about his neck and pulled his face close to hers, then kissed his lips. "I love you too, Jeb. I want us to still be spending our Christmases together when we're old and gray and sitting side by side in rocking chairs with our grandchildren playing around at our feet."

"Me too."

❧

"I'm sorry I haven't been able to come to see you more often, Sweetheart," Jeb told Aggie five months later, "but I've been afraid to leave Blackie. He's feeling weak, and his heart has been paining him real bad. He won't eat, and he can't sleep. He's sick at his stomach most of the time. I'm—I'm so afraid he's going to die, and I don't know what I'll do without him. I'd like to bring him to see a doctor, but you know how stubborn he is. He says he wants to die up there on Utopia, lyin' right in that bed I made for him. He's even made me promise to bury him near the cabin in a hole we'd dug and then abandoned when we didn't find any gold. All he talks about now is how happy he will be when he is with God."

Aggie laid a consoling hand on his arm. "He's eighty-nine, Jeb. He's lived a good, long life. You've done all you can for him." She kissed him tenderly, then stroked his cheek. "Go to him, Jeb. He needs you, and give him my love."

Despite his desire to stay with her, Jeb backed away, pulled on his coat, and headed back to Utopia.

"Blackie, I'm back," he called out as he climbed the last few feet to the old man's shack and pushed open the door. He was surprised when Blackie didn't turn to face him or even acknowledge he'd heard him come in. Thinking the older man was asleep, he carefully pulled the tattered old quilt over Blackie's shoulders. As he did so, his fingers brushed against the man's face. It was cold. Too cold. Frantically, Jeb shook him, calling out, "Blackie, Blackie, speak to me. Oh, please, Blackie, don't leave me!"

Blackie didn't move.

"God, don't take him home yet, please!" In his heart, Jeb knew God had already called His servant home. Jeb would never hear Blackie's gruff voice again, not until he joined him in heaven.

The next morning, Jeb took his shovel and trudged to the place where Blackie wanted to be buried. He stared at the hole for a long time, wondering why Blackie had seen fit to fill it with broken branches and leaves instead of letting him fill it back in with rock and dirt like he'd wanted to. Well, it'd been Blackie's choice, and whatever he wanted was what Jeb wanted.

Wiping tears away as he worked, he pulled aside the branches and leaves, then took the shovel and began to dig a little deeper and square off the sides. He was smoothing out the bottom when his shovel hit something that didn't sound like a rock. He stepped down in the hole and knelt, using his fingers to brush away the loose dirt from the top of a large metal box.

Had Blackie placed it there? Is that why he didn't want the hole filled? Jeb worked the box loose and climbed out of the hole. He carried the box back inside and stood gazing at Blackie, lying so still on his bed.

"Is this yours, Blackie? What am I supposed to do with it?" In his heart, as if Blackie himself were speaking to him, Jeb could hear a voice saying, *Open it, Boy*. He pulled loose the little metal bar and opened the lid. What he saw took his breath away.

Chapter 5

Aggie, Aggie, quick! Let me in!" Jeb shouted as he pounded on the door with his fists. "Aggie!"

When she opened the door, Jeb rushed past her and placed the metal box on the table, then grabbed her up in his arms and circled about the room, swinging her high and laughing hysterically. "Praise the Lord, praise the Lord!"

"Jeb, what is it?"

"I'm so happy and so sad I barely know where to start!" He whirled her around once more, then sat her down on the sofa, dropping on his knees before her, holding tightly to both her hands. "When I got back to Utopia last night, Blackie was gone."

Her eyes widened. "Where did he go? I thought he was sick."

Tears formed in Jeb's eyes, but he continued to smile. "Home. To be with his Lord. The place he's been praying to go."

Aggie bowed her head and began to cry. "Jeb, I don't understand. I know you loved that old man. How can you be happy?"

"He did it, Aggie! He wanted us to be together. He made it possible for us to get married." He stroked her hands with his thumbs. "You must think I'm crazy. Let me explain. When I got back to Utopia last night, Blackie—well, he'd already gone to be with the Lord." He gave her hands a squeeze. "Remember when I told you he'd already picked out the place where he wanted to be buried and had made me promise to bury him there?"

She nodded, blinking at her tears. "I remember."

"Feeling obliged to do as he'd asked, I took my shovel out to that very spot and cleaned out the hole. And you can't imagine what happened. I found a metal box. Blackie had put it there! Let me show it to you, Aggie." He grabbed the box and pulled open the lid.

Aggie gasped. Her hands went to her mouth, and her eyes widened. "Jeb! It's nearly full of gold! Where did it come from?"

Jeb pulled a paper from his pocket and began to read:

Dear Jeb,

You probably wonder why I never told you about all this gold. I had my reasons. You see, in 1848, right after I heard Marshall had discovered all that gold up near Coloma, I headed up that way and staked me out a claim and began lookin'. I worked my claim from sunup to sundown every day for nearly a month, and I found gold all right. One of the richest veins I'd ever heard tell of. I kept my find to myself, Jeb. I didn't tell a soul, and I kept finding more and more gold. It was there for the takin'.

Amazed by his story, Jeb could only shake his head.

I told myself I didn't have many more years, and the work was gettin' me down in the back, so I packed up and left Coloma and came down here to this place. My needs were small. I didn't have any use for all that gold, so I decided if I ever found a young man who was willing to work as hard as I had and loved my God as much as I did, I was gonna leave it all to him.

I took my big Bible, and I went through town, wavin' it around and shouting out Scripture. I figured if there was a young man like that around, he'd come to me and tell me he loved God's Word too. But none ever came, and I was about to give up. I didn't need any of this world's goods. Everything I needed was right up here at Utopia, but what was I gonna do with all that gold? I even considered puttin' it right back in the ground and burying it.

Then I met you, Jeb. You were the answer to my prayers, but I had to be sure you were the kind of man who could handle being wealthy and not turn away from God. I was testing you, Boy, and you passed every test. I knew there wasn't much gold there where you and me was diggin', but I had to know you'd stand by me. You worked with me every day, carryin' the biggest load, and you never asked nothin' of me. You knew your Scripture too. Almost as much as me. Then your attentions turned toward Aggie, and for awhile there, I thought I was gonna lose you. But you stayed true. And that Aggie of yours won my heart too.

Aggie leaned close and rested her head on Jeb's shoulder.

"Oh, Jeb. I didn't know. No wonder he seemed to resent me."

"That was his sinful nature coming out, Aggie. Let me read on.

> I rejoiced with you when God answered your prayers and she gave her heart to God. I could've given you this gold then, and the two of you could have been married; but I had to be sure your love would last. You two are from different worlds.
>
> And for the first time in my life, Jeb, I became a selfish old man. I couldn't bear the idea of finishing my last mile without you, so I convinced myself to keep my gold until I died. I knew my time on this earth wasn't to be long. That's why I made you promise to bury me in that hole. I knew, that way, you'd find the metal box. Inside is more than enough to take care of your beautiful Aggie and buy that house for your mother.
>
> You're a good boy, Jeb. My life has been richer for knowing you. Marry Aggie, you two have a good life together, and stay close to God. And promise you won't forget old Blackie.

Two days later, Jeb and Aggie stood over a mound of dirt and wept. After Jeb read aloud from Blackie's old tattered Bible, he placed a hand-carved wooden cross at one end while Aggie sprinkled fresh flowers across the grave.

"I'm going to miss him," Jeb said as he pulled his love into his arms. "God, in His infinite wisdom, brought Blackie and me together. His hand was upon that old man, Aggie. Now, Blackie's with his heavenly Father."

Jeb stared at Blackie's grave. "He never talked about his family, except to say his mother and father had been gone for many years. I often wondered if his mother made that old, faded quilt he keeps in that box in the corner. Sad, isn't it? That no one seemed to care if he lived or died?"

"You cared." Aggie snuggled up close to him. "I loved him too. I just wish he could be here for our wedding."

"And he loved you." A tear rolled down Jeb's face as he kissed her cheek. "He made it possible for us to be together. If it weren't for him and what he—"

Aggie put a finger to his lips. "But Jeb, I didn't need Blackie's gold. I would have married you and lived up here with you in this shack. I hope you know that."

He smiled down at her. "I do know that now, Aggie. The love we have found together is far more precious than gold."

Epilogue

Two years later

I love you." Jeb wrapped an arm about his wife and pulled her close, touching her cheek with his and taking in the sweet fragrance of her hair. "Happy anniversary, Aggie."

Aggie stood on tiptoes and kissed her husband's cheek. "Happy anniversary to you, my darling. I love you even more today than I did the day we were married. God has been good to us, hasn't He?"

" 'Abundantly above all that we ask or think.' " He took her hand in his, lifted it to his lips, and tenderly planted a kiss on the gold band on her finger. "This ring symbolizes my love for you, Aggie. I'll never forget the day I was finally able to place it on your finger. I'd never been so happy."

Aggie gazed up at him. "God meant us to be together, Jeb."

He reached into his pocket and pulled out a small velvet box. "To commemorate our two years together."

"Oh, Jeb, I don't need a gift. Just being with you is enough."

89

"Open it, Aggie. I want you to have it." He watched with anticipation as she lifted the lid. "It's a gold locket to go on that chain I gave you."

Misty-eyed, she pulled the locket from the box and held it to her bosom. "Oh, Jeb. You are so sweet. I don't deserve you."

A baby's cry quickly brought the pair's attention to their six-month-old son, who lay in the crib Jeb had made from some of the oak he'd found near Utopia.

"Shh! Blackie. Don't cry. Daddy's here." Jeb quickly bent over the crib and proudly picked up his son, cradling him in the crook of his arm. Then turning to his wife with a look of melancholy, he added, "If only Blackie had lived long enough to see his namesake."

"I know." Aggie leaned into her husband and kissed the baby's pink cheek. "I like to think that old man is looking down from heaven with those beady eyes of his and smiling at us."

"I hope you're right. I never had a chance to tell him how much I loved him." Jeb blinked and swallowed hard. "Thanks to him, we have a wonderful life here in Sacramento, and my parents are happy living in their new house. God's been good to us, Aggie."

❧

At sunrise the next morning, Jeb rode up to Utopia alone, to the place he'd buried his friend. With a heart full of gratitude, looking heavenward and holding up Blackie's old, tattered Bible, he called out loudly into the wind as he'd seen Blackie do so many times both at Utopia and on the streets of Sacramento, " 'To every thing there is a season, and a time to every purpose under the heaven: A time to be born, and a time to die.' One generation passeth away, and another generation cometh."

He tipped his hat and spread Blackie's old tattered quilt across the grave. "I love you, Blackie. May your memory live on in my son."

JOYCE LIVINGSTON

Joyce is a real Kansas "lady" who lives in a little cabin that her husband built overlooking a lake. She is a proud grandmother who retired from television broadcasting, and now keeps very busy writing stories of love and laughter. She is also a part-time tour escort, which takes her to all kinds of fantastic places. She has had books and articles published on a number of subjects. In 2000, she was voted **Heartsong Presents'** favorite new author. Two of her **Heartsong Presents** books were named favorite contemporary book of the year, in 2000 and 2002. She feels her writing is a ministry and a calling from God, and hopes readers will be touched and uplifted by what she writes. Joyce loves to hear from her readers and invites you to visit her on the Internet at: www.joycelivingston.com

Band of Angel's

by Cathy Marie Hake

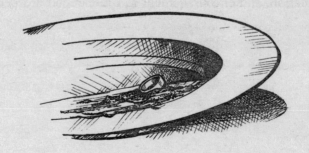

Dedication

To Deb.
We went to countless museums and libraries,
toured a mine, and even panned for gold.
The real treasure of it all has been your friendship.

Acknowledgments

I'd like to thank Knott's Berry Farm in Buena Park,
California, and Bill Jones at the Old Hundred Gold Mine in
Silverton, Colorado. They generously provided guidance,
information, and encouragement as I researched prospecting.

Chapter 1

Colorado, 1893

Gold!

Jarrod McLeod stared at his pan in disbelief. The very first time he'd slipped his pan in the creek, and he'd struck gold. Oh, this was no fool's gold. Then again, it wasn't a nugget or a few bright flakes. There, gleaming in his rusty, second-hand pan, was a small wedding band.

"Well, now I'll be!" he marveled aloud as he gently brushed away some silt and pinched the woman's ring between his fingers. He set aside the pan, carefully rinsed the ring in the icy stream, and squinted to take a closer look at the treasure. Plain it was—a wee bit lopsided from having been on the owner's finger for many a year. Sun glinted off the smooth surface of the band, making it sparkle all the more.

He read the inscription inside. "AW & JM."

A mule brayed behind him. Jarrod carefully tucked the ring into his shirt pocket, rose, and headed toward the beast. "You'll have to be forgiving me, Beulah. Prospecting fever, don't you know. A man stakes a claim, and he loses most of his sense."

The mule twitched her ears and danced to the side. The pack on her back held half of Jarrod's earthly goods. He quickly loosened a rope and relieved her of the burden. She waited as he unloaded Otto, and both mules plodded across the hard, spring ground to the stream. After they drank their fill, Jarrod secured them to a line he tied between two sturdy pines. "You beasts behave yourselves, and I'll be giving you a carrot for supper."

The bundles on the ground made for a goodly sized mess. Jarrod toed one bundle out of his way and looked about his new home. After spending the last six hours trying to locate the right claim and dealing with prospectors who thought he was a claim jumper, he had little patience for sorting through his gear, but grit and a dream kept him going. Determination would get him through the next several months. Once he coaxed enough gold dust from the claim, he'd head off and buy himself a pretty little start-up ranch. Yes, a nifty place where a man could put down roots, work his back sore and his hands raw, and smile every last minute while doing it.

A means to an end. This plot along the creek was nothing more than a means to achieve his dream. With that thought in mind, the pickax, shovel, and pans looked mighty fine. He'd work himself morning, noon, and night. No foolishness, either—he'd seen his share of men drink away their hard work or get cheated out of it at a card table. Lonely miners and placers went to town and consorted with shady women or paid unheard of sums for a decent meal. Well, not Jarrod McLeod.

He'd walked the length of the creek bank first thing. Quartz rock along it hinted that the area held gold. So did the fine-grained black sand. An occasional greenish streak in the boulders spoke of copper—another good sign since he'd read copper and quartz often lay alongside gold. Hard work and a lot of prayer, and this claim might well yield enough to put him back in a saddle.

The saddest-looking lean-to a man ever threw together sat over on the west side of the camp. Jarrod scowled at it and muttered, "Looks like the keys on a burned harpsichord." The old fellow who sold this claim to him had boasted it held a solid structure. Solid? Ha. Two logs stuck out of the ground and stood just over four feet tall. Lashed between them was a single, thick, six-foot stick. The whole affair sagged under the weight of about two dozen logs that sloped against it to form the one and only wall. A stiff gust would probably blast apart the pathetic pile.

The air smelled like rain, so Jarrod didn't spend time moaning. He'd not be able to take shelter under that—he'd best put his hand to fixing up something habitable. He stalked over to the lean-to's wall and gave the closest edge a few brutal kicks. Spiders and beetles scuttled away as three of the logs rolled and thudded into the dirt. The other logs jumped to and fro, completely unsecured to the rickety frame.

He stood back and looked at the mess, then felt the wind pick up. Another glance at the sky let him know he had just a few hours of light left, and the rain might well come before dark. "I'd best get down to business if I want to stay dry."

Jarrod tore it all apart, leveled the ground, and cut down

two lodgepole pines. By notching and stacking the new logs and adding them to the ones from the lean-to, he built a tiny, three-sided hut. He made the side walls shorter, but the seven-foot-long back wall allowed him to lie full length and stack his viands in a place that ought to stay dry. So far, the dwelling—such as it was—barely measured four feet high. Jail cells measured bigger. He'd run out of light and logs, though.

Jarrod hastily draped canvas over a pole he stuck in the center of the floor and weighted it outside the walls with handy rocks as the first raindrops fell. He strode off a few paces to take a quick look at the results of his labor. His "cabin" didn't look like a jail cell anymore: It looked more like the circus tent he'd seen back East.

Back sore and hands blistered, Jarrod sat beneath his newly constructed shelter. Rain pattered off the canvas and slid outside the cabin. He warmed his hands around a cup of scorched coffee and stared at the flickering lamp. Other men might find it odd that a wee chain of daisies danced about the globe, but Ella had loved that lamp, and it was all he had left of her other than his memories. She'd shared his dream of the ranch, and he wanted to put her lamp on the kitchen table someday in her honor. Until then, with Ella's memory in his heart and God in his soul, he counted himself a rich man.

❧

Angel Taylor stood by the boiling pot and shaved one more curl of homemade lye soap into the water. She shoved four shirts into the water, thrust in a wooden paddle, and agitated the smelly contents of the cauldron. A few more pokes, and she set down the paddle. Mud caked the pile of britches at her side. She dragged them down to the river, rinsed the worst of the dirt from them, leaned over her corrugated washboard, and scrubbed stubborn dark spots on the seat and knees of each pair.

"I'm hungry, Girl. What're you fixin' to do? Starve me half to death?"

Angel gritted her teeth to keep from snapping back at her stepfather. Not once had he asked how Mama was faring. Her cot had creaked all night because of her wracking cough. Nothing Angel did seemed to lessen Mama's misery, but Ben's callous disregard certainly made it worse. At least he'd caught fish this morning, so they'd have something more than rice and beans to eat.

"Girl, I asked you 'bout dinner!" His pan clanged on the rocky ground as he tossed it down.

"Rice is boiling. Soon as I rinse out the shirts and hang them to dry, I'll fry up the trout."

"Shoulda seen to my meal afore you got them shirts started."

Wiping back a damp curl that fell on her forehead, she called, "It won't be long."

Half an hour later, several garments hung on the clothesline, and Angel handed a pie tin of rice and fish to her stepfather. If she changed into her other skirt, this one would have enough time to dry by nightfall; but she dismissed that fleeting thought. She refused to risk waking Mama by slipping into the tent. Besides, as soon as lunch was over, Angel would be knee deep in the water again. Days like today, she felt sure she'd never be warm again.

"Ten shirts, six pair of britches, and five balbriggans." Her stepfather spoke with his mouth full and pointed his fork at the laundry neighboring prospectors dropped off. "I reckon that'll barely keep us in beans and coffee for a week or so. Ain't you got a couple of flour sacks you can stitch into a shirt to sell? That'll give us some fatback."

They'd had this conversation two weeks ago. Angel's jaw hardened. "I need one more sack so I can make myself a new skirt. I only have two, and they're both ragged."

"Nobody here to see and court you. A new skirt's a waste. A man's shirt—well. . ." He drew out the word with relish. "A shirt, that could bring in enough to make a real difference 'round here. Gotta pull together, Angel. We're family."

"This wouldn't be a problem if you'd have grubstaked us for the winter."

"I ain't begging others for food, and I won't be beholden to any man."

Angel tugged at her wet sleeve. "Since today is the third day in a row that I've done laundry, we have money. You could take it to town and get Mama medicine. She needs tonic and a cough elixir, and we need—"

"Enough!" He stood and stomped toward the river.

Angel sand-scoured and rinsed the plates. The wind shifted, and she caught a faint whiff of coffee from a neighboring claim. The scent made her mouth water. She remembered how she used to have parties with Mama and Grandma where they'd set the table with fine linen and china. As a treat, they'd allow her to have coffee with plenty of cream and sugar. When she'd come to Colorado with Mama and Ben, she'd learned to drink it black. The next year, she'd watered it down to stretch their meager supplies. This past winter, they'd run out.

During the winter, folks didn't have laundry done—they wore every last garment they owned in an attempt to stay warm. As a result, her stepfather had run out of money, and they were perilously low on supplies. Now that spring had arrived and she was doing laundry again, it stood to reason they could spare some money for Mama's medicine.

Harvey Bestler and Pete Kane came back for their laundry. Pete paid her stepfather the laundry fee and wandered off. Harv went on into the tent, took off his only other pair of britches, and tossed them out. "Go on ahead and scrub those today. I'll just take 'em wet and hang 'em from a tree."

"I'd better not." Angel bit her lip and looked away. "The britches on the line need mending."

"I can wait."

She scrubbed the grimy pants and rinsed them, then hung them close to the fire in hopes that they'd dry a little while she mended the others. Her sewing box already sat on a stump because she'd had to stitch on a button. She sat down and applied her needle to the threadbare pants. As she jabbed the needle into the fabric, she promised herself, "I'm only staying to take care of Mama. I don't have to stay after. . ."

Chapter 2

"A ngel, I've spent half the day here and given you good cash money. Now give me back my pants."

Jarrod heard the baritone from inside one of the two tents and turned to leave. He wanted nothing to do with a shady lady or her customer. The dainty wedding ring in his pocket couldn't possibly belong to this woman, whoever she was.

"A man's always glad to keep company with a pretty gal like you, but I really do got to go. A fella's gotta work."

"Here you go," a sweet voice said. "They're mended, but I don't expect that patch to hold for long. Next time you're in town, you'd better get some cloth. I'll stitch you a new pair for cheaper than you can buy them."

Jarrod stopped in his tracks. Guilt rushed through him. Maybe he'd been wrong in his assumptions, and if so, he'd been wrong to judge and condemn the woman. He tromped back around the stream side of the camp and spied several garments fluttering on a clothesline. From the variety in size, he deduced she did laundry as well as sewing. Yes, he'd been wrong. It was a good reminder not to judge.

Jarrod glanced around. The campsite rated as Spartan as his own. Two sun-bleached canvas tents sagged near a stand of trees—undoubtedly located there in hopes that they would provide a windbreak. An outdoor cook fire seemed to also double as the laundry site. Stumps served as seats, yet not a single felled tree lay about or formed a structure. They must have used the rest of the wood for fuel. They were panning at the creek side instead of using a rocker box. Perhaps these folks were new arrivals too. If so, this woman was quite enterprising to start up a business right away.

Jarrod patted his pocket and determined to see if this was the ring's owner. She'd probably be delighted to have it back. Women put stock in sentimental things like that.

"You need help, Mister?"

Jarrod turned around and froze. An unkempt man stood all of four feet away, and he had the business end of a rifle aimed right at Jarrod.

"Just what're you doin', skulking around here?"

"I'm, um. . ." Jarrod cleared his throat. "I'm your new neighbor. I have the adjoining claim. Downstream."

"You take me for a fool? Pete Kane was here today already, and Charlie has the claim just beside us on this side of the creek. We don't want no trouble, and we don't cotton to claim jumpers, so you can just hike right back outta here."

"Hang on, Ben." A man came out of the tent, adjusting his suspenders. "Charlie told me he was cashing in. Could be this man's not trying anything fast."

"I have the deed." Jarrod didn't move an inch. Hostility shimmered in the eyes of the man holding the gun, and he hadn't lowered the weapon.

"Father," a pretty blond woman said as she rounded the tent and stopped next to the grouch. She cast a quick glance at Jarrod and pushed the barrel of the rifle toward the ground. "He's not armed."

"Could have a gun back behind his belt." The rifle jerked back upward, its aim directed at Jarrod's midsection. "Might be he has a knife strapped to his leg."

"A fella would be ten times a fool to go 'bout unarmed," the man from beside the tent agreed.

"So he's either a claim jumper or a fool. Some fine howdy you men give to a new neighbor." The tiny woman stepped directly in front of the weapon. "I'm Angel Taylor. Behind me is my stepfather, Ben Frisk, and over by the tent is Harv Bestler. Sorry for the poor welcome. Folks here tend to shoot first and ask questions later—if they bother to ask at all."

Jarrod gave her a grateful smile and dipped his head in greeting. "Jarrod McLeod. It's a pure pleasure to be meeting you, Mrs. Taylor." He didn't lie and say he was glad to meet the two men. Neither seemed the neighborly type. "I came as far as the pine with my weapon but left it there as a sign of good will."

Harvey rose on the toes of his battered boots and craned his neck. "I don't see nuth—what in the world? A bow? You sound funny, but you don't look like no redskin I ever saw."

"You in league with them?" Ben asked. "We got these claims legal. You ain't takin'—"

"Now hold on. I'm a placer, just like the both of you. Bought my claim, aim to work it, and hope to make a go of things."

While he spoke, Jarrod noticed how Angel's jaw hardened. He didn't know what he'd said wrong, but he'd stepped amiss again. These folks were bristly as hedgehogs.

He shrugged. "I can see you folks are trying to settle in too."

"We been here three, almost four years now." Ben finally took his finger off the trigger.

Jarrod tried not to show his surprise. Other than the tents, no shelter could be seen. "So you're seasoned placers. It's good to have neighbors who know the ropes."

"Wasted 'nuff time jawin'." Ben swished his hand in the air as if he were swatting a bothersome gnat. "Git along."

Harv slapped a battered gray felt hat on his greasy hair, picked up a small bundle of clothes, and nodded at Angel. "You done a fine job, Gal." He then tromped straight across the creek and into a tiny shack that leaned precariously toward one side.

Jarrod jammed his hand in his pocket and felt the smooth gold ring. He didn't want to waste a lot of time tracking down the owner, but he'd worn out his nonexistent welcome.

Ask. Just ask, a small voice inside urged.

He cleared his throat. "Um, I was wondering if you could be so kind as to tell me—are there other women upriver?"

Angel's cheeks went scarlet.

Horrified that she'd misconstrued his meaning, Jarrod yanked the ring from his pocket and held it out. "I found this. I'm wanting to return it to its rightful owner. I'm sure the lady is heartbroken at the loss."

For a brief instant, unmistakable recognition lit Angel's eyes. In a spontaneous move of joy, she began to reach for the ring, but Ben's growl halted her move. Every speck of color bled from Angel's face. Jarrod watched her flinch and immediately shoved the ring deep into his pocket. "If you hear anything, please let me know."

Ben turned to Angel. "Is that what I think it is?"

"I'm sure hundreds of women wear wedding bands just like it." Jarrod realized he'd managed to get the woman into trouble and strove to say something to let her off the hook.

Angel's stepfather wheeled back around and blustered, "Lemme see that ring."

Jarrod noticed how she folded her arms around her ribs and subtly shook her head. Her wide hazel eyes pleaded with him. He didn't understand what was going on, but he refused to act against the lady's wishes.

When Jarrod didn't hand over the ring, Ben Frisk banged the butt of his rifle into the ground in a show of rage. "Girl, that was worth money. Coulda had us coffee all winter if I'd pawned it."

"Miss Angel, if you're the rightful owner, I'm more than willing to return it."

"She's the owner, all right! Letters scraped inside it'll prove I'm right."

Angel shook her head. "It's not mine anymore. I don't want it."

"If you change your mind—"

"Oh, she's a-changin' it right this very minute!"

Angel shook her head again. Sunlight glinted off the strands of her hair, making her glimmer. "Mr. McLeod has rightful claim on that gold. Whatever a man finds on his claim is his."

Chapter 3

G al, yore stupid as you are stubborn."

Angel ducked her head and scrubbed the frying pan a little harder. Ever since her grandma's wedding band had come loose from where Angel tacked it to the hem of her ragged skirt, she'd been heartbroken. It took everything inside of her not to take it back when that new neighbor offered it to her—but the minute her stepfather found out she'd gotten it back, he'd take and pawn it.

Ben had been in a terrible mood since she refused to take back the ring. Three days of listening to his grumblings and rants left her nerves as tightly strung as a new clothesline. He cared more about gold than anything or anyone. Lung fever had hold of Mama; gold fever claimed Ben.

"Coulda had a nice hunk of fatback and coffee for weeks, but you ruint it all. Got yourself of a mind to have a conniption. I'm a-tellin' you, Missy, yore gonna use them flour sacks to make a shirt. After what you done, you don't deserve no new skirt. Took the food right outta my mouth."

"I'm not making a shirt." She stared him straight in the eye. Standing, she spread out her skirt. "Take a good look. I've patched this as best I can, but the hem's ragged and it has dozens of little burned spots from embers. My other one is even worse."

"Ain't no fancy cotillion here. You got what you need."

"No, I don't. With Mama's help, we barely got everything done and pulled in enough gold to keep going. She listened to your dream about striking it rich and said a woman had to follow her man. Well, look what your big plans did to her—she's deathly ill." She swept her hand toward the tent, then gestured toward the creek in utter disgust. "Instead of thinking about how to help her recover, all you can do is squat over there, lusting for more gold."

"Enough!" He bolted to his feet. "Your mama knows her place. Good thing she's not out here to see how yore behavin'." He snatched his hat off a stump, spanked it against a thigh, and slapped it on his head.

Tears obscured Angel's view of her stepfather's back as he knelt and began to pan for gold. "How could you say such a terrible thing?" she whispered. "If you loved her, how could you think it's a good thing she's so sick, she can't even get up anymore?"

Smoke from the cook fire blew into her face, causing the tears to overflow. Angel didn't want her stepfather to witness her tears, so she plodded to the water's edge. She favored this spot because she could turn her back to her stepfather and let the wind blow his mutterings the other direction. A few deep breaths and a swipe of her hand, and all evidence of her teary moment was gone.

An eddy of water swirled into the tiny curve of the shore, and she plunged her pan into it. No matter how often she did this, the icy water came as a shock. Angel shivered as she agitated the pan. Neck, back, arms, and legs all cramped from working to coax anything of value from the creek. The weak spring sun rose higher in the sky, and she shifted a bit to lessen the glare from the water.

"Miss Taylor, you make doing that look easy."

Angel twisted to the side as she gasped.

"I didn't mean to startle you," Mr. McLeod said in his rich Scots burr. He gave her a rakish smile. "If you're of a mind to forgive the intrusion, I was hoping we might come to an agreement."

Angel set aside her pan, carefully covering the tiny dish containing the flecks she'd gotten during the long morning. A quiver full of arrows over his right shoulder reminded her of one of the tales Mama used to tell her. . .*Robin Hood*, she remembered. The brace of rabbits he held made her stomach rumble in the most unladylike way. "What kind of agreement?"

"Whilst building my shack, I ripped the knee on my britches. If you have a dozen nails, I could surely use them too."

"You've built a home?"

He chuckled. "Home is a fancy description. 'Tis a wee place, but it'll serve."

"I heard your ax biting through logs, but I presumed Charlie didn't leave any firewood."

Bootfalls announced they had company. Her stepfather came up, put a proprietary hand on her shoulder, and scowled. "What do you want?"

Mr. McLeod casually repositioned the beautiful bow on his shoulder. "I came to barter. I'd like Miss Taylor to mend the knee of my britches and would appreciate a dozen or so nails from you."

Ben squeezed her shoulder, telling her to stay silent. "Nails? They're dear out here."

Mr. McLeod nodded. "In town, they were seven cents a pound."

"It'll waste half a day, you going to town and comin' back. Even if I figgered two cents apiece on those four rabbits, you ain't got enough to trade for the nails and my gal doing your mending."

Angel choked back a cry and plastered a smile on her face. She wriggled away from her stepfather and clasped her hands behind her back. "But those look to be plump rabbits—especially for it being spring. Besides, Mr. McLeod isn't just anybody; he's our nearest neighbor. I think three rabbits, and we've struck a fair bargain."

"Four," Ben rasped angrily.

"Four," Angel repeated as she stepped forward and reached for the rabbits. "And Mr. McLeod joins us for supper."

Mr. McLeod's bright blue eyes twinkled. "Now there's a bargain made in paradise."

❧

Jarrod hiked back over for supper after sunset. Ben had made it clear he wasn't about to waste any daylight with socializing. How pretty Miss Taylor managed to endure her stepfather's sour disposition rated as a true mystery. In the past few days,

Ben's strident voice had carried in the crisp air, and most of what he said revolved around wanting meat and coffee. *And I made it worse by letting him know she lost that gold ring.*

Jarrod marveled at the fact that they were out of such essential supplies. Miners got paid an hourly wage; placers who panned their own claims didn't have reliable income, so they usually got the mercantile owner or a townie to grubstake them. He'd had two offers from business owners, and the man at the land office even offered the names of a few more. Though no one seemed to become rich overnight along this creek, the claims produced enough to keep merchants interested in a cut of the take.

Savory aromas wafted past him. So did the sound of someone coughing. Jarrod called ahead to keep Ben from grabbing his rifle. "Oh, something's smelling wonderful!"

"Pull up a stump," Angel invited as she stepped out of one of the tents. She held a spoon and tin mug. "Supper will be ready in just a few minutes."

"Go dip your mug in the creek, McLeod," Ben mumbled. "Ain't got nothing better or stronger to drink."

Jarrod collected the three mugs by the fire and filled them with bracingly cold water. He paused for a moment on the way back, then handed one to Ben. "Looks like you're starting a garden."

"Angel's messin' with it." He snagged the first plate Angel dished up.

Angel's cheeks went a beguiling scarlet as she gave Jarrod an apologetic look. He continued to stand until Angel had food on both of the other tin plates. "You're a clever lass to be gardening, Miss Taylor. Why, canned vegetables and fruits were higher than ten cats' backs. I bought me some seeds, hopin' to come up wi' sufficient to keep my slats apart."

She tried to give him his plate, but he still held a cup in each hand. Jarrod chortled as he turned his palm upward and held both cups in that one hand. "There, then. I think we can make a go of this."

Once Angel sat on an overturned crate, Jarrod perched on the tree stump and smiled at her. She lowered her lashes in an innately modest reaction, but it wasn't for prayer because she grabbed her fork. Ben was already eating, so Jarrod came to the realization that they didn't bless their food. He quietly bowed his head and said a silent grace.

"These are the first dandelion greens for the year," he said in appreciation.

" 'Bout time we had something different." Ben scooped up a forkful of food. "Sick of eating this rice."

"To my way of thinkin', rice always tastes good—but this gravy on it makes it better still." Jarrod helped himself to another bite. "Looks like you used some kind of herbs on the rabbit."

"I had a little basil and rosemary dried from last year."

"The mercantile owner's wife insisted I take a packet of herbs," Jarrod said. "Only thing I know to do is use cayenne to keep animals from digging into the garden or henhouse."

"I could give you a few pointers on what herbs are suited to different things," Angel offered.

"I'd be much obliged. I figure since my cabin's finished, I'll pan for a few days, then put in the garden."

Angel leaned forward. "Did you hear that, Father?" Her voice sounded a bit strained. "Mr. McLeod has already built himself a fine little log cabin. It'll be so warm and safe."

"I tole you afore, no use wastin' time on those projects when we got us our tents."

Jarrod looked at the pair of tents. The canvas looked old and tired. He seriously doubted it could last through the sun and snow of another year without rotting clean through. "I'd be willing to spend a day or two to help you. If we gathered a few other men, we could have a wee place—"

"Not interested," Ben interrupted. "Satisfied with how things stand."

"Well I'm not." Angel clenched her hands in her lap. "Mama needs better shelter, and I don't want to be cold and hungry anymore."

"You ain't cold. You already changed into your dry skirt. Got plenty of blankets, don't you?"

Jarrod gave her a startled look. "Your mother is here?"

Angel stared at Jarrod pleadingly. "She's sick—terribly sick—and needs decent shelter. What could I trade you? I'll sew for you. I'll do your laundry forever—"

Ben raised his hand. "Hold on here. You git paid for them chores so's we can buy vittles. Cain't go givin' away valu'ble work."

"I'm making a fair barter."

Jarrod frowned. "I shouldn't think it would cause discord for me to lend a hand so your wife has decent lodging."

"It's been a sore point between us since the day we arrived," Angel said. "I'm sorry you're having to hear this—"

"You ain't sorry atall. You're stirrin' the pot so's it'll boil over and you can git what you want."

"I'm trying to make a fair trade so I can get what Mama needs." Angel turned back to Jarrod. "Please—just tell me what you think would be fair."

Ben lifted the piece of rabbit and bit off a huge mouthful. His glower could start a bonfire. "Go ahead. Me? I don't need nothin' other than what I got. Build them somethin'. Mebbe then she'll quit her whining."

Chapter 4

"A ch! Now will you be lookin' at what I did?" Jarrod lifted his right arm and stuck his left forefinger through the rip in his sleeve.

Angel walked over toward the home he'd been working on alone. Never once had her stepfather offered a hand. Every log felled, notched, lifted, and fitted testified to Jarrod's kindness. Her father insisted he'd never step foot in such a folly and demanded it only be big enough for a bed for Mama and her. She'd agreed—all they needed was a warm place to lay their heads. Jarrod insisted that cutting the logs two or three feet shorter wouldn't save him any labor, so what she'd thought would be a bitty shack was turning out to be a sound little cabin.

Jarrod's callused finger wiggled through the ripped fabric. "I did a royal job of tearing this to kingdom come."

"It's not so bad." Angel inspected the damage. "Just a bit of stitching, and it'll be serviceable for a long time yet."

"Easy for you to say such a thing. You've needles, thread, and talent aplenty. Me? I'm beggared on all three accounts."

"It's my cabin you're making; it's only right I repair your shirt. I'll have it done in a trice."

"Nae, Lass. We already struck a fair bargain for my labor."

She whispered emphatically, "It's far more than we agreed upon. I was to have a roof over Mama's head, and you're making me a—a—a rainbow!"

He chuckled. "If 'tis a rainbow, the both of you'll be swimming inside at the first rain if I don't get that roof on it." He pulled his finger out of the hole and moved the arm with the torn sleeve behind his back. "You'll not take a single stitch unless we come to an understanding. Just as your stepfather refuses to be beholden, so do I."

"Piffle! It's nothing!"

He pulled away and gave her an indignant look. "Angel, you need to value yourself and your work. God created a wonderful, talented lass in you. Modesty is a fine quality, but denying the value of one of His gems is pure silliness."

Angel looked up at him and felt an odd glow. How long had it been since anyone told her she was special? Long ago. . . back before her stepfather moved them here. Her cousins, Philip and Gabe, for all of their teasing, still treated her like a princess. When the day came for her to depart, each of them had managed to pull her away for a moment and say something dear to her. In the everyday scramble and hardship of settling and surviving here, the niceties of compliments disappeared.

Niceties. That was it. Jarrod McLeod managed to bring a touch of gentleness and decency along with him. His rich burr made each word sound important and sincere. Oh, and how he spoke! He'd gone in to meet Mama, and never once did his kind face reflect dismay or disgust at how sallow and frail she was. The big man no more than reached Mama's cot, and he'd gone down on his knees instead of towering over her. He'd paid his respects as if she were an important lady and the tattered tent were a fine mansion. He'd murmured quietly, given Mama a few sweet moments of pleasant company, then held up her head and given her a sip of broth. Touched to the core of her being at his incredible kindness, Angel barely managed to choke back her tears when he tucked the blankets up as if Mama were his very own.

Better still, each time he came over, he paid Mama a short visit. Ben refused to allow any Bible reading, but Jarrod got around that by quietly reciting a few verses he'd memorized, then he'd whisper a brief prayer that invariably left a smile on Mama's face.

Now. . .now he stood here, smiling at Angel and calling her a gem. She'd thought God had forgotten about her. In all of the ugliness of the past years, she'd let her spirits sink. Her relationship with the Almighty had practically dwindled away to nothingness. But here Jarrod stood, calling her a gem of God.

"I'm not a gem," she blurted out. "Mama and I sometimes pray together, but I don't think God even listens to us anymore." She hung her head and wished she hadn't ruined everything with that confession.

"Lass, our heavenly Father hears you." Soft as a breeze, Jarrod's voice reached her, but underneath the quiet tone was rock-solid certainty. "His children aren't spared hardship, but He stands beside them in their trials. Your faith might have withered a bit on the vine, but a bit of tending, and it'll flourish."

"I wish I had your faith."

"Faith is for sharing." He tilted her face up to his. The kindness in his eyes sparked something deep inside. "I'll gladly share mine with you."

The rip in his sleeve caught her attention again. "Then I'll share my needle with you."

Jarrod's brow furrowed and his eyes narrowed as he gave consideration to the matter. Suddenly his eyes brightened and he gave her a cocky grin. "I have it."

"What do you have?" *Oh, why did I ask? I wanted to mend his shirt as a favor—not for gain.*

"Well now, I'm hoping you'll not be offended by my paltry offer. Seeing as you're restoring wear to my shirt, what if I barter a used skirt for it?"

"A skirt?" What was he doing with a skirt? The very question made her cringe. She'd simply assumed he was alone and unmarried. Could he have a wife waiting for him somewhere?

"My Ella, God bless her soul, was sick a good long while. After she passed on, I just bundled her clothes up."

"I'm so sorry for your loss." *No wonder he's so good with Mama even though she's ailing.* "How long were you married?"

"Married?" He chuckled. "Oh, no. Ella was my sister. We had grand plans to start up a ranch."

"Then why are you prospecting instead?"

His face went pensive. "After payin' the doctor's fees, my pockets were pretty nigh unto empty. I'm not going to spend my whole life standing knee-deep in chilly water, Angel. My dream hasna changed one iota. I'll stay here only 'til I have enough to buy me a sweet plot of land."

"Plenty of men say that, but then they succumb to gold fever."

He positioned another nail, then hammered it in place with a single, solid whack. "The forefathers of this fine country might hae said all men were created equal, Angel, but that doesna mean they were all created the same. Money isn't wealth. It canna buy love or happiness or health."

She stared at him in silence as he worked.

"So?" He turned and looked at her. "Are you willing to accept the barter of a skirt? I've three shirts, and I canna afford to lose this one. Sure as the sun rises and the river flows, this rip will race all the way up my poor sleeve. I need the shirt; I certainly dinna have any use for a skirt!"

"Oh, Mr. McLeod, I'm sure you could barter it for more than getting a small tear sewn back up."

His brows veed. "Miss Angel, you're the only lady hereabouts—excepting your mama, of course. I dinna know a single man who can sew worth sneezing at. Seems to me, since you're the only one who could barter for the skirt, you can set the price to suit your fancy, and I'd not complain a bit."

"Mr. McLeod, I don't believe I have yet to hear a single complaint come out of you."

He shrugged. "God provides what I need. I've a roof o'er my head, clothes on my back, and my daily bread." He flashed her a smile that made her heart do an odd flip-flop. "And on top of all of those blessings, you're makin' that bread, and that means I see a beautiful woman each day."

"Flatterer." She knew from the heat that flashed from her bosom to her hair that she must be three shades of scarlet.

"Nae, Lass. 'Tis the honest truth. A fact is a fact, e'en when the telling may cause a comely blush. Now tell me, where are you wanting me to set a wee window in this place?"

She blinked at him in surprise. "A window? I've no glass!"

"We can still make do, if you want. I'd just grease paper to fill the hole—it'll let in light and air on fair weather days, and I'll make a tight-fitting set of shutters to hold out the cold of winter."

Her stepfather stomped up. His scowl could scare away a bank of thunderclouds. "Just because he's here is no excuse for you to slack off. Get on down there and pan."

"But you said I could work on the garden today!"

"That was 'fore you wasted the whole mornin' simpering around this fool. We're gonna go hungry, and he'll not have a single grain of gold in his pouch if I leave you two together."

Angel whirled about and ran to the bank of the creek. Tears blurred her vision as she dipped her pan. Water and silt slopped over the edge as she gave the pan a savage jerk. *Thanks to that dreadful man, Mama and I have gone without a roof, wear rags, and skimp on food. Did he have to humiliate me too?*

Lord, give me wisdom. I want to slug this man into next year for treating the lass that way.

"The fault was mine. I ripped my sleeve and—"

"She don't work for free." Ben glowered at the tear and a

spark of greed lit his eyes. "She stitches that up, and you pay."

"I agree. We came to a fair price."

"Since when did you have my permission to conduct business with her?"

"You told us to come to an agreement about me building the cabin." Jarrod slapped the nearest log with the flat of his hand twice. "You can see I've been a man of my word."

"It's taken you long enough. Whole thing's foolish. We done just fine without no cabin. Dumb thing's takin' up timber I'm gonna need, come winter; and Angel's wastin' half her time, tryin' to fix up fancy vittles since you're eatin' with us. She ain't gotten that garden patch planted and ain't panning as much. I can't do all the work myself. We're gonna go hungry. All 'cuz of this. . ." He angrily waved his hand toward the cabin. "This dumb thing."

The man's a selfish lout. He's not caring for his dear wife as he vowed he'd do. He expects that poor lass to launder and garden and pan, but he won't even put a roof over their heads or give Angel a length of cloth for a skirt. Jarrod straightened his shoulders and clenched his hands into angry fists. He couldn't abide any man mistreating a woman. Then again, if he took out his temper on Angel's stepfather, there was always the possibility that Ben would turn on them when Jarrod was gone.

Turn the other cheek, my son. Walk the extra mile.

Jarrod slowly relaxed his shoulders and uncurled his fists. "I'd not want to have my help turn into a hardship. I'll turn o'er the rest of the gardening plot for you."

Spluttering in surprise, Ben backed up a step and quickly

recovered. Tugging at the hem of his sleeve, he grumbled, "That makes us just about square."

As Angel's stepfather walked back to the stream, Jarrod turned back to work. *I've given my word, and I'll keep it, Lord. Give me patience and let me be a good witness. But God? I need to be working my own claim. I know I just told Angel that money isn't everything, and Thou knowest every word I spoke was sincere. But I'm never going to get enough gold to buy my ranch if I let Ben badger me into doing everything here.*

He glanced over his shoulder at Angel. Sunlight glinted off her tawny hair. *Father, I'd be thinkin' she's the real treasure here, and just about any man would be proud to take her to wife. I'm not any man; I'm Thy son. I'd spoil my witness by romancing her heart for myself instead of tending her spirit for Thee. Let me be a light to her and Ben, but don't let me forsake wisdom because I let my heart run away.*

Chapter 5

R eady?" Jarrod's eyes sparkled as he gently scooped Mama into his arms.

"Mama, just wait and see." Angel hurriedly folded up Mama's cot and rushed out of the tent. A stone's throw away, the new cabin promised sound shelter, and she hastily set the cot in the back corner where it would be warmest and the sunlight could shine through the window to give Mama brighter days.

Jarrod followed along. Cradling Mama as if she were his very own mother, he murmured, "Here you are, now."

Mama rested her head on his shoulder and managed to whisper, "Oh, thank you, Mr. McLeod. God bless you." Those few words started her coughing and stole her energy.

"You're more than welcome, and God does bless me." He turned sideways to fit Mama into the doorway without bumping her and chuckled. "I've never carried a woman over a threshold before. I'm supposing you'd best start calling me by my given name."

Angel wanted to thank Jarrod again, but as soon as he settled Mama on her cot, he headed back to work his own claim. Maybe that was for the best. She and Mama spent a few moments of peace and joy together, and for the first time in ages, Angel took Mama's hand and said a prayer of thanks.

Ben hadn't bothered to offer his help with anything at all; he snorted and snarled the whole while from his place by the creek. Bless his heart, Harv Bestler had crossed the creek and helped Jarrod lift the last logs on the walls and put on the roof. Angel didn't know whether to be thankful for the help of her neighbors or angry at her stepfather for his black-hearted ways. Though it didn't seem possible, he grew more surly with each passing day. He'd netted a fish for supper, but if it fed two children, they'd both leave the table hungry. Still, he'd declared he'd done his fair share and caught his own supper. To her mortification, he hadn't just said it, he'd bellowed every last word.

Harv looked across the stream at the little fish. His voice, rich with sarcasm, boomed back from the other side of the creek, "Now there's a nice change. I always like to hear good news."

Though Jarrod had gone back to his own claim, she knew he had to hear the selfish, mean-spirited boast too. All of an hour or so later, Jarrod returned. His knees and sleeves were wet, and a few wood shavings freckled his hair. Without saying a word, he set down a rope-handled bucket and left. The two modest-sized trout he'd brought now sizzled in the frying pan.

She crossed the creek and asked Harv to join all of them for supper, but he whispered, "Ask me some night when Jarrod isn't there. He's a fine man—don't get me wrong—but I'd rather you had one or the other of us with you at two suppers than both of us at once. That way, you don't have to get indigestion by eating alone with Ben."

So here she was, holding her new skirt off to the side, careful not to let it drag near the edge of her cook fire. The flames made the russet and gold leaves in the calico print glow, and Angel twirled a damp wisp of hair around her finger, hoping it would stay in a tendril to make her look soft and feminine. She wanted everything to be perfect tonight—as an expression of her deep gratitude.

"Ah, a pretty woman and a pan of fish." Jarrod stepped into the ring of firelight. He wore an endearingly crooked grin. " 'Tis a sight to warm the heart."

Her stepfather snatched the largest fish, dumped it on his tin, and plopped down on a stump. "It's gold I want in my pan."

Jarrod put a small bundle off to the side and sat on what had become the stump he usually used. "How is Mrs. Frisk?"

Her stepfather snorted, so Angel softly said, "I fed her earlier, and she's fallen asleep. She hasn't looked this comfortable in years."

He smiled at her, accepted his supper, then bowed his head for a quiet moment. He always did that—praying before he ate. At first, it seemed so oddly out of place. Soon, Angel expected it and it gave her a bittersweet flood of memories. Back home, Grandpa Monroe always said grace at meals. She scarcely remembered her own father, but one of the memories she held was of him holding her on his lap, his big hands enveloping hers to form a steeple, and the feel of his chest rumbling against her back as he'd pray.

Fork poised over his fish, Jarrod said, "Angel, I'm a mite thirsty. Could I trouble you for a mug of water?"

His request startled her. Jarrod always saw to the minor details for himself. Then again, what kind of hostess was she, expecting a guest to go stoop at the creek and fill his mug—especially since she had no coffee to offer? "I'll be right back with it."

The tin mug went cold at once from the water, and her fingers felt nearly numb in the scant minute it took for her to dip it and return. Angel handed it to Jarrod, then turned and stopped. He'd switched their pie tins and taken the smallest fish for himself. When she sat down, he calmly boned his supper and made an appreciative humming sound.

"What's in the parcel?" her stepfather demanded.

Though guilty of wondering the same thing, Angel wished he'd not be so rude as to ask—especially in that tone.

"A few traditional things." Jarrod finished his last bite and set his tin down on the ground. He lifted the cloth bundle and unknotted the corners. "I had to make a few changes, owing to what's on hand. The Scots usually give bread, wine, salt, and a candle when blessing a new home." He pulled out a small bag of flour. "So you never go hungry."

Angel accepted the flour and mentally calculated it would make bread for three days.

"Being that I dinna imbibe, I have no wine. I gathered some berries, though, in hopes that your life is always sweet."

Angel accepted the bowl and ignored Father's snigger. "We'll enjoy these as dessert tonight."

"Salt, so there's always spice in your life. . .and a candle, so you'll always have light." He gave her a paper twist that felt grainy and an ordinary tallow candle.

Angel looked at the four simple things and felt rich beyond compare. His sincerity in wanting good things for her shone through. He couldn't give her expensive, fancy things, but he gifted her with shelter, a pretty skirt, and blessings for her home. Safe and provided for—she hadn't felt either of those things for so long, yet both feelings flowed over her. Tears blurred her vision.

"Our family tradition is to bless a home with a reading from the Word. I brought my Bible, and I—"

"Put that away." Her stepfather shot to his feet. "You don't, and I'll feed it to the fire."

Jarrod rose and held the black leather book to his chest. He said nothing.

"I'd like a blessing," Angel dared to stand and say.

"Not out of that, you won't." Father pointed at Jarrod's Bible.

The rippling water and night sounds filled the air, but silence still crackled along with the fire. Jarrod finally broke it. "An Irish couple on the ship over gave my sister and me a blessing. 'Tisn't from the Bible, but I think it's fitting. I'll share it, instead."

"Please do." Angel moved a step closer. Why did her stepfather have to spoil everything?

Still holding his Bible close to his heart, Jarrod looked over her shoulder at the cabin, then into her eyes. His delicious baritone filled the air. "May God grant you always a sunbeam to warm you, a moonbeam to charm you, and a sheltering angel so nothing can harm you."

"Oh, that is lovely."

"It's pure drivel. Supper's over. Time you left, McLeod. No reason for you to be coming back, either."

Angel watched Jarrod walk away. As he stepped past the illuminating circle the small fire cast and into the shadows, she felt like the only light in her life had been extinguished.

Days and weeks passed. Jarrod spent little time in his cabin. After surveying his claim with a pick and pan, he'd wanted to repair the dilapidated shaker box Charlie left behind. Using the shaker box would be far more effective than kneeling at the bank and panning. Pete Kane came upriver to have Angel do his laundry, and he'd helped Jarrod replace a few parts on the rickety-looking equipment so it worked like a charm. He'd taken a fistful of coffee beans in trade, and Jarrod set to work with the box at once. Afternoons and evenings, he prospected. Mornings, he tried his hand at a bit of gardening.

He'd put in a fair-sized garden, and some of the truck came up beautifully. He'd discovered if he asked Ben about giving or bartering some of it, he'd always be rebuffed. On the other hand, Angel and he managed to deal well. He'd planted more cabbage than he could eat; she traded him for lettuce. She had bush beans by the pint; he had radishes and onions. They'd each planted herbs, carrots, and different varieties of squash. She also had beets, butterbeans, cucumbers, and tomatoes. Both gardens suffered from the wild animals' plundering, but Angel had warned him, so Jarrod planted far more than he'd need.

It wasn't long before prospectors would float messages down the creek or walk up it and want to buy or trade. Jarrod learned to give Angel his surplus. She could sell it for him, especially when men came to get laundry done. Most of the men didn't have cash money. They'd either come up with half a pinch of gold dust or something to trade. With winter over, a fair number of them had empty flour or sugar sacks. She'd accept them, then sew shirts from them. He'd never seen a more industrious woman. If she wasn't shaving lye soap into the wash kettle, she was scrubbing things on a washboard, sewing, gardening, or panning for gold.

Even with all of that to do, she cared for her mama with great tenderness. Jarrod slipped Angel some Rumford pocket soup so she could fix broth for her mama on days when she couldn't eat anything else. He'd tried to give her a bit of his Underwood deviled ham to share with her mama after a five-day rainy stretch where hunting and fishing hadn't been possible, but Ben pitched a fit.

Harv Bestler crossed the creek that night. He and Jarrod shared a cup of coffee and conversed in low tones. Harv said, "That God-fearing woman followed her husband here, only to have her health go as sour as Ben's disposition."

"Have things been this bad all along?"

"First year wasn't too bad. It's a hard life, but they managed. Second year, things took a bad turn." After gulping one last mouthful of coffee, Harv confessed, "I offered to send word to Mrs. Frisk's brother to come fetch her and the girl, but Mrs.

Frisk feels a woman should stay with her man. She wanted Angel to go, but she was too weak to write; the gal refused to leave her mama, so she wouldn't pen the note and I can't write none."

Jarrod listened somberly. It galled him to think these women had been enduring this at all, but the sheer length of time they'd suffered made it even worse. He let out a deep sigh. "Let's make a pact to keep an eye out for Angel and her mama."

Not many days thereafter, a man slogged up the creek past Jarrod. Even from a few yards away, Jarrod could smell the reek of whiskey on him. Jarrod wasn't about to let things slide any closer toward danger. He grabbed his bow and an ax and hastened through a small break between the bushes separating their claims. Exaggerating his stride until he swaggered a bit, he walked straight up to Ben and announced, "I'm here, so we'd best go ahead and decide where to put that smokehouse we'll be sharing."

Ben gave him a baffled look.

Under his breath, he said, "You're about to have bad company."

Ben pivoted. He sized up the man coming out of the river and reached for the shotgun he always kept at his side. "Don't want strangers here. Be on your way."

"I got hard cash." The stranger craned his neck to look about the site. The tents partially blocked his view of the cabin. When he staggered to the side a bit and spied it, a lecherous smile lit his face. "Heard tell you gotta woman here."

"My daughter's busy." Ben waggled the business end of the shotgun at him. "Now git."

The stranger lazily sat down on the nearest stump. " 'S'okay. I'll wait my turn."

Footsteps sounded from behind them. Jarrod's heart sank. He'd hoped Angel would stay out of sight, but here she stood. Breathlessly, she said, "Jarrod?"

Jarrod shoved Angel behind his back.

"Hoo-ooey! She's got yaller hair." The stranger stood and started to yank one of his suspenders from his shoulder. "Purty thang."

Jarrod stepped forward. He gripped his ax in his right hand and slapped it back into his left hand a few times for emphasis as he growled, "There's no lightskirt here."

"Y'all kin share. I ain't had me a woman—"

"Ben, you wanna shoot him before or after I heft my ax?"

"I'm not patient. I'm givin' him to the count of three to be off my claim, else he's gonna have more holes 'n a harmonica. Nobody comes on my claim without my say-so."

"No use getting all het up." The stranger started to back up toward the creek.

"We'll consider it an honest mistake." Jarrod continued to thump the ax in his palm. "You don't come back, and we'll all forget this."

After the man left, Angel sank onto the ground. "Oh, my."

"You're just fine." Ben shot her an impatient look. "No use havin' a fit of the vapors. He's gone."

Angel looked up at Jarrod with huge, frightened eyes.

He smoothed her hair back from her forehead. "I was just talking to Ben about a smokehouse. We ought to put up some meat for the winter, and we could build something right here, along the property line, to share. Why don't we work on that today? You can sit right there and pan by the bank, and we'll be right here by you."

"Smokehouse is a waste of time." Ben spat off to the side.

Angel raised a shaking hand to her throat. "Only because you don't have any ammunition for your rifle."

Chapter 6

"We're going to town tomorrow—the three of us."

The set of Jarrod's jaw made it clear he wasn't going to put up with any refusal. Angel watched as he stared down her stepfather.

Finally Ben kicked the ground. "I was already plannin' to go. If you wanna, you can tag along."

"Good. Be ready by sunup."

"But my mama—"

"I'll ask Harv Bestler to keep an eye on her for the day."

Ben spat off to the side. "You think you got everything all worked out, don'tcha, Scotsman?"

Jarrod made no reply, but from the way he stared at her stepfather, he clearly wasn't willing to put up with any nonsense. Finally he turned and met her eyes again. "Angel, pack up your extra truck. We'll tie it to my mules, and you can sell it." He spared her a smile, but his eyes still held fire. "Maybe you can get yourself a little something with that."

"She's buying coffee."

Angel allowed Jarrod to help her to her feet. The feel of his big hand wrapped around her arm, steadying her, made her long for more. She wanted to lean into him and absorb his strength. She hadn't been to town for two years. A day where she didn't have to plunge her chapped hands into the cold water—it was almost too marvelous to believe, and Harv would be gentle with Mama. Jarrod was responsible for this. He'd made it possible. "Coffee sounds wonderful."

"Since we won't be panning tomorrow, we gotta do more today." Ben tugged Angel away from Jarrod's side. "Get busy."

Jarrod tacked on, "Bring your pan to the edge of the claim. We'll keep you betwixt us just for good measure."

Angel panned for the rest of the afternoon, but she did it reflexively. She'd dip her pan, swirl and shift it until all of the silt washed out and all that was left was the black, fine pay dirt. Until that color showed in her rusty pan, she didn't have to pay attention at all. Then, she'd rinse it carefully, shake and coax and wash off the last until the only things left in the pan were the few precious grains of gold. Pan after pan after pan. . .

She wondered how much gold dust they had. Her stepfather always took her findings for the day and hid them away. She had no idea precisely where he kept the hard-earned treasure. It never seemed right that he took it all. Then, too, when he'd go to town and come back empty-handed, she'd swung between being irate and hopeless. Had he wasted it all, or had he only taken a portion? Tomorrow, he'd have her along. She'd be sure they went to a mercantile and bought staples first. If only Father would walk out of the range of hearing for a moment, she'd turn and plead with Jarrod to help her force Father into that plan. It shamed her, but she decided her pride wasn't half as important as the dire need to restock her empty larder.

How much does a bag of flour cost? A pound of coffee? Oh, and sugar. Beans and rice. They'll store well in the back corner of my cabin. She studied the little dish she kept fingering her gold dust into. *What will that much gold buy?*

Ben muttered under his breath, but Jarrod anticipated his attitude and took coffee to share the next morning. It served as a potent reminder of what they could get in town. After a cup, Ben's penchant for the scalding drink made him stand up and smack the dust off the seat of his britches. "We'd best not wait all day. Get a move on."

Angel quickly handed two full sacks of her garden truck to Jarrod to tie onto Otto's back. While he secured them, she did one last check on Mama, then thanked Harv for the kindness he showed by staying with her for the day. Within minutes, Jarrod lifted Angel onto Beulah, and they'd all set out.

Jarrod held Beulah's halter and walked along at a fair pace. He wanted to get into town and back before the sun went down. Squinting at the horizon, he estimated if he kept up this pace, they'd make it.

"Are you sure I'm not wearing out Beulah?" Angel leaned toward Jarrod from her perch. "I'm going to want her to carry a lot of supplies back."

"You're just a dab of a lass." They'd barely finished crossing Pete Kane's claim, and Jarrod didn't want her to start fretting.

They had a long day ahead of them. "Beulah's happy to carry you, and it'll keep your hem from gathering dust."

She let out a bit of rusty laughter. "Wouldn't that be a sight? Me telling the men they can bring me their laundry while I have eight inches of grime around my hem!"

The hair on the back of his neck prickled as Jarrod stopped dead in his tracks. "You're not going to tell them you'll take on business. 'Tisn't safe."

"I'm gettin' more ammunition," Ben growled. The bags of produce on Otto's back jostled as Ben led him ahead. "She'll be plenty safe."

Greed. Jarrod had a strong hunch gold was the one thing that motivated Ben. Jarrod unashamedly took advantage of that sad fact. "To my way of thinking, with the late runoff, this is the best time to be panning. Angel can keep her laundry business going to earn money from the locals, but if she does much more, you'll miss out on everything she's panning because she'll have to make more soap, spend more time scrubbing and wringing, and—"

"You're already wasting good pannin' time, gardening and such," Ben mused. "Cain't miss out on much more. I ain't goin' through another winter without coffee."

Relieved, Jarrod set a slightly faster pace. Colorado rated a close second to the most beautiful place on earth. Scotland headed the list, but a man couldn't live in the past, so he appreciated the fresh pine scent, the loamy earth, the birdsong, and the endless blue sky surrounding him now. Most of all, he appreciated the one piece of scenery that surpassed anything he'd ever seen: the sight of Angel smiling.

When they got to town, Ben licked his lips, dropped Otto's halter, and headed straight toward the saloon's batwing doors.

Jarrod reached over and caught his arm. "We'd best go to the mercantile first."

A soiled dove leaned over her balcony from the upstairs of The Watering Hole and called out with notable enthusiasm, "Benny! C'mon up and pay me a visit!"

Jarrod didn't turn loose. He gave Ben's arm a squeeze and said, "You have ammunition and coffee to buy."

"Sometimes a man's gotta—" Ben glanced at Angel.

Jarrod looked up at her too. Her face had gone white with shock. She stared at him with glistening eyes that ached with all of the betrayal she felt on her mother's behalf. She slowly turned her face to the other side of the street. Jarrod wanted to comfort her, but this wasn't the time or place. He directed a scalding look at Ben.

Ben lowered his voice to a raspy, man-to-man whisper. "You know. A man's gotta take care of things. Manly things."

Purposefully mistaking him, Jarrod started traveling down the rutted street with Ben in tow. "I agree with you. Taking care of supplying your wife and Angel is the manly thing to do. A man always takes care of his loved ones."

While Jarrod helped Angel off Beulah, Ben stomped into the mercantile. Jarrod didn't let go of Angel at once. Instead, he continued to hold her waist and gave it a reassuring squeeze. He refused to lie or to make excuses for Ben, so he opted for a different tack. "Take the opportunity to stock up. Beulah and

Otto wilna be happy if they made this trip for a mere bag or two, and I'm not of a mind to deal with three stubborn mules on the way home."

"Three?"

He waggled his brows. "There's no changing Ben's disposition, so help me make Beulah and Otto happy."

A flicker of a smile let Jarrod know he'd managed to handle the awkwardness so Angel wouldn't feel ashamed around him. "I'd guess we'd best take our vegetables inside."

As Jarrod untied the first bag off Otto, a head of lettuce escaped. A well-dressed man bent and snatched it up. He cradled it to his vest and eyed the other bags. "Do you have more of this?"

"Yes." Angel went to reclaim it. "Beans and—"

"I want it all," he interrupted. "I'll pay cash money."

Jarrod chuckled as he hefted one bag. "I'm doubting you'll be wanting it all."

"But I do! I own Fancy Pans. I'm always ready to buy quality truck. If those bags hold anything similar to this, I'll be more than happy to snap it all up."

By the time he'd looked in the second bag, the restauranteur didn't even bother to inspect the other two. "Four dollars for all of it."

Jarrod felt Angel jump. She looked to him, and he shook his head. Staring at the man, he demanded, "How much is a meal at your establishment?"

By the time Jarrod held the door of the mercantile open, he couldn't help smiling at Angel. She positively skipped over the threshold. The bargain they'd struck and the promise of a free meal in a nice restaurant made Jarrod want to jig right alongside her.

They'd been paid in coins, and he promptly gave Angel her half. She hurriedly handed back one of the silver dollars and whispered, "Please keep it for me. It's not much, but I'll need it someday."

He'd slipped it into his pocket and added one of his own. When the time came, she'd need all he could spare her.

Chapter 7

B en shot them a dirty look as they entered the store, then thumped a can of Wedding Breakfast coffee onto the counter and set three tins of chewing tobacco next to it. " 'Bout time you got in here. Bring in that truck so's the store-keeper can tell me how much credit I'll get."

"We already sold it," Angel said. "Jarrod and I each have three and a half dollars cash and lunch at a restaurant!"

The lass acted like a child at Christmas in the mercantile. Every last thing held her enthralled. The first thing she did was choose a cough elixir and a health tonic for her mother. Bless her soul, she didn't even look at the cost. Jarrod knew she'd sacrifice anything for the sake of her mother.

The most pressing needs seen to, she then agonized over which flour and sugar sacks she liked best, stood by the huge barrel of coffee beans and inhaled the aroma as if she were a bride appreciating the most beautiful bouquet a groom ever gathered.

Seeing how she relished each and every scent and item, Jarrod lollygagged as he selected things and formed a small stack of goods on the counter. The storekeeper's hair glinted oddly in the sunlight streaming in through the window. At first, Jarrod thought it was merely the pomade casting a reflection. Upon second inspection, Jarrod realized the truth. He was a sticky-fingered proprietor.

Oh, he'd read about such men—just never met one. Sure enough, the storekeeper would run his fingers through his hair, then reach into a miner's poke to pull out a pinch of gold flakes as payment for something. Most of the dust went into the receptacle behind the counter, but some clung to the storekeeper's fingers—which he'd run through his hair or wipe off on his apron. By panning the wash water from his bath and laundry, the man undoubtedly pulled in as much gold dust as any of the local placers who worked by the cold streams.

A pair of Cornish miners played draughts over between the stove and the cracker barrel. "Smashed Oliver McKnight like a June bug," one said grimly.

The other shook his head. "He was always talking about coming to the mine to earn a nice nest egg so when his sweet little Charlotte was of age, he'd be able to 'give her the world along with his heart.'"

"Three-fifty a day sounded like a lot, but seein' Ollie all bloody and squished—" The first shook his head.

"Superstitious cowards," the storekeeper whispered disparagingly to Jarrod and Ben. "They had another cave-in—just a little one. Only killed one man. Still, the mountain's making some noise, so they're sure the tommyknockers are warning them to stay out of the mines."

Ben snorted. "Don't need pretend creatures to warn me off.

Couldn't pay me 'nuff to crawl inside a mountain and haul out gold for another man."

"Your claim doing well?" The shopkeeper gave both men an assessing look.

Ben scowled, and Jarrod knew better than to give a direct answer. They'd be fools to admit anything, so he shrugged diffidently. "I just bought the claim off someone else. I'm supposin' it'll take me awhile to be any good at it. Came to stock up on some staples."

He specifically chose his flour sack to match Angel's. Truth be told, he'd look mighty silly to be walking down the street with his flour in pink fabric with wee daisies sprinkled all over it, but he didn't much care. The lass could use the extra fabric to make herself a frock instead of a skirt, and she'd be pretty as one of her blushes in this color.

Angel's stack of supplies at the counter nearly made Ben's eyes pop. "Now hold on. No use gettin' extravagant," he protested as she set a small box atop the bags and tucked a metal pail of lard beside them.

"Baking powder, baking soda, and salt aren't extravagances," she said quietly, but Jarrod detected the firm undertone. "I've stuck to basics: flour, sugar, beans, lard, and coffee. Did you get your ammunition?"

Ben rapped his knuckles on a box of bullets he set next to a slab of bacon and scowled. "Money we got from the truck ain't gonna be 'nuff."

Jarrod slipped a few last things on the counter with his selections. He drew his gold dust pouch from his pocket. "Ah, but there's satisfaction in knowing we earned every speck of what we eat." When he'd finalized the transaction, he said, "Speaking of eating, I'm ready to go to that restaurant."

He and Angel spent time savoring the fine meal. Her gracious manners made it clear to Jarrod that though she'd never said much about her past, she'd obviously grown up in drastically different circumstances. Ben wolfed down his meal and plowed out of the restaurant so he could get to the saloon. Jarrod stayed behind and savored the food and company.

Ben ambled along next to Otto. He hummed under his breath—no doubt, the time he'd spent bending his elbow in the saloon was responsible for his uncustomary merriment.

Angel walked between him and Jarrod and daintily held up her skirt a bit. She'd worn the one Jarrod had given her, and she fretted over the hem as if the dust wouldn't ever wash out. Every few minutes, she kept glancing at the burden on Otto's sturdy back. Each time, her smile grew. Jarrod had whispered to her to estimate generous quantities, and the packs tied to the mules gave her a sense of accomplishment and even a flicker of hope. *I'll be able to give Mama medicine and feed her well.*

Ben and Jarrod were discussing the smokehouse as if it were already built. That heartened her further. Ever since Jarrod arrived, things had improved. He'd shown her kindness and courtesy, seen the longings in her heart and bettered her life in every way. She and Mama had a roof over their heads, and after today, they had medicine, plenty of staples, and the promise of sufficient meat—if Jarrod continued to be as adept at hunting as he'd been thus far.

But for how long?

Jarrod said he would stay only as long as it took for him to pan enough gold to buy his dream ranch. She didn't know how much gold that would require—or how long it would take. Jarrod hadn't wasted a single cent in town. Every last purchase rated as a necessity. Some might consider that parsimonious, but she didn't. After her stepfather's previous forays to town where he spent everything—from today's events, Angel had a mortifying notion of just how he'd squandered their gold—she had a deep appreciation for a man who exercised self-discipline and frugality. A deep contentment radiated from him, making it clear he didn't need a lot of material things to keep him satisfied.

Her stepfather dragged her and Mama here and hadn't put himself out at all in any way for them. Even after Mama got sick, he'd not lifted a finger to ease things by getting medicine, chopping wood for heat, or providing adequate shelter.

For all others might say about love, Angel decided few people knew what it truly meant. They saw love as taking, not giving. In that light, love would prove to be vastly overrated and empty. She'd turned down many a proposal out here—none of the men who asked cared a whit for her. She vowed to stay for Mama. She couldn't fool herself into believing Mama would recover because Mama had lost too much weight and slept most of the time. At least that was a blessed escape from her pain and cough. For now, they had food aplenty, clothes, and shelter—humble as it was.

She owed it all to Jarrod.

And he'd be leaving.

Chapter 8

Arms full of branches, Angel walked to the smokehouse. Her stepfather had agreed with Ben and Harv about building it, but when the time came to do the work, he balked. Jarrod and Harv decided to build it near the bank on Harv's side of the creek. Neither of those men said a word about why they'd chosen that location. They didn't have to: Angel knew full well why. Her stepfather wouldn't do his share of building or filling it, but he'd gladly help himself to whatever the smokehouse contained if it were on his claim. When Jarrod left, he'd not want to rob Harv of his fair share. Hardworking as Jarrod was, Angel knew he'd not be a placer for long.

Angel nimbly crossed the log bridge Jarrod had constructed, and she dumped off the wood. Though she couldn't hunt, she'd do her family's part by helping dress out and cure the meat.

Harv grinned at her. "Jarrod went a-huntin' this mornin'. Got hisself a passel of squirrels. I set out a sieve last night and netted 'leven fish. Pete brought over a few fish he wants smoke cured too."

Jarrod rested his hands on his hips and tilted his head to the side. "I was just telling Harv and Pete about what a good cook you are. Think we could talk you into making squirrel stew and dumplings? Then Harv will fillet and smoke the fish for us to have some other day."

"I'll bring coffee," Pete offered.

Warmth rushed through her. Jarrod had been complimenting her cooking to someone else? Angel smiled. "Squirrel stew and dumplings it is, gentlemen."

Jarrod nodded, then gave her a chiding look. "You'll not be carryin' wood again, Lass. 'Tisn't fitting."

She shrugged. "I do it all of the time for the wash pot."

"We know," Harv grumped. "Makes me wonder which Ben uses less—his ax or his head."

All of them exchanged a glance, and the men burst out laughing as a smile tugged at the corners of Angel's mouth. Harv had a way of looking at life and speaking his mind that managed to lift the spirits.

"We're partners in this venture," Jarrod said, "and we men already agreed you're not responsible for any of the wood, so that's how the vote stands."

"But if you both hunt and dress the meat, I—"

"Will be filling the air with the aroma and our bellies with your fine squirrel stew." Jarrod took her arm and started back toward the bridge. When they reached it, he cupped his hands around her waist to help her step up. She didn't need the assistance, but his gentlemanly ways made her feel dainty and special, so she didn't protest.

He didn't lift right away. He stared down into her eyes. "I have the ring. I'll slip it to you, and you can stitch it back into your hem."

She cast a glance across the creek and shook her head subtly. "He'd find it. Every night, he searches to be sure I didn't keep any of the gold for myself."

A muffled sound of outrage rumbled in his chest.

"The day Ben gets his hands on my grandmother's ring, it'll be lost to me forever. My cousins, Philip and Gabe, are to receive Grandma Monroe's locket and get Grandpa's pocket watch. The ring is my one worldly treasure. Grandpa made it for her out of the first gold he ever mined. I trust you to keep it for me, Jarrod."

"You deserve better, Lass."

Lass. He called her lass as if it were an endearment. His rich, deep burr made that word and her name both sound like caresses when he said them. Before she let him know where her mind was wandering, she shook herself free and scrambled onto the log bridge. "Bring the squirrels as soon as you can. I'll want them to simmer 'til tender."

She made it all of a few steps when he hopped up and fleetly followed behind her. "I've carrots aplenty. I'll pluck them up along with a turnip or an onion for the stew."

"No, no," she denied as she finished crossing. Relief flooded her that he'd left the sore subject behind and chosen to discuss something so practical and mundane. "Feed the carrots to Beulah and Otto. I have a bumper crop of carrots too."

"I've been thinkin' on digging a root cellar."

Angel spun around and looked at him. "For a man who said he'd stay only long enough to pan out enough to buy a ranch, you sure are putting down roots."

Lines around his eyes crinkled as he threw back his head and chortled. "The roots are already planted, Lass. I'm just hoping to save me a fair bunch of them for when the harvest is over."

"If you keep hunting and gardening, it'll take you years to pull enough from the river to buy that ranch."

Jarrod's face took on a pensive air. "Whatever happens, it's all in God's time, according to His will."

She gave him a flicker of a smile. "Once I told you I didn't think God listened to me anymore. I was wrong. He took His time to answer my prayers. Because Mama and I had to do without for so long, it makes all I now have seem far more precious. It's as if He's showering me with blessings."

"Sure and enough, He is, Angel. Of that you can be certain."

"I need to go see to Mama."

"We'll talk more about this later."

She pressed her lips together and cast a surreptitious look to the side. Her stepfather would make Jarrod stop seeing her if he found out they discussed anything religious. She couldn't take that risk. "I have to go." Before he could say another word, she dashed off.

The elixir really did help. Mama's breathing didn't carry that rasp if she had a dose four times a day. Maybe it wasn't as much the medicine as the company. Jarrod came over about noon each day and carried Mama to a pretty spot where he and Harv had slung a length of canvas to form a hammock. Fresh air, sunshine, and gentle companionship put the slightest tinge of pink into Mama's cheeks.

Jarrod and Harv made a show of having an argument over who got the privilege of feeding Mama lunch each day. Ben never sat with them—he'd grab his food and stalk off. While Angel sewed, one of the men would feed Mama and the other would gut fish or dress out whatever they'd hunted. The camaraderie between Jarrod and Harv reminded Angel of how her cousins, Philip and Gabe, used to act with one another. Some days, it made her homesick; other days, it was such fun, she'd lose herself in the joy of their nonsense.

"I've decided on a spot to dig my root cellar," Jarrod announced one day just as the air started to take on a decided nip that warned the season was changing. He pointed at a site.

"That spot is all rock. It's as hard as your head," Harv teased.

"It'll keep creatures from burrowing in and helping themselves to my food." Jarrod nodded to himself.

"Everybody knows you have the second-best carrots around," Mama said in her shaky voice.

"Second best?" Jarrod gave her a look of mock outrage.

"Seems I'm the only impartial judge hereabouts." Harv swiped a part of a carrot Angel had been cutting to dehydrate and chewed it. He then wandered over, picked a carrot from Jarrod's garden, and rinsed it in the creek. He took a bite and made a wry face. "Hard to say. Maybe I ought to eat a couple more to make up my mind."

"What mind?" Jarrod asked Mama in a stage whisper.

They all laughed—Mama included. Later, as Jarrod carried her back into the cabin, she tapped his chest. "You've got a good heart, Jarrod McLeod. I prayed God would pour out His joy and love, and you're the answer to my prayer."

❧

Jarrod decided prospecting for gold held absolutely no charm whatsoever. The sun glaring on the water hit his eyes and burned his skin. Hot as it was, he wouldn't remove his shirt out of deference to Angel's sensibilities. He'd used his pickax at a particularly promising black streak on his claim and fed it through his shaker box. Some days, he managed to find several tiny nuggets and a gram or so of little golden grains. Other days, he'd garnered nothing more than flakes that caught along the rusty spots in his pan.

Silver miners were paid twenty dollars a week. Most weeks, Jarrod knew full well he'd have made more working in the dark bowels of a mountain with other men, but the very thought of being closed in like that made him break out in a cold sweat. He'd spent almost all of the voyage from Scotland up on deck because he couldn't bear being crammed so tightly with everyone else in the dim steerage compartment.

He cupped his hand and scooped up a drink of cool water, then stood to stretch his weary back muscles. *Lord, I'm sorry for having a complaining spirit. Thou art showering me with sunshine and fanning me with a fresh breeze.* Just then, Ben shouted something unintelligible at Angel. *And Father, I'm thinkin' Thou hast planted me here for more of a reason than funding my dream.*

Angel broke into his prayer by marching straight across to his claim. Temper set her hazel eyes aflame and lent vivid color to her cheeks. She carried a gunnysack over her shoulder, but Jarrod knew it couldn't contain her belongings. She'd never leave her mother, and if death had come, Angel would be in tears, not in a roaring temper.

Angel didn't say a thing until she stood right before him. "I'm going to town. Mama's out of cough elixir, and she needs it bad. Will you keep an eye on her while I'm gone?"

Ben stomped up and made a grab for the gunnysack. "You ain't going nowhere, and this food ain't yours to sell."

"I planted and grew it!"

Ben thundered, "On my claim!" He yanked the sack from her grasp.

Jarrod steadied Angel so she wouldn't fall. He pursed his lips and looked up at the scudding clouds for a moment, then back at Ben. "So 'tis your claim, is it?"

"What kind of fool question is that? Of course it is!"

"Not your family's?" Jarrod gritted his teeth together so hard, he could feel the muscle in his cheek twitch.

"Mine." Ben thumped his chest with his free hand. "My wife's useless, and whatever Angel does, it barely pays the keep on the both of them."

"Families pull together to make ends meet," Jarrod said softly, but then he injected a steely undertone to the rest of his words. "A man's place is to provide for his kin."

"Ain't none of your business. Besides, Angel ain't my blood kin."

"No, she's not your family," Jarrod agreed with a steely glare. "You agreed Angel should work the land. She's sharecropping. Rightfully, a portion of the yield is Angel's to do with as she pleases."

While Ben dropped the sack and let out a bellow at that pronouncement, Angel took the next mental step. "Part of the money I earn with laundry is mine from now on too. And so is a portion of the gold when I pan!"

Ben shook his finger in her face. "You stop it right there, Missy. You ain't got any call on nothin' of mine. You're workin' so's you and your ma can eat. You start challenging me and making fancy demands, and you can keep off my land."

Jarrod could feel her shudder and wilt. Everything within him railed at this cruelty. He tilted her face to his. "I'll let you and your mama live in my cabin."

"My wife ain't goin' nowheres."

The trapped look on Angel's face and the tears in her eyes nearly tore Jarrod's heart from his chest. He gently fingered an errant golden tendril back behind her ear and urged, "Go take care of your mama, Lass. I'm needin' to go to town, myself. You just tell me what to get."

"It's a waste of good money. No matter what you give her, she ain't gettin' better."

A wounded cry spiraled out of Angel. Jarrod clasped her to his chest as she shook with nearly silent weeping. He glared at Ben. "The elixir eases your wife's cough and gives both comfort and rest. 'Tisn't a waste at all; 'tis a necessity, and a merciful one at that."

"Ain't your business, and it ain't your money." Ben swiped the sack from the ground, made a sound of disgust, and walked off.

Jarrod continued to hold Angel as she cried. They'd never said a word about how her mother was losing ground and growing more fragile with the passage of each week. Ben had been cruel, and Jarrod despised that fact. But he knew he couldn't lie now and reassure Angel that her mama would improve.

Lord, help me get Angel away from that black-hearted man.

From behind him came the sound of a man clearing his throat. Harv's voice broke in to Jarrod's thoughts. "Mrs. Frisk— she didn't. . .um. . ."

"No." Jarrod stroked Angel's back as he watched his friend circle around them. "We're concerned because she's worsening. I'll be going into town to fetch more medicine. I'll be askin' you to keep an eye out for Angel and her mama for the day."

"I'd be right proud to. I could use a thing or two, since you're making the trip." Harv's brows beetled in a dark, questioning frown as he tilted his head toward Ben's claim. When Jarrod nodded subtly, Harv gave Angel's shoulder a clumsy pat. "Maybe our missy can have a sit-down for a few minutes and write out a list for me."

Angel shimmied from Jarrod's hold, wiped her face with the backs of her chapped hands, and said in a small, choppy voice, "Of course I'll scribe your list."

"Be much obliged." Harv rocked from toe to heel a few times, and an impish twinkle lit his eyes. "First thing I want is the strongest purgative you can buy so's I can slip it into Ben's coffee."

Angel forced a pitiful excuse for a laugh and grabbed each of their hands. Squeezing them tightly, she asked, "What would I do without you?"

Jarrod cupped her jaw with his other hand and captured her gaze unwaveringly. "You've no need to ask the question, Lass. You'll not be finding that out."

Jarrod stood in the mercantile and looked about. He let the storekeeper gather the items of Harv's list while he made careful choices for himself. He'd taken about half of his placer gold to the assay office and sold it, but for all his hard work, the financial results left his spirits flat and his pocket far too light.

Prices in town had gone up. Jarrod grimly determined to get the root cellar dug, dehydrate vegetables and berries, and hunt as much as he could. If the prices made him wince, they'd send Ben into a fury.

Angel had wisely been gathering berries and drying some of her vegetables. She even filled a big crock with a dill brine in which she'd been making pickles. At her suggestion, Harv donated a barrel, Jarrod gave her cabbage, and she'd made sauerkraut that would be done curing in the late autumn. Truly, he'd never seen a more industrious woman.

The sales lithograph over the display of Dr. Jayne's expectorant that Angel told him to buy made Jarrod's heart lurch. Little Red Riding Hood huddled in a doorway in her cloak—it seemed oddly, sadly appropriate. His Angel and her mama had suffered far too much, and even if it took every last cent he had, Jarrod was going to make sure they were cared for.

He studied the other patent medicines. Supposedly, Seeley's Wasa-Tusa cured most anything, but he set it back on the counter when he read the boast, "87 percent alcohol." Since Angel thought Dr. Jayne's worked well, he'd trust her judgment—but he didn't buy just one bottle.

The trip home in the dark was treacherous. Thanks to Beulah and Otto's surefooted walk and Harv's beacon-sized fire, Jarrod made it back. "Coffee smells good."

"Have a cup."

"After I take Mrs. Frisk her elixir." He took out what he needed and headed toward Angel's cabin. From halfway across the campsite, he could hear her mama's harsh cough. "Angel?"

The door flew open. A tiny flicker from the kerosene lamp glowed around her like a halo. "You're back!"

His nose wrinkled at an awful smell. "Sounds like your mama needs this." He handed her two bottles.

"I made an onion and mustard plaster for her chest. It helped a little, but this will make all of the difference. Thank you so much!"

He held out a crushed cone of paper. "Horehound drops."

Angel's jaw dropped and she blinked at him. "You bought candy?"

" 'Tis said it helps with coughs, but I want you to have a piece or two yourself."

"I don't need—"

"Life's not always about needs, Lass. Sometimes, it's about little pleasures and tiny joys. Give me your word you'll have one tonight."

Tears misted her pretty hazel eyes and lent a throaty quality to her voice. "Yes."

"There now. That's a fine promise. The night's goin' chilly. You latch the door now and bundle up soon as you've given your mama her elixir."

"I put aside some supper for you. Harv has it."

"Then let me give you a Scripture before I go." He looked at the beautiful, careworn lass as she clutched the medicine and candy to her bosom and felt a glow, knowing she'd still thought of his needs and set aside a meal for him. " 'Tis in Psalm 34, but I canna recollect the exact verses. 'The angel of the Lord encampeth round about them that fear him, and delivereth them. O taste and see that the Lord is good: blessed is the man that trusteth in him.' "

&

Angel watched Jarrod walk away, then latched the cabin door. She turned and set his offerings on the little shelf he'd built into the wall. She carefully set it so Mama could still see her carved wooden rose. Just as Angel treasured her ring, Mama cherished that rose Grandpa made when he'd courted Grandma. "Mama, Jarrod brought you some of Dr. Jayne's expectorant. Wasn't that nice of him?"

Once Mama swallowed a spoonful and caught her breath, she patted Angel's hand. "Good man."

Angel turned away from the meaningful look in her mother's eyes. Mama cottoned to Jarrod, and for good reason. He showered her with affection and respect. Harv did too, but in a different way. Harv was a sweet, bumbling, jester of a man.

He'd tried to help out when he could, but Jarrod—well, Jarrod had a way of stepping in and getting a lot done with a minimum of fuss. Angel didn't want Mama trying to play matchmaker just because Jarrod believed in putting his muscles behind his faith.

The brown paper drew her attention. Horehound. Just the thought of it made her mouth water. Grandpa used to slip her a chip of it in church when the preacher got a bit longwinded. She took the tiniest drop for herself and gave one to Mama. "Here. A special treat. I think you'll have sweet dreams tonight, Mama."

"Some days, you live on dreams. Some days, you live on blessings."

Angel stooped, gave her a kiss, then closed the shutters. She'd left them open in the hopes that the dim light would help lead Jarrod home. When the sun set and he'd not yet gotten back, she'd been worried. It was her fault he'd gone to town. Now, with him back and a spoonful of medicine in Mama, relief poured through her. She curled up on her cot and sucked on the horehound. . .and the flavor lingered long after the candy dissolved—just like Jarrod's comfort lingered even after he went back to his own claim.

Chapter 9

The pickax barely made a chip in the hard rock. Jarrod broadened his stance and hefted the pick again. It came down in a mighty arc and made a small divot. Almost an hour later, he had a hole the size of both of Angel's fists. He leaned in an arc to ease his back and arm muscles, then waved at Angel. "How's your Mama today?"

"She slept like a baby, thanks to you."

He chuckled. "Good thing. As much noise as I'm makin' now, she's probably thinkin' the walls of Jericho are tumbling down."

"What if you used a metal tent stake as a chisel? Would that help?"

"Why, yes, I do believe it would." Half an hour later, Jarrod grinned at his progress. By chipping away at the edges, he'd managed to almost triple the size of the opening. If he worked at this all day for the next three days, then the mornings for a few more, he'd have a nice-sized, secure root cellar. Grayish granite chipped away, and Jarrod halted. Green. He'd hit a streak of green. It meant he'd found some copper, and copper often ran alongside— *No. I'm not going to let my imagination run away with me.*

He struck again. More green. Then more. The stripe widened. Time passed, but he lost track. Finally thirst made him halt. He walked to the creek and took a big, long drink, then splashed the refreshingly cold water on his face and neck.

Ben glanced over at him. "Never seen a man waste as much time as you—wandering off to town, messin' with a garden, diggin' a root pit."

Jarrod shrugged. "Bible tells of Joseph setting by food for the lean times. From what I hear, a man gets hungry in winter here if he doesn't plan ahead."

"You sayin' I didn't plan ahead? You callin' me a fool?"

"I have no idea how you supplied your family. Rain might have spoiled supplies. Creatures might have gotten into the bags and barrels. I'm just saying I'm trying to exercise wisdom on my own behalf."

"Hmpf." Ben plunged his pan into the water again.

Jarrod stopped in his cabin for something quick to eat. He didn't want to waste time cooking. After eating a chunk of jerky and taking a quick glug of apple cider from a jug, he was back out at the root pit.

Curiosity made him want to dig deeper, but common sense told him to widen the opening. If all he did was drive straight down, Ben would suspect he was digging a sample core. Not wanting to give Ben any reason to get snoopy, Jarrod tamped down his own feelings. He needed to stay calm. *Might be, nothing is here at all. Even if I don't strike gold, I'll still have a fine place to store my garden truck.*

Light began to wane. Jarrod served a few more blows on the chisel. All day long, he'd carefully taken the coppery earth off and slipped it in the hollow of a rotting log. The secrecy of the action went against his grain, but safety demanded he do just that. He set a board over the opening and started to walk away.

"You've been busy today."

"No more than you, Harv. What do you have there?"

"That net you set out caught this beauty." Harv held up a sizable trout. He hitched a shoulder and added, "I didn't catch nothing today, and I thought maybe you'd feel like sharing if I cook."

Soon, the men sat by a small fire and ate the trout. Harv stretched out his legs and studied his boots. He bent over and thumbed a crack in the old leather. "These ain't gonna last me another winter. I'm of a mind to bag me a buck. Injuns wear buckskin boots. Figure I could too. Eatin' something other than squirrel, fish, or rabbit would suit me fine."

"For all of the berries, I haven't seen many deer."

Harv shook his head. "Thimbleberries this time of year. Deer don't favor them. They was fine, eating the whortleberries and bilberries in July, but whatever we didn't gather, the gray catbirds, quail, and squirrels ate. The back corner of my claim is part of a deer run. What say we stake it out at daybreak and try to get us one?"

Jarrod didn't want deer—he wanted gold. The pit called to him, drew him. In that instant, he understood the seductive, insidious pull of gold fever. He cleared his throat as a flicker of compassion for Ben kindled in his heart. "Harv, I'd be proud to hunt with you. Are you wanting me to leave my bow behind?"

He pursed his lips and pondered on the matter. "Bring it. May be that some other critter happens by. You can take it down all quiet-like, and the deer won't be spooked away."

"The smokehouse can handle a buck, no problem. I'd like to see us fill up on as much as we can. I've decided to start setting more snares—all of the beasts have been fattening up over the summer, so they're of good size."

Harv agreed and headed for the log bridge. After he left, Jarrod put some gravel in his shaker box and worked by firelight for another hour or so before turning in.

After he read his Bible and prayed, he stacked his hands behind his head and stared up at the roof. A realization struck him. *Even if I hit gold and have enough to go buy my ranch, I'm not leaving until I can take Angel with me.*

"Mama! You're the one who always told me to be grateful."

"I never served you deer liver."

"It won't keep. Jarrod and Harv are smoking almost all of the rest of the deer. They butchered it into pieces no self-respecting cook would recognize, but we'll have plenty of fine meals from it. Here. Eat some."

"Did Ben at least help them butcher it?"

Angel shook her head.

"I can help." Mama rose on one elbow. "I'll wash the tripe and we can make sausage."

"No, Mama. You save your strength. We'll do just fine.

Truly, we will." Horror streaked through Angel at the thought of her mother doing anything at all. The minute she attempted even the smallest task, Ben would take that as a signal that she ought to be panning again.

As Angel gently nudged her to lie back down, Mama said, "Ever since Jarrod came, we've been eating better."

"He said Harv shot the deer. Harv's proud as a peacock. While they were waiting, Jarrod used his bow and brought down a wild turkey. It's months early, but we decided we're going to celebrate Thanksgiving day after tomorrow."

Mama's lids drooped, but a sweet, weary smile chased across her face. "Lord knows, we have plenty for which to be thankful."

❧

Two shirts. The nip in the predawn air demanded Jarrod put on two shirts. Even working to go through solid rock, he'd not work up enough heat to keep himself warm if he wore but a single shirt.

His breath condensed in the air as he stirred the banked coals from last night's fire. While coffee and oatmeal cooked, he carried some of the gravel from the pit over to his shaker box. He'd begun to see little glimmers last evening, so he'd decided working it would be more promising than working the creek silt. Then, too, it would quell any curiosity from Ben—as long as Ben didn't realize he'd carried the gravel from the area where he was digging.

Because he didn't particularly care to get in and out of the water all day, he'd taken to scooping a score or more of the sixteen-inch pans full of creek bottom and piling them by the shaker. He'd never dreamed when he started that habit would stand him in such good stead now.

A bowl of oatmeal and a cup of much-too-strong coffee later, Jarrod started to operate his shaker box. Pan after pan, he shook gravel through the grates.

Muscles heated from the hard work and the rising temperature as the morning sun climbed, Jarrod removed the outer shirt. He squinted at what he'd coaxed from the shaker box: several specks and flakes that amounted to about the size of his thumbnail. *Better than what I'd normally get, but still not much. I'll dig back there a bit deeper and see if there's more to be had.*

"Jarrod?" He looked over his shoulder and smiled at Angel as she picked up his shirt from the stump where he'd flung it. "I'm doing laundry today."

He nodded. They'd tangled over this a few times, but he'd finally relented. They'd made a deal—he made the cabin for her; she did his laundry and occasionally cooked for him. Just as he didn't want to be indebted, neither did she.

"We still have a bit of turkey left. I thought I'd make pasties for lunch."

He headed for his cabin. "Only if I give over some flour." When he came back out, he held a small bundle of laundry under one arm and a bowl of flour in the other and winked. "I'll carry this back so I'll have an excuse to visit your mother."

"You don't need an excuse. Mama looks forward to seeing you." Angel fell into step alongside him. "How are you doing on the root cellar?"

"It's taking a lot of time. I chose rock because I'm tired of creatures burrowing and eating the roots. I suppose I could have sunken a barrel, but being a hardheaded, stubborn Scot, once I started, I refused to change my ways."

They'd reached her fire. Jarrod set down his laundry and flour and wordlessly lifted the big iron wash cauldron. He carried it to the stream, filled it, and carried it back to the fire.

Harv and Pete were crossing the log bridge with their laundry. Pete dumped his sorry-looking pile of clothes and scratched his elbow. "That turkey you folks shared surely sat fine in my belly. Harv'll tell ya I make a purty fair corn bread. I even got me two eggs to make it, so how 'bout if I invite myself to lunch?"

"I got cornmeal," Harv offered.

Jarrod tucked Angel's braid behind her shoulder. "See there? You'll not have to cook at midday."

"I don't mind at all—"

"Laundry's hard work." He gave her a stern look. "You've got plenty to keep you more than busy."

"How'd you get eggs?" Harv asked Pete.

"Angel, get busy." Ben's interruption made them all turn around. He glowered. "You ain't getting anything done, standing 'round with this pack of lazy men. They might not have nothing to do, but you shore do. The rest of you, git."

"We'll eat at high noon, my claim," Harv whispered.

Just as the other two men headed toward the bridge, Ben swaggered back over. "You two best pay up now for your wash."

"Left my money over on my claim," Harv said.

"Me too." Pete gave Ben a look of owl-eyed innocence.

❧

Gold. Jarrod squatted down and reached in to touch the nugget he'd just chipped free. The front of it was copper, but the whole back gleamed with promise. Instead of lifting it, he paused and caught his breath, then shoved it aside and touched the rock face he'd just bared. Gold.

He chipped out a piece and placed it in his pocket. Someday, when he had a ranch, he still wanted a keepsake from this moment. *Lord, I prayed Thou wouldst help me get Angel away from that black-hearted stepfather of hers. My heart knows Thou hast placed this gold here. Let me be wise in what I do with it.*

Chipping away at the stone, Jarrod uncovered the colorful vein. He scraped the granite, quartz, and copper out of the pit to form a heap that would fill a lard bucket twice over. He stared at the widening yellow streak and wondered how deep it ran.

"Chow time!" Pete yelled from Harv's claim.

Jarrod crossed over to Harv's claim and sat next to Angel. She handed him a steaming pie tin. "Harv already fed Mama some. She said Pete's corn bread is so good, it'll be served at the banquet table in heaven."

"There's a fine recommendation." Jarrod took the food and frowned. "Your hands—"

"Washerwoman hands," she interrupted in a matter-of-fact tone. "I have my hands in and out of water so much, it's a miracle I haven't sprouted gills."

He wished he'd not said anything. The lye soap had her hands all red, and they'd been chapped already. Angel wasn't a vain woman, but she surely didn't need a man pointing out any of her flaws. He forced a chuckle, then took a taste of the corn bread and hummed his appreciation.

Secretly he kept thinking that the golden corn bread was disappearing fast, but the real gold of the day was just starting to make an appearance. That gold would buy Angel's freedom.

Chapter 10

Jarrod had gone to town again. Angel would have loved to accompany him, but Ben refused to let her go. In fact, Ben wouldn't listen to a word she said about supplies she wanted. He shouted that she'd spent far too much the last time she'd been in town, and he wasn't breaking his back every day down at the creek so she could squander his gold on foolishness.

Angel barely kept from asking him about *her* gold—the gold she slaved to get from the cold creek's bottom. He'd continued to take her findings each evening, and she'd seen him go through the hems of her skirts and her shoes before bedtime each night. He invariably muttered that she'd steal him blind if he didn't check. It had gotten worse since the men who paid for laundry started giving her the pay instead of handing it to Ben. Ben thought he'd take it back, but she'd entrusted it all to Jarrod, and that only made Ben more livid.

The paltry sum she counted as her very own wouldn't be much. She had no choice, though. Once Mama passed on, Angel knew she'd have to leave. Ben wouldn't give her a cent or a blanket when she left, either. If she could scrape together enough, she'd send a telegraph back home to Uncle Blackie and ask him to wire her enough money to buy a ticket on the stage. She should have thought to see how much a room in the boardinghouse cost. She'd need to stay there at least a few days. A telegraph would be three dollars for ten words, but she had a grand total of $1.81. Perhaps she could convince the owner of Fancy Pans to hire her for the time she'd be in town. He'd seemed nice enough.

The thought of Mama dying wrenched Angel's heart, but Mama often spoke of going home to be with Jesus and how happy the thought made her. Knowing Mama would be at peace softened Angel's grief, but it didn't take it away. On the other hand, the notion of leaving Ben filled Angel with nothing short of relief. Her mind skipped to Jarrod. He was rarely out of her thoughts these days. When she left, she'd be leaving Jarrod behind. The tremendous ache intensified inside of her— she'd lose Mama and Jarrod all at the same time.

At first, she'd been worried that Jarrod would strike gold and leave her behind when he went off to his dream ranch. He and Harv sometimes spoke aloud of ranching together—they'd make good partners. If they both left, she'd never survive here.

But now, she had come to the conclusion that even with them splitting the costs of buying a ranch, the men would have to stay at the creek for years—and Mama wasn't going to last that long. The irony of Angel leaving the men instead hit her. She couldn't laugh, though. The whole situation was just plain awful.

Jarrod had been wise to tell her to load up on supplies.

Especially with the smokehouse full, she didn't have to worry that Mama and she would go hungry. Even so, she would have enjoyed the opportunity to walk along the path to town, wander past the storefronts, and watch the rich panoply of folks in town. She might have been able to take in a shirt and sell it. Chances were good, she wouldn't even reach town before she sold it—prospectors and placers were eager to stay on their claims. They'd be interested in bartering for a new shirt she'd made from some of the sacks she'd gotten in return for her produce and laundry.

Instead, she watched as Jarrod tied a small keg of sauerkraut to Beulah so he'd have something to barter. He'd set out at daybreak, and a terrible sense of loneliness lapped at her with every panful she swirled. From the day he'd come, Jarrod somehow managed to insert himself into her life—to extend his friendship, his help, comfort, and his strength. Just knowing she could look over and see him or call out if a problem arose had given her a sense of security.

Last night, he'd come over to spend a few minutes with her and Mama. He'd recited the fourth chapter of James. Some of the words spun in her mind over and over again in the same cadence as she revolved the pan. *"God resisteth the proud, but giveth grace unto the humble. Submit yourselves therefore to God. Resist the devil, and he will flee from you. Draw nigh to God, and he will draw nigh to you. . . . Humble yourselves in the sight of the Lord, and he shall lift you up."* Humble yourselves. . . . Humble. . .

Lord, how much more humble can I be? I try so hard not to sass my stepfather. My hands are chapped, and my hair is straggly, and

170

I have nothing of value.

The pan held no gold whatsoever. She dumped it, scooped another panful, and continued to work. *God, I think I have the humility part down. How about Your part where You give grace and lift me up?*

❧

Jarrod headed for the assay office. He wanted to be the first man there for the day. Along the way, he'd been stopped twice by thirsty, armed men who wanted the contents of his keg. They hadn't accepted the explanation that it contained sauerkraut until he pried out the large cork stopper and gave them each a whiff. Disappointed, neither of the men were further interested in the keg when they discovered it held no spirits.

Hitching Beulah to the post outside the assay office, Jarrod whispered a prayer of thanks. He'd worried he'd not make it here with his precious load. To be sure, he doubted anyone had ever hefted a keg of sauerkraut into the place; but once he entered the office, pried off the lid, and pulled out the lard can, he said in the quietest tone possible, "This isn't an ore sample with lots of rock. I believe it's what the fables say leprechauns guard at the end of the rainbow."

Sooner than Jarrod could sneeze, they'd locked the assay door and put up the "Closed" sign. He'd secretly hoped they'd do just that. If anyone discovered he'd struck gold, his life and dreams would be in danger. . .and the most important dream was for him to be able to sweep Angel away from here.

"Never had such a stinky sample." The assay man wrinkled his nose. His expression changed to open-mouthed astonishment when he accepted the lard pail from Jarrod. The weight of it spoke of an appreciable load. He quickly thumbed off the lid.

Jarrod grinned. "I know you don't normally let a fellow stay and watch, but it'll take dynamite to make me leave."

"Uh. . .yes, well. . ." The assay man choked, "Feel free to stay. Jimmy, forget the sledgehammer. Put this on the bucking-board and use the muller."

Jarrod watched him take several crucibles from a shelf and cleared his throat. "I've also brought a coffee tin that's full too."

The clerk and the assay man exchanged startled looks.

Quirking them a grin, Jarrod offered, "If we get hungry while you work, we can always eat some of the sauerkraut. Best you ever tasted. My Angel made it."

"Mister, if this turns out to be real, that angel of yours is going to be walking the streets of gold."

"We'll still want to do splits on this," the assayer said as he pulled a device to the fore that would divide the pulverized gold into three separate sample splits.

"Don't bother. When I leave, I'll be giving away the claim, so I don't need to establish an average yield or prove the ore is high grade."

The assayer shook his head and put some of the pulverized gold into a crucible. He selected litharge as the flux and mixed it in to help the metal melt. The crucible went into the D-shaped upper door of the combination furnace and came out a half hour later. Carefully he poured the melt into pointed-bottom molds and whistled. "Hardly anything but color here."

While that cooled, he filled several more crucibles.

Jarrod knew he had to stay on the far side of the counter, but he leaned forward to watch the assayer empty the molds and shatter away the glasslike slag to get to the metal that had sunk to the bottom. He placed the metal into heated bone ash cupels and placed them in the other door of the furnace. The litharge burned away, leaving nothing but the metal button-shaped dore. Once freed from the cupel, the dore was painstakingly weighed, then dipped in nitric acid to remove any silver. All that was left was gold—which, of all things, looked like a black button.

The dore was weighed again, and the assayer murmured, "You're losing almost no weight here. Your sample is nearly pure gold."

The clerk and assayer listed each dore, added up the weight, and independently calculated the value of Jarrod's bonanza. They conferred and showed Jarrod their ciphering. "At $20.67 per Troy ounce, Sir, you just struck it rich. Never saw anything like it. That is a vein of pure gold."

" 'Tis a miracle. God put it there." Jarrod shook his head. "I'm blessed."

❧

Angel tossed the hot potato from one hand to the other. Its warmth felt wonderful. Jarrod had brought back two gunny-sacks of potatoes. "You're going to have to dig that root cellar even bigger now."

He grinned. "It'll be worth it."

Ben snorted. "Why bother? Weather's turned. It'll be cold enough to keep them in your cabin."

Jarrod ignored him. "I sold the sauerkraut. Since the keg was yours, Harv, and Angel did all of the work with my cabbage, I reckoned we all ought to get something out of it."

"Kraut's not worth much." Harv scratched the back of his neck.

"Worth plenty," Ben said as he leaned forward. "How much didja git for me?"

"Winter's coming." Jarrod gave Angel a smile that warmed her heart every bit as much as the potato warmed her hands. "I brought back kerosene and wicks for our lanterns."

Ben shot to his feet. "You had no right. Wasn't your money to spend."

"It was mine, and I'm delighted." Angel looked up at her stepfather. "You're in the tent with a lantern. Mama and I will need to use the other, so the extra kerosene—"

"This is your fault, Scotsman. Built that stupid shack, and now it's costing me."

Angel wanted to cry. Her stepfather was a miserable, selfish lout. Just yesterday, she'd seen him swipe the horehound candy, leaving none at all for Mama. Now he wanted to rob Mama of the comfort of a lamp.

Harv banged his plate on his knee. "Aw, pipe down, Ben. The way I see it, he did you a favor. Now you got an empty tent to work in all winter. Sure beats freezin' outside like you done last winter."

"This ain't none of your business."

Jarrod folded his arms across his chest. "The business was his, Angel's, and mine. Harv helped raise the uppermost logs and roof. The deal didna involve you at all."

"Forget dealin' with the man, Jarrod." Harv glowered at Ben. "He ate your taters and my venison, but he didn't put a morsel on our plates. Something for nothing—and even that's not good enough. Plain and simple, he's a leech."

Ben blustered, "Angel cooked that food!"

Jarrod nodded. "Aye, she did a fine job of it too. I doubt there's a harder workin' lass on the face of the earth. If you were her father, you'd have call to be proud."

His words of praise made Angel's heart sing. So did the fact that he stood up for her. Ben was the one who disavowed any blood tie to her. Jarrod simply underscored that now.

"Speaking of parents, Angel, is your mama feeling well enough for me to pay her my respects?"

"She'd love to have you visit."

"Sickly old women and root cellars," Ben sneered. "Never saw a man waste so much time."

"What a man counts as important is between him and God."

Two months later, Jarrod slipped the section of log back into place inside his cabin. He'd chiseled about a foot free, hollowed the core, and filled it with more gold. Once mortared in place, it made a perfect hiding place.

The vein of gold had narrowed to a mere thread, but he didn't care at all. He had more than enough now to take Angel to a modest ranch and provide for her. God had blessed him with all he needed in a material sense. *Lord, open the Lass's heart fully to Thee. The bloom of her love took a bad frost. Winter's here,*

and yet Thou canst make a flower bloom at any time. Tend her
spirit, and then let me tend her heart.

He put on his jacket and tromped through the snow to
Angel's cabin. "I chinked a few places between my logs and
have extra mortar, Angel. Do you have a few areas that need a
wee bit of attention?"

"You built it soundly, Jarrod."

"But there are bound to be a few spots." He walked around
and dabbed a few places here and there. Angel accompanied
him, and he waited until Ben's back was turned and handed her
a bottle.

"Boveril?"

He nodded. "If you get snowed in, you and your mama can
dilute it and heat it over the kerosene lamp to have beef soup."

His eyes narrowed as her hands shook when she slipped the
bottle into her skirt pocket.

"Lass, I've an early Christmas present for you. 'Tisn't much,
but I'd rather you have it now. Come with me."

"Jarrod! You don't need to give me a thing!"

He ignored her protest and took hold of her elbow. As soon
as they reached his cabin, he let go. She'd not come inside, and
he'd not have it any other way. He ducked in and reappeared.
"Close your eyes."

A beguiling flush filled her cheeks as her lashes fluttered
shut. "This isn't right, Jarrod. I don't have anything for you."

"Hush." He unfolded the fawn-colored cloak and draped it
about her shoulders. The thick wool swept around her. He was
sure the cloak would match the brown and golden shards in her

eyes, as he fumbled to fasten the button at her throat. "Merry Christmas."

Her eyes opened. A glistening of tears turned them into molten gold. "Jarrod, it's so beautiful!"

"The woman who's wearing it is beautiful." He pulled up the hood and gently tucked strands of her soft hair inside the dark fur trim. "There."

She slipped her hands out and clasped his. "Thank you."

Pete wandered up. He chuckled. "Now will ya get a gander at that. Our Angel's wearin' new duds. I was in town yesterday. Came by to drop off a letter and pass on the word: Sunday, they're holding a Christmas tent meeting. Circuit rider's scheduled to be here."

Jarrod's heart jumped. He smiled down at Angel. "I'd be pleased to take you."

"She ain't going nowhere with you, Scotsman." Ben's bellow split the cold air. "Least of all to church!"

"I want you to go with Jarrod," Mama said. "I'm giving you my permission."

Angel sat on her cot and stared at her mother in surprise.

"I heard Ben shouting. I made a terrible mistake marrying him, Angel. I was so lonely, and he was the first man who paid me any attention after years of widowhood. I knew he wasn't a believer, but I ignored God's Word and married him anyway. Foolishly I was sure I could change him. All it did was cause you and me both misery. I won't have him ruin your life anymore. Go. Go to church. I'll tell Ben I'm letting you."

Ben's dark mood couldn't ruin Angel's excitement. The beaming smile on Jarrod's face when she gave him the news warmed her every bit as much as the cloak. Harv volunteered to come over to feed Mama stew for lunch, and for the next three days, Angel thought of almost nothing other than the fact that Jarrod would be taking her to church.

Saturday night, she boiled water, bathed, and washed her hair. After it dried, she sat on the floor, and Mama helped her roll the back of it in rags so she could arrange her hair in a suitable style for Sunday. When they were done, Angel went to the shelf to get Mama's medicine.

It was gone.

Chapter 11

Jarrod heard Mrs. Frisk's cough as he walked to the cabin. Angel opened the door, but she wasn't ready for church. Pale faced and red-eyed, she stepped outside and shut the door. "I can't go."

"Not with your mother sounding like that," he agreed. "What happened? She was stable."

Tears spilled down Angel's cheeks. "Her elixir is gone— there was still almost a full bottle yesterday afternoon. I know it's Sunday, but when you're in town, could you see if the store-keeper would open just long enough for you to buy some?"

Jarrod wrapped his arms around her. "No need to weep, Lass."

His jacket muffled her whisper. "Use the money you're keeping for me."

He dipped his head and brushed a kiss on her temple. The dear woman in his arms was willing to sacrifice her own escape for her mother's sake. "There's no need. I've two bottles of Dr. Jayne's at my cabin."

"I still want you to go to church without me."

He cradled her face and said in a soft growl, "We'll be havin' our verra own church right here."

"Oh, I'd like that. Mama would too."

"Go on inside and keep warm. I'll be back in a trice."

Jarrod went to his own cabin and quickly collected several things in a gunnysack. Just as Angel opened the door for him, they heard a loud roar and looked just in time to see Ben fly through the air and splash into the nearly iced-over creek.

Harv stood at the bank where Ben had been. He wore a thunderous scowl as he stared at the hole in the ice a good four feet away and waited until Ben surfaced. "Served you right," Harv bellowed as Ben started to climb out of the frigid water. "I shoulda done that months ago." He stomped up to the cabin and demanded, "How's Mrs. Frisk?"

"Jarrod brought her some elixir." Angel pulled them both inside and latched the door. "There's not much space. Please take a seat on the other cot."

Harv ignored her. He stood over Mrs. Frisk and nervously rubbed his knuckles. "Don't like how you're a-coughin'. I aim to lift you a tad higher so's to ease your breathing. Angel, stick something 'hind her shoulders. That ought to help a mite."

It took but a few moments to situate and medicate Angel's mother. By then, the poor woman was exhausted. Harv waited to be sure she'd fallen asleep, then growled to Jarrod, "That no good varmint met me at the bridge. Said I didn't need to come check on her. Bragged he'd made sure Angel wouldn't be going no place. Know what he did then? Poured out Mrs. Frisk's medicine."

Angel went white and turned away. Jarrod longed to speak with her privately, but he didn't want to leave her mother alone, and Harv needed to be calmed down. Then again, Jarrod wasn't sure he was the man to pacify anyone at the moment.

"I shouldn't have planted him a facer; I shoulda filled his hide with buckshot." Harv rocked back and forth in agitation.

"The Bible says to do good to them who hurt you." Jarrod shook his head. "Right about now, that's about the furthest thing from my mind."

Harv snorted. "Yeah, well, I was thinking of another verse. Told me just where to aim my buckshot: Turn the other—"

"Enough!" Jarrod silenced him.

"Sorry, Angel," Harv said. "I have a bad habit of letting my temper get ahead of my sense."

Angel reached up, but from his vantage point, Jarrod couldn't tell whether she was rubbing weary eyes or wiping away tears. He softly said, "We're not going into town, but that doesn't mean we can't have our own Christmas service right here. Why don't you nap a bit, Angel? Harv and I'll go fix a nice meal. When you and your mama wake up, we'll all break bread and worship."

"Could we?" She turned around, and a tiny bit of hope glimmered in her sad eyes.

"Absolutely."

Harv cleared his throat. "I'm not 'zactly a Sunday-go-to-meetin' kinda fella, but I'd be proud to join you."

"There you have it then. We'll be back after awhile." Jarrod gently turned Angel to the side and smiled at her baffled look. He reached up and teased free the knot holding a length of rag.

A satiny soft ringlet unwound and curled about his fingers.

"Oh!" Embarrassment colored that small sound.

"A woman's hair is her crowning glory, and I'm thinking you're quite a princess." He lifted her off her feet, laid her on the cot, and as Harv luffed a blanket over her, Jarrod brushed her curls on the pillow. "Rest, Lassie-mine."

"Make up your mind," Harv teased. "Is she a princess or is she a mere lass?"

Jarrod walked past him and waited until the second he was shutting the cabin door to say, "My lass is a princess."

"Do good to them who revile you for my name's sake." The instruction played through Jarrod's mind. He didn't have a right to welcome Ben into the women's cabin. Yes, Angel's mother was Ben's wife, but his neglect and outright abuse gave ample cause for the women to be insulated from him. Even so, Jarrod tried to do the right thing. He dished up a portion of the meal and took it to Ben's tent.

"Ben?" The tent flap was loosely tied back, so Jarrod stepped inside.

"Get out!" Ben wheeled around and roared.

Jarrod stood rooted to the ground. The dirt bore an arc-shaped scrape from a small chest having been pushed aside. In the earth beneath where the chest had stood was a hole—and in it were stacked several of the small leather pouches placers used to hold their flakes.

"You've starved your kin and wanted to pawn off a family treasure, yet you have more than sufficient to provide for them?"

"Ain't none of your business." Ben shoved the chest back over his stash.

"I'm making it my business."

"Not a week after I married what was s'posed to be a rich widow-woman, I found out the house she was a-livin' in belonged to her uncle and she only had fifty stinkin' dollars to her name. I figgered to leave her a-hind with the excuse that I was going prospectin', but she took a mind to tag along. Said a woman belonged with her man. You got no call to be judgin' me. She made her bed, and she's lyin' in it."

With painstaking care, Jarrod set down the plate. "Esau sold his birthright for a meal. I'm thinking you sold your soul for gold."

Ben rose and stood toe-to-toe with him. "Then I'll sell my family too. You keep yer mouth shut about my stash; I'll leave them alone and let you come on my claim to provide for them."

❧

Angel smoothed the russet shirt, took a deep breath, and reached for the door. She'd slept hard; so instead of forming orderly ringlets she could style, her hair spiraled in an impossible commotion she'd tried to contain in a ribbon at her crown. *Mama's in her nightdress, I'm a mess, and we're entertaining for Christmas. I didn't even cook or—*

"Let them in, Dear," Mama whispered. "It's cold outside."

"Happy Christmas." Jarrod smiled at her with enough warmth to melt every snowdrift in Colorado.

"Yeah, Merry Christmas. Now git inside afore I drop something." Harv nudged Jarrod inside.

In a matter of minutes, the men dragged in a small bench, tossed a towel over it as a tablecloth, and set several dishes on it. Harv sidled between the "table" and Mama's cot, scooped her up, and sat down with her on his lap. "Beggin' your pardon, Mrs. Frisk, but I want you to have a good meal; and you'll waste all of your strength trying to sit up on your own. I mean no disrespect."

Jarrod sat next to Angel. "I'd like to say grace." He said a simple, heartfelt prayer, then lifted the Dutch oven's lid with a flourish. "M'ladies, Christmas dinner is served."

Angel smiled at Jarrod. "Roast duck and baked apples—you and Harv put together a wondrous feast."

Awhile later, Mama said, "I can't eat another bite."

Jarrod wiped his hands and reached into a bag. He pulled out his Bible. "I thought to read the Nativity from St. Luke. 'Tisn't just a fairy tale or a birthday story. The King of Creation sacrificed His Son to ransom us—each one of us—back into His family. Divine love paid the price."

Grandpa used to read this passage, then Uncle Blackie did. Angel hadn't heard it for years. She closed her eyes and listened to Jarrod's rich, deep voice as the words of Christ's birth filled her tiny cabin.

"We oughtta sing a carol or two," Harv decided aloud when Jarrod shut the Bible. They sang "Hark! The Herald Angels Sing," then managed to mix up all of the gifts in the "Twelve Days of Christmas," and ended with "Silent Night."

Mama glowed with joy, but her weariness was unmistakable. They tucked her in, then cleaned up the supper mess.

Angel insisted, "I'm doing the dishes."

Harv chortled. "Won't hear me complain. I hate that chore."

As they worked together, Angel quietly confessed to Jarrod, "Hearing the Bible does something deep inside of me. Until you came, Mama and I had gone years without the Word or church at all. I'd nearly lost faith, thinking God forgot us."

"God never forgets His children."

"I suppose not, but this child sure lost sight of Him. You tell me I'm a princess, but—"

"No buts. You're the daughter of the King of kings. Might be that your faith got weak, but that happens when you don't have the Bible or any Christian fellowship. God's here with you, and His arms are open wide. He's glad to have you run to Him."

"When you were reading the Christmas story, I was thinking about what you said. Divine love—God ransomed me back with His sacrifice of love."

"That He did. I'm leaving my Bible in your cabin so you can read from it for yourself each day."

"Jarrod! You can't do that. You treasure your Bible."

They'd finished the dishes. Jarrod cleared his throat and folded her chapped hands in his. "We need to have a talk, Lass. Things are changing."

She dipped her head. *He's leaving. I should have known.*

"I told you from the start that I didn't plan to stay here for long."

Lord, I've started to lean on Thee again, and with Jarrod leaving, Thou art the only way Mama and I will make it.

"But your mama's doing poorly."

Give me strength, God. I'm not just losing my mama, I'm about to lose the man I've come to love.

❧

Jarrod watched the color drain from Angel's face and slid his arm around her waist. He drew her into the shelter of his arms. "I know losing her will grieve you. I'll miss her too. She's a dear woman."

Angel remained silent. She nodded, and tears slipped down her cheeks.

Jarrod tenderly brushed them away. "I'll be staying 'til she goes home to be with the Lord." His heart wrenched when Angel let out a small sob. He cradled her head to his chest, but used his thumb to tilt her jaw up so she'd still face him.

Somewhere in the span of months he'd been here, the time that he was ministering to her in God's name had also become a courtship. At first, he'd been wary of that fact because he didn't want Angel to think he'd used God as a tool to work his way into her heart. She'd needed spiritual restoration, and he didn't have a doubt in his mind about the strength of her faith. Love had blossomed alongside faith—and that boded well for marriage. He looked at her and knew the time had come to speak from his heart.

"I'm wanting you for my wife, Angel. Will you come away with me on that day? We've a future waiting for us together. I've fallen in love with you, Lass. I'll cherish you as the Bible tells me to."

"You love me?"

He chuckled softly. The dazed look in her eyes might have

hurt him, but the wonder in her voice and the hope in her smile charmed him. "Heart and soul. Will you be my wife?"

She clutched his jacket with both hands and burrowed close. "I kept telling myself not to fall in love with you because you'd leave. I couldn't help it, though. I prayed God would send someone to help, but I never thought He'd really hear me. You're the answer—not just to my dreams, but to my prayers too."

Jarrod finally allowed himself the kiss he'd waited and longed for. He sealed their engagement with a kiss that held the promise of a bright future.

When they parted, Angel took a few moments to catch her breath and gather her wits. "But Jarrod, you were going to stay until you'd have enough gold for a ranch."

"Lass, I've had enough gold for a ranch now for a whole season. God blessed us with a sweet little pocket here on my claim. We've gracious plenty to meet our needs."

"Then why did you stay?"

"Because the gold in your eyes was more precious to me than anything else. The real treasure wasn't what the current of the river swept my way. It's what the path of God brought."

"You sacrificed your dreams to stay with me?"

"No, Dearling. I realized my heart's desire when God set me down here next to you. 'Twas no sacrifice—'twas a joy." He pulled her ring from his shirt pocket. It sparkled in the weak winter sun. "This band was a token that God used to bring us together. It even had my initials inscribed inside—see here? JM. I want you to wear it now as a symbol of our engagement. Your grandpa made this band for your grandma from gold he found, and I thought it was a fitting tradition. I've had gold from my claim made into a band of your verra own. 'Twill fit alongside this the day we take our vows."

"Ben will take it from me."

"Nae, Lass. Ben willna ever bother you again. You and your treasure are safe at last."

Epilogue

Christmas morning brought no more than a light dusting of snow. Jarrod stopped by the root cellar that he'd emptied. Once it held God's gift of gold for him to ransom Angel from this place. Now a cross stood over it. Angel's mother had been delighted with the news of their engagement. She'd given her blessing and said a sweet prayer for them. The very next day, she'd simply failed to awaken from her midmorning nap. Jarrod rested his hand on the cross and promised softly, "I'll be takin' your daughter to a nice little place, and she'll be cherished. God keep you until we meet again at His banqueting table."

He nodded at Pete and Harv. They stood off to the side. Jarrod's things took most of the space on Otto and Beulah, but one gunnysack held Angel's things. Ben had blustered last night about Angel trying to steal his supplies, but she'd packed nothing but her clothes and the little wooden rose her mother passed down to her. All of Harv's possessions formed a haphazard lump on the back of a placid-looking mule. He'd been happy as could be when Jarrod and Angel asked him to join them on the ranch Jarrod bought.

The men each held the halters of a trio of horses. Pete and Jarrod had gone into town yesterday so Jarrod could quit claim his place over to Pete. Jarrod then bought the horses so they could travel on to the ranch he bought.

The day he'd heard of the Christmas service, he'd been sent a telegram from a widow whose ranch he'd admired. They'd kept in contact, and with the silver panic and the devaluation of land, she'd decided to sell. Now, that spread would belong to him and Angel. He didn't want his wife having to walk out of here—he wanted her to ride like a queen.

Jarrod crossed Ben's claim one last time. The hour had come for him to collect his bride. He patted his pocket. Angel's band nestled there. Soon it would glitter on her hand, always to remind her she was his true treasure. He knocked on the cabin door and called out from the second chapter of Song of Solomon, " 'Arise, my love, my fair one, and come away.' "

CATHY MARIE HAKE

Cathy Marie is a southern California native who loves her work as a nurse and Lamaze teacher. She and her husband have a daughter, a son, and two dogs, so life is never dull or quiet. Cathy Marie considers herself a sentimental packrat, collecting antiques and Hummel figurines. She otherwise keeps busy with reading, writing, and bargain hunting. Cathy Marie's first book was published by **Heartsong Presents** in 2000 and earned her a spot as one of the readers' favorite new authors. Since then, she's written several other novels, novellas, and gift books. You can visit her online at www.CathyMarieHake.com.

A Token of Promise

by Rebecca Germany

Dedication

To all those family members who came before me
and left not only wonderful heirloom reminders of their lives
but an unshakable faith upon which I could build my own
Christian faith. I thank God for you.

Chapter 1

San Francisco, California—October 1897

Red! He appreciated the color in a sunset, in a strawberry pie, and in a woman's blushing cheeks, but tomato red did nothing for Gabe Monroe's freshly polished top boots. Would the beaver cloth forever be stained?

He looked from the mess of seeds and tomato pulp up the length of long skirts in front of him. *She must be the one. Yes, she'll do nicely.* With her slight frame and golden flecked brown hair, she favored his late sister-in-law.

"Oh!" The young woman's market basket dropped to the ground as she knelt and swiped at the mess with her hands.

Gabe touched her shoulders, coaxing her to stand. "It will wash up."

"I'll get you a rag."

"Don't worry about it. I'll clean up back at the hotel."

Her gaze darted toward the well-tended yard until she braved a look into his eyes. He returned her study of him with his head tilted to the side, admiring her blue eyes and blushing cheeks.

"I really. . .am. . .am sorry," she stammered in apology.

"Are you Reverend Chiles's ward?"

"Umm, yes."

"Well then, I'll return for you on the morrow next. Good day." He touched his hat and strode to a fine carriage and horse that waited in the shade of a tree. *What luck! It is a most uncanny resemblance.*

❧

Charlotte Vance hurried in the side door of the large home of the Rev. and Mrs. Chiles. Weaving between several barrels of packed china, she willed her racing heart to return to normal. What business could a handsome man of some obvious wealth have at the reverend's home? She didn't recognize him as a parishioner, and if she understood him correctly, his visit seemed to have something to do with her. . .and two days hence. Questions and possible scenarios vied for attention in her mind.

From the kitchen came the high-pitched voice of the lady of the house. "Charlotte, where have you been? Oh, there is so much to be done, and my poor legs are already weak with the tension."

Charlotte took a deep breath as she rounded the doorway to the kitchen and placed her groceries on the table. "The market was busy today, Ma'am, with the last of the harvest having come in. I saw Mrs. Morgan, and she sends her regards and prayers for your health."

Mrs. Chiles rummaged through the basket, seemingly ignoring Charlotte's words. "Is this all you got? The reverend specifically asked for tomatoes."

"Yes, Ma'am, those—"

"Tsk. I'd send you back, but there is too much to do here." The woman thumped her cane against the polished floorboards. "You must get things packed and ready for the movers. Now that you are leaving, the reverend says we will start for my niece's home in just four days—after Sunday's church picnic of course."

"Leaving?"

"Get the lunch together, then I believe you should start with the parlor knickknacks." The old woman sank to a kitchen chair. "Oh, how I ache. I so look forward to settling in Phoenix. Retirement must be a lovely thing. No more ridiculous expectations placed on an old woman. . .and man." She sighed.

"But Mrs. Chiles, about where I am to go in two days. . ." Charlotte choked on the fear that suddenly rose in her throat. For two years she had relied on the Chileses' generosity to give her a home in exchange for her work as a housekeeper. She had no means to support herself.

Raising a frail hand as if shooing a fly, the old woman said, "Oh, Child, the Lord is blessing you with a ready-made family. Though love escaped you when your dear Oliver was killed, you are going to be comfortably provided for all in perfect timing for our departure."

Charlotte's heart went back to race speed. "Family?"

"Why, yes. A man with a child is in need of a wife." She smiled. "And he's a Monroe. I met his grandmother Aggie back some thirty years ago. What a dear lady." Mrs. Chiles's body slumped against the chair as she seemed to tire of the topic. "The man will be here on Friday to take you to the boat."

Arctic blue eyes and wavy, dark brown hair rushed to her memory. She covered her warm cheeks with her hands and asked, "Boat?"

"Girl, must you persist with these one-word questions? Of course a boat. You will be living in Alaska with half the rest of the country who have been struck with gold fever." Mrs. Chiles rose to her feet, aided by her cane. "I must survey what needs to be done. Oh, so much work remains."

Left alone with still more unanswered questions, Charlotte quickly found a chair to drop into. Though she was twenty and without parents, did that give others the right to decide her future?

This couldn't be happening. She knew she would need to find a home and a job when the Chileses moved to Arizona, and she had been praying for an answer to her problem. But this didn't seem natural—marrying a stranger, mothering a motherless child, moving to Alaska.

Still, what choice did she really have? If Rev. Chiles had approved of the man and the marriage plan, it must be worthy of her trust.

Four and a half years ago she had promised to marry Oliver McKnight, but could she really be ready to be a wife—and mother—in two days?

❧

Alaska. It seemed like another world to Charlotte. A place of wild and sensationalized stories. But it was where she was bound with all her worldly possessions stuffed into two large trunks along with new purchases of wool-lined boots and fur-lined gloves.

She sat on the edge of the berth, happy to have a small sleeping compartment to herself away from the three other women onboard who were rumored to be adventuresses. She could feel the stress along her shoulders, the consequence of the morning's rushed activities.

With all the shopping, packing, and good-byes to be done in two short days, there had been no time for Mr. Monroe to come to dinner and give Charlotte a more clear idea of what to expect from her new home. She still didn't know if the man's child was a boy or girl. And worse, she didn't know exactly when her nuptials would be performed.

She didn't know if she'd ever learn to demand answers from her elders. It wasn't in her upbringing. She just assumed that Rev. Chiles would perform the wedding vows Friday morning when Mr. Monroe came for her.

He arrived while she finished the breakfast dishes, and her trunks were promptly loaded into his carriage. When Charlotte ventured to ask about the wedding, Mrs. Chiles made her feel like a child.

"Don't slow the man down, you have a boat to catch. Mr. Monroe has all the marriage fixings worked out for when you reach Alaska. Don't you, Sir?"

Mr. Monroe only frowned at the old woman and stepped closer to Charlotte. He towered over her, and she had to look up into his eyes. Eyes the color she could only guess an Alaskan glacier might reflect.

He cleared his throat. "Miss Vance, please accept this locket as a token of your engagement."

As he placed the fine, oval-shaped locket in her hands, she noticed his own hands were rough—not the hands of a high-society gentleman. They were strong hands, testifying to honest work.

No more was spoken on the subject as good-byes were said, and Charlotte left the fresh flowers she had gathered for a bouquet in a vase for Mrs. Chiles. Mr. Monroe had remained quiet all during the drive through the long, steep streets to the wharf, and Charlotte had concentrated on keeping her tears behind a dam.

She fingered the gold locket that hung around her neck. Though heavy and ornate, its beauty charmed her.

Oh, Lord, give me strength to do as Thou wouldst lead. I've done as my elders have told me, but, Lord, if I should get off this boat now and fend for myself, I will. I'm scared of the unknown— but mostly of being alone. Oh, dear Father. . .

Suddenly Charlotte felt the need to get out of the cramped room and go on deck to view the docks and city. She threw her cape over her shoulders and made her way to the top deck. Rushing to the railing, she clung to it as she felt the small steamer shift and pull away from the dock. She scanned the crowds of people on the wharf who cheered on the Klondike stampeders even as they hurried back to work in preparation for another boatload to leave. A few dozen men lined the *Dawson*

Belle's decks to wave back, but the hull of this boat mainly carried supplies to sustain those already living in the northern regions.

"Wouldn't you be more comfortable below deck and away from the chill wind off the bay?"

Charlotte already recognized the deep baritone voice as Mr. Monroe's. She closed her eyes and tried to relax. This mellow voice would greet her every morning.

"Miss Vance?"

Slowly she turned to face him. She couldn't explain how, but she already liked him. He exuded confidence yet with a bit of bashfulness. "May I ask your name, Mr. Monroe?"

"My name?"

"Yes, don't you think we should be on a first-name basis now?"

He cleared his throat and leaned against the rail. "Well, it's Gabriel, but friends just call me Gabe."

She liked it and couldn't stop a grin, but as she looked up into his face, she saw something in his expression. A question? A regret?

He looked away. "Would you like me to walk you to your room?"

"No, thank you. Not just yet. Please tell me a little about Alaska."

"Well. . ." He cleared his throat again. "It is large and wild. Majestic mountains tower around the little valley where Dyea sits with only a small opening out to the ocean. It rains a lot."

"Is Dyea a large town?"

"Sure. It's been fast doubling in size. It's located just south of Chilkoot Trail, which so many are using to get to the Klondike."

"But there is gold in Dyea too, right?" The reports she heard made it sound like gold was all over the ground in Alaska.

"Nah. You gotta get over the mountains to start looking for gold." He crossed his long legs, throwing more of his broad weight on the rail. "I'll be heading there before long myself—after you're settled, of course."

Suddenly it seemed like her lungs couldn't draw air. "You mean. . .you are going to leave me in Dyea. . .alone?"

He stared at his boots. "Philip will take good care of you. You'll know that as soon as you meet him. He has a real prosperous store there. In fact, he leases this steamer for hauling his goods." He smiled at her; though as she kept staring at him, his brows began to pucker.

"Who is Philip?"

He drew himself up straight. "What? He's my brother. . . younger brother." He began to relax. "I'm sorry if I forgot to give you his name in all the rush and excitement of finding you. I know you'll like him fine, and everyone can't help but love his little Sarah."

Charlotte swallowed hard against the tightness in her throat and chest. "His daughter?" she whispered.

"Yes, that's Sarah." His tone warmed at the mention of the child. "She just turned two. Her mother died of a fever."

She turned back to the rail, clinging to it for support. *Lord, it was bad enough that I have no other option than to marry a stranger, but to marry a man I haven't even set eyes on is. . .*

Charlotte gazed out at the shrinking harbor. Her heart sank

as she knew her destination had been confirmed. She would go to Alaska and become Mr. *Philip* Monroe's wife.

The silence of a woman could be such a deafening noise. What had he said to stifle her questions and dim the light of interest in her eyes?

Gabe lifted his hand. He wanted to touch her shoulder. He wanted to offer her comfort and reassurance, but. . .this was his brother's bride. Right now his feelings weren't very brotherly.

She drew him like a moth is drawn to candlelight. It was a crazy sensation. Gabe had had his one true love and watched her be taken from him. He knew Charlotte had also lost her fiancé. Love like that didn't strike twice.

He sat down on a nearby crate. The deck had cleared of all but a few men who were smoking together. He gazed at Charlotte's back, so stiff yet so delicate.

Gabe swallowed hard and searched for something to say. . . anything. "Lottie, would you like to sit down?"

She turned her face toward him. "What did you call me?"

"I thought since you asked for my first name that I could call you Lottie," he mumbled.

"Charlotte is my name."

"I know. I just thought Lottie was fitting." He looked up to gage her mood.

She sighed and moved to sit beside him. "I've never had a nickname. My father always called me Charlotte, and I was always the proper preacher's daughter."

"You don't think Lottie is a proper name?"

She gave a laugh as she leaned back against the steamer. "It's fine."

"When did your father die?" he asked, enjoying the relaxed tone the conversation had taken.

"About two years ago."

"And your fiancé?"

She turned pain-filled eyes to him. "Four years ago, in Colorado while mining for gold." A tear suddenly sprang down her cheek, and she dashed her fingertips against it.

"I'm sorry. I'd. . .um. . .offer you a handkerchief, but I don't carry anything decent for a lady." Silence cloaked them for a couple minutes as they gazed at the water around them, then he offered, "I can understand your loss. I lost my fiancée."

Charlotte looked at him, and somehow he relished having a connection he could offer to her pain.

"She died?"

"Well, no. She. . ." How could he explain such a painful event? "Aileen's father and mine did business together. My father has full or part ownership of a lot of businesses in and around San Francisco—even Philip's business in Dyea. He got the bulk of my grandfather's wealth that came out of the '49 gold rush."

Gabe took a focused breath. "Anyway. Aileen's father got into a tight business situation, and my father initially helped him. But then my father withdrew all his money when the Panic hit, and Aileen's family went broke. They lost everything, and her father has even been under question of the law. He refused to let us marry and made her marry another wealthy man. Someone who wasn't Blackie Monroe's son."

He chanced a look at Charlotte. Her blue eyes reflected his pain. Her soft features held understanding and sympathy. It gave him strength to continue.

"If I make money in the gold fields, I can pay back what my father owes the family. . .and do it without my father's money supporting me."

She nodded. "It's not your debt, but I understand."

"I can accept now that marriage isn't for me with the loss of Aileen," he continued. "Just as you have resigned yourself to marry someone you have never met after losing your love."

She stared at him with her mouth agape. Then seeming to shake herself, she closed her mouth and looked away. She pulled her cape closer around her neck.

Again he felt like he had not worded things right. "Lottie?"

She shook her head but turned to him. "Do you think God would allow love to be stolen away from us and never give us something to fill the hole?"

"I don't know if God gets all that involved in how we feel."

"Oh, but if you believe in Jesus Christ and the Holy Spirit, you must believe that God wants us to know His love and cares about even the smallest part of our lives. Only through His comfort have I managed my grief over losing Daddy and Oliver." Her eyes pleaded for Gabe to understand her faith.

"I believe and all, but. . ."

An icy wind whipped around the steamer. This conversation weighed on his soul more than talking about Aileen. It took too much effort to ponder God's role in his daily life, and he just wasn't ready to think that deeply about it.

"Perhaps we should go below deck and get settled in before the lunch hour," he suggested.

She gave a resigned nod and rose. He tucked her arm around his. She fit comfortably alongside him. He knew he could get used to her presence. This woman and her role in his life must be handled with care.

Gabe spent the next several days both trying to avoid the feelings Charlotte sparked in him and reminding himself of why he was taking her to Alaska. A man—his younger brother—needed the comforting presence of a woman, and an adorable little girl needed a mother to hold and love her. Still he was drawn to Charlotte's company and lured into more talks about relationships with others and God. He didn't want to think about these things, yet the conversations seemed to come naturally when he was with her.

For two days he found enough excuses to stay away from her, hoping the time and space would clear his thinking. Then they entered the Inside Passage. The waters were calm, protected by islands to the west. Rocky, forest-covered shorelines stood sentinel on the east. Occasionally she pointed out to him a bald eagle, a sea lion, or a pod of black-and-white killer whales. He took excursions off ship at Victoria, British Columbia, and Mary's Island.

One day, though, four kegs of beer fell and broke in the hold, and crates of goods had to be shifted, sorted, cleaned, and dried. He smelled like a brewery, and he couldn't understand why his brother agreed to supply the foul stuff to numerous saloons.

Then just north of Fort Wrangell a storm churned up the waters and blew rain and sea water in against the small vessel.

Chapter 2

Charlotte lay on her bed trying to keep as still as possible. The steamer tossed back and forth on the waves, up and down, back and forth. With each dip of the boat, the walls of her room seemed to bend closer to her. Her cape and dressing gown swung away from their hooks. Her trunks slid into her small walkway.

She had never experienced seasickness or claustrophobia before, but the combination of motion, illness and enclosure tore at her sanity. She threw back the blanket and searched for a means of escape. The room had no window to open, only a glass-covered hole for light, and no storage areas in which to contain the shifting items on every inch of space.

It seemed to take several minutes for her to pull herself off the bed and secure a footing on the floor. She tried to straighten her skirt and blouse, then reached for her cape. The pitch of the ship hurled her against the door, and she knew she would be sick. As soon as the ship settled again, she threw her door open and stumbled into the passageway. Gripping the handrails, she tugged herself up the stairs to the deck level.

Water ran everywhere, from sky to deck, from sides to sea. Charlotte shuffled to the railing, and the sight of rolling sea brought her sickness out. She clung to the railing with each pitch of the boat. Then someone slid into her back, and his long arms came around her.

"Lottie, what on earth are you doing out here?" Gabe nearly yelled against her ear.

He smelled like fermented yeast, and she became sick again. He held her as she recovered. "I'm so sorry you're sick, but you have to go below. The storm isn't safe."

Only a moan could get past her throat. He pulled her tightly against him and moved them away from the rail. Getting her back to her room took several minutes of zigzagging their path with the roll of the steamer. He not only smelled like a drunk, he walked like one.

Finally he helped her ease down to the edge of her berth, removed her wet cape, and wrapped her blanket around her. He brought her washbasin to the bed and rearranged some items that had been tossed askew. Then he went to the door. "I'll come back in an hour or so and check on you."

"Nooo," she whined. "Don't leave. I. . .hate to be sick. . . alone."

Slowly she moved her aching head to look at him. He drew his hand across his face and into his wind-tossed hair, seemingly deep in thought. In time, his shoulders relaxed, and a smile tugged at his mouth when he looked at her clinging to the edge of her bunk.

He tried to help her lie down, but she resisted. "I n–need to sit up." She tugged at his arms. "Sit down. . .hold me."

He jerked back. She couldn't look at him. Her head swung like a weighted pendulum. She plucked his arm again, and he eventually settled down beside her.

"You stink," she said.

Sharp laughter filled the small space, and his body shook. "I got caught in a spill—not a binge." He removed his jacket and tossed it to the far side of the room, sending the majority of the smell with it. Then he leaned back against the cold wall of the steamer and tucked her against his side.

Gradually she felt herself begin to relax. The heat radiating from him soothed her battered body. She even felt sleep teasing her senses. Perhaps the storm would pass.

When she awoke, she was alone and cold. The boat had ceased its erratic pitching, and with it, her stomach had settled; but her heart beat a dangerous staccato rhythm of unwarranted emotion. She missed Gabe, missed their conversations. *Oh, Lord, how can I marry his brother with these feelings warring in me?*

❧

Gabe took his breakfast coffee to the deck. Through the morning fog he could see chunks of ice on the water and land to his right. The familiar sight of Haines Mission brought welcomed relief. They should reach Dyea's tidal flats before sunset, which came ever earlier as fall deepened.

Though silent, he felt Charlotte come to stand alongside him before she placed her hand on his arm. She had recovered well from her bout of sickness, but his attraction to her still threatened to drown all his good intentions and determined goals.

Her simple touch reached his heart. He took a deep breath. "We'll be home by dinnertime."

"Home. . ." She stood pensive, taking in the mountainous view. "What will be there for us?"

The word "us" echoed through his mind. It seemed as if she had asked if their friendship could have a future beyond that of the brother and sister they would be once she married Philip.

He forced himself to ignore it. "Dyea isn't much, but it's home for now. Sarah will be shy at first to meet you, but she'll warm up quick." He purposely left out mention of his brother's welcome.

"We live in a small room and lofts at the back of Philip's store," he continued. "Dottie created a homey little space back there—"

"D–Dottie who?"

Dread rose in Gabe's chest. "Sarah's mother."

Charlotte withdrew emotionally and physically from him, backing toward the door to the stairs.

"She has been gone well over six months," Gabe said, reaching out toward her. "Lottie, I'm sure Philip will let you make your own home out of the place and with Sarah."

"Don't!" she snapped. "Don't ever call me Lottie again!"

Gabe was taken aback, but as he quickly reviewed what he had just said, he realized his late sister-in-law's name was similar to Lottie's. "I'm—I'm sorry. I never meant to use the name to change you into someone you are not."

"Yes, you did!" she gasped. "You wanted me to replace Philip's wife. You changed my name so you wouldn't forget—so I wouldn't forget—what I'm intended to be." She shivered. "Another man's wife."

She disappeared into the ship before he could offer another word. Her statement held truth. Something as simple as a nickname had become a wall between them—a sobering reminder of their individual places in the pattern of life.

When the *Dawson Belle* anchored in Dyea's deeper waters, Gabe dreaded finding Charlotte. He wouldn't blame her if she refused to go ashore and demanded to return to California. Much still lay ahead of her, not the least of which was the unpredictable way Philip would react to her.

After stalling long enough with preparations for going ashore, Gabe found Charlotte's room empty. She already waited atop deck with her luggage, watching the scow being loaded with other passengers.

"Let me go first to help you aboard," he offered.

She raised her chin and stared straight ahead, but she allowed him to guide her down the ladder onto the other boat that bobbed in the gathering dusk.

The trip to shore seemed to pass too quickly. Gabe felt confident that he had done the right thing bringing Charlotte here as Philip's wife, but still a nagging sensation made him uncomfortable and edgy.

He stepped off the scow and helped Charlotte onto the beach. Around them lights shone from windows of unpainted wood-planked buildings, tents, and combination wood-and-canvas structures. The streets flowed with people, horses, and dogs. In the mix of noise, music rang out from numerous businesses of entertainment even at this early hour.

Charlotte tried to take in all the activity, but her mind nervously focused on the introductions yet to come. She took a few steps and promptly stuck her shoes in mud.

Gabe immediately acted upon her plight. "Here. Let me carry you?"

"What?" Barking dogs, shouting men, chopping axes, and now this ringing in her ears as Gabe swooped her up into his arms and against his broad chest. She gasped and wiggled in an attempt to loosen his grip.

"Stop it," he said, clenching down on his jaw. "Just don't. . . just rest."

Charlotte obeyed. His touch calmed her and created a shelter amidst the ruckus all around them. Gabe gripped her close to him as he walked through the wharf area. Men leered at her, and she tucked her face into his neck, focusing only on the leather and musk scent of him.

Soon she felt him take a step up, and she looked above her to read a large sign painted in bold blue letters—MONROE'S GENERAL MERCHANDISE.

She thought of putting her feet against the doorframe and begging Gabe for more time to prepare herself. No time, though, could erase the fact that her heart wanted one brother while her words and actions had pledged her in marriage to another.

The door swung open, and Gabe strode into the middle of

a large room filled from floor to ceiling with every imaginable type of saleable goods. He proceeded with her to a back corner where a small table sat beside an imposing stove and the walls were covered with shovels, rakes, picks, and all manner of long-handled tools. Here he finally let her settle onto her own feet. She eased away from Gabe toward the heat from the stove.

A tall man with a dark head of thick hair came out from behind a long counter. "Well, my brother," his voice boomed, "I hardly recognized you with that lovely piece of jewelry draped around your neck. Welcome to Monroe's, Ma'am."

Gabe frowned and offered his brother a somewhat reluctant hug. "Philip."

Charlotte removed her cape in the heat from the stove and tried not to stare as she considered the man named Philip. He looked much like Gabe, though leaner with darker eyes of gray-blue.

"How was ol' Californy?" Philip asked.

Gabe cleared his throat. "Just fine. Much the same."

"And Father and Mother?"

"I saw them only briefly, but they are the same as always."

"Gabe. . ." Philip held in check what would likely have turned into a rebuke of family affairs. Instead he smiled at Charlotte. "Where did you meet this fine lady? Whoa now. . . what's this?"

Philip stepped closer to her. "Why, Gabe, she has a locket like. . . Gabe. . . This *is* grandmother's locket. *Dottie's* locket!" He swung around to face Gabe with an unspoken demand for answers.

213

Gabe shuffled his feet. "Yes. Well. . .Miss Vance." Gabe sighed. "Philip, this is Miss Charlotte Vance."

Charlotte recognized the stress he put on her full name. She held her breath.

"She has come to. . ." He rushed on. "Well, she has agreed to marry you and be a mother to Sarah."

Philip looked like Gabe had struck him as he took a step back and shook his head. "What on earth. . .have you done?"

"Now, Philip, Charlotte—I mean, Miss Vance—comes upon the recommendation of Rev. Chiles. She is a preacher's daughter, orphaned, and in need of a home."

Charlotte reached for the back of a nearby chair, nearly burning her hand on the stove in the process. She took a tight hold on the arched wood.

"I don't care who recommended her," Philip spat.

The conversation had drawn the attention of customers in the store. Gabe lowered his voice. "You said it didn't matter who you had for a wife as long as Sarah had someone to raise her well."

"Hah! Sure, I could use a wife. Yes, Sarah needs a mother. But I was talking out of my grief. I didn't expect you to go snatch a woman off the streets—pardon. . .church pews."

Gabe looked like he wanted to hit him.

Philip gave a short, bitter laugh. "Don't go trying to fix my problems, big brother. My problems are bigger than even you can manage. Stick to your own issues."

The brothers stared at each other.

Quietly an older man approached. "Perhaps you gentlemen

would like to take this out back and air it away from your customers."

Gabe raised an eyebrow.

Philip shrugged. "This is Michael Stanton. I've hired him to help out around here—since you're never around." He spun on his heel and stomped through a rear door through which Charlotte glimpsed a smaller room and another door that seemed to lead outside. Gabe followed.

Charlotte took a tentative step, but Mr. Stanton held out a deterring hand. "You best let them handle this."

"But. . .but it's my future they're debating," she whispered.

"Oh, I believe it is much more than that." He pulled a chair out from the table. "Can I get you anything, Ma'am?"

Charlotte didn't know what to do, so she sat down. "I don't think so."

❧

Philip leaned against the back of the wooden building, facing a row of tent houses. Gabe stopped on the bottom of three narrow steps.

"You know it's funny, Gabe. When I saw you with that woman, I thought you had finally gone and put the past behind you, accepted things that can't be changed, and found someone to love."

"You know there was only one love for me," Gabe choked as his heart thumped. "I'm not going to up and marry someone else—especially when I've got so many wrongs to right."

"If—and I mean *if*—Father has wronged Aileen's family, then it is his place to confess the corn."

"Hah. And you think he would. The man barely spent two days with us while we were growing up. We don't know half of the business he's cooked."

Philip glared at him. "You could have jumped in there and found out for yourself. Father offered you half the business."

"I'm not going to let him put a leash on me and lead me around. He's got enough puppies in his holdings. He doesn't need me, and I don't need him."

"Is that what you think of me because I took his money to set up this place?" Philip asked.

Gabe sighed. Arguing about their father never got them anywhere. "Can we just keep to the issue at hand?"

"I am!" Philip snapped. "You're so much like Father, yet you won't admit it. You want everything to go your way. You make a rash decision and expect everyone to fall in line with your idea. Well, I won't!"

Gabe paced the rain-soaked patch of yard. "Just give Charlotte a chance. Look at her. Talk to her. You'll like her. I promise."

Philip just stared at him.

"She's pretty. She's a good listener."

"If she really knew us, she'd run far away from us blokes," Philip said with the first hint of a smile.

"She already knows most of the important things about us. Even about Father."

"You told her about your clash with our father?"

Gabe nodded.

Philip seemed stunned. "Then you told her about Aileen?"

"She seemed to understand. She was once engaged herself." Gabe suddenly felt warm and clammy despite the brisk wind.

"Well, my brother, I think you should marry her if she got you to say that much about yourself."

"I can't."

"And I won't—so I guess you'll have to send her home." Philip turned to take the steps back inside.

Gabe grabbed his arm, looking up at him from ground level. "Just give her a chance. She doesn't have a home or job to return to. Just take a few days to get to know her. Let her help you with Sarah."

Philip sighed and leaned back against the doorframe, studying him. "You really do care what happens to this woman."

"I feel responsible for her."

"And you care."

Gabe started to protest.

Philip raised a hand. "Don't bother. We'll see how things go."

"Where can we have her stay?"

"She'll stay here."

"But. . ."

"What do you think this is, high society San Fran? This is lawless Dyea. Her situation will hardly draw notice, and we'll, of course, treat her like a *sister.*"

Sister, for certain.

Chapter 3

C harlotte wandered the narrow aisles of the crowded store. Goods of all varieties lined shelves and tables or were displayed in open crates and barrels. Large piles of gold pans sat in one front corner. Above them hung several hooks full of snowshoes, which looked like misshapen tennis rackets. Hooks also hung from beams under the peaked roof, suspending large items like sleds and even a small bathtub. One little table boasted sturdy Indian moccasins, while another exhibited the best in factory-made, dual-buckle, rubber boots.

Sleeping bags, camp stools, fishing tackle, and knives awaited the outdoorsman. Nothing much held feminine appeal. Even the foodstuffs were practical. The basics filled shelves behind the counter, including odd-looking squares of dehydrated vegetables. Sacks of carefully weighed miner's rations formed a low wall down the middle of the store.

Several men crowded the counter, attempting to dicker with Michael for the lowest prices and arguing among each other about the best ways to navigate the treacherous Chilkoot Trail.

No one paid Charlotte any heed, and she soon meandered back to the corner stove. A Sears, Roebuck, and Company catalog lay open in the middle of the table, and she sat down to flip through it. If she were staying, there were some things she might need to have ordered.

A breathy whisper soon caught her attention. "Daddy."

Where the rear door had not been tightly shut, a small pixie face peered out. Near-black ringlets dangled over dark eyes that were lined with long lashes. A pink gown in rumpled state hung down to tiny stockinged feet.

Charlotte's heart twisted at the angelic sight.

"Daddy." The child rubbed her eyes.

Charlotte stood and stepped toward her. "Come here, Child."

The little girl's eyes widened. She looked behind her, then around the store at the men, who paid her no notice. Charlotte knelt down to her level. "My name is Charlotte. What's yours?"

Stepping tentatively from the doorway, she said, "Sarry."

Charlotte smiled. "Is that Sarry or Sarah?"

The adorable child just nodded and stepped within arm's length of Charlotte. She studied the adult before her, then reached out. "Pwetty." Her tiny hand clasped the locket at Charlotte's neck.

"Oh, Honey. . ." It had been the child's mother's. Could she possibly remember?

Charlotte scooped up the lightweight tot and took her to the chair by the stove. She combed her hair with her fingers while the child continued to turn the locket over and over in her hand. "You got more pwetties?"

"Hmm, no, I guess I don't have any other jewelry." Charlotte leaned toward the child's ear. "This is very special, and I promise it will be yours one day."

Heavy footsteps came from the back room, and soon Gabe and Philip entered the store, filling the room with their presence. Charlotte sought Gabe's gaze for a hint to the outcome of the brothers' conversation. She didn't know what to expect. She didn't even know where to place her hope.

Gabe's eyes widened when he saw her with Sarah. He smiled warmly, then quickly turned away.

Sarah spotted her father and squealed, "Daddy!"

She reached up to him, but Philip seemed frozen. He stared at Charlotte and Sarah for a long moment. Gabe scuffed his boots against the wooden floor and coughed.

"I hold you, Daddy." Sarah reached for her father.

Philip propelled himself to pick up his daughter. He smiled as she hugged him and swung her around. "See, your uncle Gabe is back. You wanna give him a hug?"

The child pulled back bashfully, then suddenly she flung herself toward her uncle with arms wide open. Gabe deftly caught her in a big hug. "How's my big girl? Well, I do believe you've grown while I was away."

Charlotte enjoyed the family scene. It touched her to see grown men making such a fuss over a child.

Philip stepped away from Gabe and Sarah, approaching Charlotte. She stood.

His guarded look appraised her. "I apologize for my rather rough greeting earlier. Welcome to Alaska."

Charlotte dipped her chin and waited.

"Gabe will give you a tour of the accommodations while Sarah and I dish up the stew I have simmering." He gave her a curt nod, then retrieved his daughter.

As the two entered the back room, Gabe gave Charlotte a rather sheepish look. She would have laughed if her situation hadn't seemed so serious.

"Sorry. I have a way of acting on some things before I fully think them through."

She drew back. "So it would seem." What did that mean for her?

He looked at the floor. "Philip is mad that I've tried to push him to move on for Sarah's sake. He'll get past it and come around soon enough."

She raised her brow, waiting.

"You'll stay. You can sort of be Sarah's nanny while you and Philip get to know each other." He turned his blue eyes to her. "It'll work out. Trust me."

Trust him? He had dragged her hundreds of miles on a whim, caused her heart to hope for love with him, and now would leave her future dangling until who knew when.

"Perhaps I should go back to California?"

"Back to what? Rev. Chiles told me you have no family, and he had not been able to secure any position for you in these hard times. Just give Philip a little while. It won't take him long to lo—like—you as I. . .as I know you deserve."

Charlotte searched his expression, but any emotion hid behind a stoic face. He extended his arm, allowing her to precede him into the back room.

Lord, hast Thou taken me into this remote land and put me through tortures of the heart just so that Thou canst use me here? I want to be able to help that child, but I so long for some of my own happiness.

ॐ

Over the next several weeks, Charlotte developed a morning routine. She put the oatmeal on the stove to simmer and checked to make sure Sarah was contentedly playing at dressing her rag doll for the day. Then Charlotte took her Bible to the kitchen table that had been fashioned from a large crate and drew the rocking chair up to it. The living quarters were tight with the makeshift table and chairs taking up most of the space the small cookstove and cabinet didn't occupy.

Oddly enough, she had gotten out of the habit of daily readings while living with the reverend and his wife. Still she knew her source of true strength could only come from praying and reading God's Word.

The month of November had passed, and with it Thanksgiving Day. No one had made any noticeable effort to celebrate the American holiday.

Dyea had seen a few snow flurries the first two weeks of December, but then it rained, making the ground a treacherous mixture of mud and slush. Snow pummeled the mountain passes, and no trail over the peaks would be navigable until the snow packed. The town teemed with men who were putting together their Yukon outfits and taking in a lot of amusement before their trip. Even some from points along the trail like

Canyon City and Sheep Camp had come to enjoy Dyea's culture for awhile.

Charlotte rarely ventured out into the lawless streets—and never alone. Just last week a man had been murdered in the street two buildings away from Monroe's. Shots were heard any time of day, be it for celebration or dispute.

Charlotte kept to herself and out of the way of the Monroe men. Gabe headed into town every day on what seemed to be missions to learn more about the trail and what lay beyond the mountain range from those who were headed there and from some who had returned. He had even taken overnight trips to Skagway four miles away at the base of White Pass. He brought back a few hair-raising tales that made Dyea's troubles seem tame in comparison.

Philip spent his days in the store on the other side of the wall from her, but they rarely spoke. He always treated her kindly, but she had no indication that he thought about her becoming his wife.

She spent her days preparing meals, reading to Sarah, and tending to the living area and laundry. Everything was as neat and orderly as possible in the tight quarters—not that she had a compulsion for neatness. The idle days dragged on, long and tiresome. Though she gratefully accepted the roof over her head in such foul weather, shouldn't a maid get some pay?

She pulled her shawl snug to her as she rose from her readings. It was hard to concentrate on the writings of Solomon, who lived in grandeur yet wrote about dissatisfaction in his life.

The damp cold seemed to seep clear through, keeping her

shivering all the time. At night she would climb the ladder to the loft at the rear of the store. Crates of supplies lined the low walls, and a mattress just fit under the eaves. She would tuck herself between Sarah and the stovepipe, but still she could find no warmth. If the cold bothered the child, she didn't show it.

"My, it's warm in here," Gabe remarked as he and Philip came in from the store where they kept their sleeping pallets near the heating stove. "I didn't know that little cookstove could put off so much heat."

"I'm sorry. I—I hadn't noticed," Charlotte stammered.

Philip chuckled. "You'll get used to the damp cold here soon enough. Though I can't promise it will get any better until at least April."

Charlotte served up the oatmeal with thick slices of toasted bread.

Sarah pushed her bowl back toward Charlotte. "Mine sweet, Lottie."

Gabe came to attention on his stool. "What did she call you?"

Charlotte felt blood rush to her cheeks. "S—she's just taken to shortening my name. I—it's easier for the child."

"Ahhh, well. . .I never. . ." Laughter rumbled from deep in Gabe's chest, and Sarah clapped her hands, giggling.

His brother just stared at him.

Gabe quickly sobered. "Oh, I'm sorry."

Philip's brows came together. "For what?"

Gabe shot a look at Charlotte. She waited for Philip to display outrage at the nickname, so like his wife's. His grief had ways of surfacing unexpectedly in conversations or routine tasks.

Then Gabe relaxed. "Well, if you don't mind. . ."

"I mind that you're keeping me from my breakfast."

Charlotte sprinkled Sarah's cereal with a small amount of brown sugar, then she silently blessed the food while the men dug right in. It bothered her that the Monroes didn't make giving thanks a part of each meal, but it didn't seem her place in the household to point it out. She just continued to pray for God to make Himself real to each man in every area of life.

"Does anyone realize that Christmas will be here in three days?" Philip asked as he sipped his coffee at the end of the meal.

Gabe shrugged.

"A man came in yesterday asking about Christmas decorations." Philip laughed. "With so many real necessities to haul up here, why would I give thought to stocking such baubles?"

Heaviness settled on Charlotte. "Don't you celebrate Christmas—Jesus' birth and all?"

"Oh, sure," Philip responded casually. "Back home Mother would deck the whole house in Christmas finery, throw parties, and give out grand gifts. But up here, what's the use?"

Charlotte bristled. "Christmas is a reminder of how Christ came so humbly to redeem us. Lavish or not, wherever we are, we should do something to show thanks for what the Lord has done for us."

"He hasn't done much for me lately," Philip muttered.

Gabe interjected. "He's just saying that up here without parlors and families, there's little call for all the fuss, but we can still have Christmas." He pushed his stool back from the table and stood, his large frame dwarfing the others and filling the small room. "In fact, I'll go into the forest today and see if I can't find a small tree and some spruce boughs for you to liven up the place with. How would that be, Charlotte?"

His face held such childlike expectation that she had to smile, and her heart did a flip. She truly appreciated his efforts to give her a Christmas celebration.

"I'd like that very much."

She watched as Gabe bundled himself into his heavy brown duck coat, admiring his muscular shoulders and strong hands. His big heart seemed to extend to those hands as he ruffled Sarah's curls and tweaked her nose on his way out the back door into the dark, misty morning.

Charlotte sighed.

When she turned back to the table, she was surprised to see Philip still sitting on his stool. He leaned against the wall with his hands clasped at his waistline, watching her. His eyes held a new sense of curiosity. Could this be interest?

She couldn't return his odd look. She had tried not to worry about her future or pine for solutions to her awkward situation. But she would rather be a maid in Philip's home than his wife. When she gave him any real thought, he reminded her of what a brother should be.

"Charlotte." He waited until she looked at him. "I've failed to say thank you for all your work around here and the attention you give to Sarah. You are appreciated more than you may know."

He rose and flashed her a grin as he went into the store to open for the day.

A Token of Promise

She slumped back against the simple rocker she always sat in at the meagerly furnished table. She fingered the locket that still hung around her neck. Maddening emotions battled for her attention, but the day wouldn't be long enough to sort them out.

Chapter 4

The next afternoon, Philip stuck his head into the rear room and asked Charlotte to help out in the store while his assistant, Michael, went across town on an errand. Charlotte had spent her whole morning arranging pine branches on the two windowsills and cabinet top. Gabe had left them at the back door along with a skinny little spruce tree he had cut down. She would wait to bring it indoors tomorrow—Christmas Eve.

Grateful for another diversion from her mundane days, Charlotte followed Philip into the store. Smoky lanterns lit the room even in the middle of the day.

She arranged Sarah near the stove with some playthings, then eased behind the counter, awaiting instructions. He asked her to start by unloading a small crate of canned fruit onto a low shelf behind the counter.

The flow of customers seemed to be extra heavy for this wintry day.

A large woman with a manly frame leaned over the counter.

"Ma'am, would you help us? Your man doesn't seem to know nothin'."

Charlotte straightened from her task and glanced around for Philip. He had moved to the end of the counter to help a man weigh a purchase.

"Umm. . .certainly, if I can," she replied.

"I need spices for cookin' a goose, and he," she jerked her bony thumb toward Philip, "says he stocks no rosemary. Then he tells me there is no pure white sugar. What then do you have so I can make a proper Christmas dinner?" Her voice rose with exasperation.

Charlotte searched her mind. She knew very little about what Philip stocked.

"Well, I'm cooking a roast with lots of onions and baking a butterscotch pie. Can I show you our onions?"

The woman clucked her tongue like a hen that had lost an egg. "I must find some rosemary or sage or thyme, something worthy of the Christmas palate. We can have onions any day here. I thought this was supposed to be the best-stocked store in town. I have been sorely deceived," she stated with gusto.

Charlotte sighed and looked toward Philip. Should she interrupt him? But what more could he offer the woman? He would still lose a customer, and she wouldn't go quietly.

Then Charlotte had a sudden thought. "Please wait a moment, Ma'am. I may have something that will do."

Charlotte wove her way to the kitchen area of the back room and opened the small cabinet. She took out a little cloth packet she had noticed before. Pockets of muslin were sewn together along one side like a booklet. Each pocket had a button flap and stitched labels that read *oregano, parsley, thyme, sage, rosemary,* and *chives.* They looked like they'd never been used. Philip's wife might have received the packet of herbs as a gift.

Charlotte fingered the beautiful packet for a moment, then strode back to the store and handed it across the counter to the gruff woman. "We don't stock herbs and spices, but you may have this."

The woman seemed shocked. She took it and read each label. "I never. . ."

Another woman, dainty with a pointed nose, approached the counter. "Don't take it Mrs. Sheever." Then barely lowering her voice, she added, "You don't know what that Jezebel has been using those for."

Charlotte lurched backward against the rows of shelving.

Mrs. Sheever dropped the packet and turned to the other woman. "Do tell."

"This may well be the most popular store in town because of the men who come just to catch a peek at the woman Mr. Monroe and his brother generally keep locked in the back room. She lives there with them. . .*both,*" the woman hissed with a twitch of her sharp nose, "but she's not the sister or wife of either one, and God is surely disgraced."

Unshed tears threatened to choke Charlotte. "How dare you make accusations about my situation when you know nothing about me. There are plenty worse things. . .and *people*. . .in this town who need *your* kind of god's attention more than me and my. . .family. Merry Christmas!" she spat as she turned on her heel and raced past Philip, who apparently had given the incident his full attention.

She would have slammed the door behind her if Sarah hadn't followed her.

If Charlotte had been back in any small town in the States, the women of the church probably would have given her an old donkey and told her to load up and be gone by dawn. Her father had told her of just such a happening in the Illinois town where he first pastored.

Charlotte dropped into the rocker as tears came like a tidal wave. Sarah wiggled up onto her lap and sat patting Charlotte's cheek. "It be okay, Lottie. Chwistmas is comin'."

It hurt to smile, but Charlotte finally did.

Lord, help me be more like a child and trust Thy protection and guidance.

❧

Later as she began to put supper fixings together, Charlotte heard Michael's voice in the store. Soon Philip came into the kitchen. He paced a bit before saying, "I'm sorry, Charlotte, about that scene. I personally escorted the ladies out."

Charlotte kept her back to him as she worked at the little stove. *They were no "ladies."*

"I know things are hard for you, and you must get frustrated wanting things to come together." He became quiet for so long that Charlotte thought he must have slipped back to the store. She glanced over her shoulder.

Philip stood rubbing his chin while Sarah silently clasped

her father's leg in a bear hug. The child must have sensed the tension.

"Perhaps I should move out," she suggested. "Is there a minister and his wife in town who'd take me in?"

Philip gave a half chuckle. "There are no churches in Dyea. We do have one minister who lives in Bailey's Hotel and preaches hell fire and brimstone down at the waterfront. You're much better off staying put. Just give it a bit more time," he said; then kissing his daughter on her head, he returned to the store.

Time. Time for what? If Philip knew he planned to marry her, why didn't he just do it and give her his name? Time could be dangerous. More time to soil what name she had. More time to worry. More time to fall deeper in love with Gabe.

In a town that had no churches and barely took time to sleep even under nearly eighteen hours of darkness per day, Philip kept his store open on Sundays. While the men treated Sundays like any other day, Charlotte used the time to teach Sarah hymns. She missed being in church and gathering with other believers.

So it rather surprised her when Philip announced that he would keep the store closed on Christmas Day. Her joy quickly faded when she wondered what the four of them would do all day cramped into the tight quarters.

After a breakfast of flapjacks, Gabe and Philip went outside together. Charlotte started the roast and rolled out her piecrust. She had little gifts for each of them, which she would give at dinnertime.

232

The sun had already begun to wane when the men returned. Philip set something covered with a blanket on the table while Gabe placed a small cradle on the floor. Sarah sprang to his side. "What's it? Mine?"

Gabe coaxed her to pull the little blanket out of the cradle. Sarah tugged at the blanket like something underneath it might bite her. But her face filled with delight when she saw a new, porcelain doll lying in the cradle. It had lovely long brown hair and a painted face with brown eyes.

"Hello, Mary!" Sarah exclaimed.

"Who's Mary?" Philip asked.

Sarah gave him an exasperated look. "My dolly, Daddy."

Gabe chuckled. "Well, I wonder where she got that name?"

Charlotte hesitated. "Probably from the Bible stories I've been reading her this week."

Gabe nodded approval, and Philip just shrugged.

He turned to the object on the table. "This is for you, Charlotte."

Charlotte stepped tentatively to it and pulled the blanket away. There sat a new china pitcher and bowl set. "Oh, why thank you." She knew Philip didn't stock such breakables in his store, only special ordered them for some hotels.

"I figured you and Sarah might be tired of washing with the pail," he mumbled.

Charlotte almost wanted to laugh. The gift was thoughtful, yet practical.

"Let me get your gifts." Charlotte opened the cabinet, glanced at the herb packet that had mysteriously returned to its place, and pulled out three small packages she had hidden on the bottom shelf. She gave one to each person.

Sarah tore right into the brown paper. She squealed over her new knitted slippers and tugged them on over her shoes. Philip thanked her for his wool mittens. Gabe took his time opening his package, unnerving Charlotte. She gripped the back of the rocker as his package revealed two hand-stitched and monogrammed handkerchiefs.

"Oh." He met her gaze. "Thank you very much," he said, adding softly, "Lottie."

Charlotte felt the blush flame her cheeks and turned to the oven to peek in at her pie.

As she cleared the table, she noticed that Philip had sat down on the floor with his daughter to play with her. Again, Charlotte marveled at what a good father he was, and she could understand how he didn't want to be separated from his child.

Gabe stepped to Charlotte's side, trapping her in the small area between the table, stove, and cabinet. "I, uhh...well, I have something for you. Just something little." He practically shoved a paper envelope into her hands.

Charlotte's fingers shook as she unfolded the paper. A necklace lay in the center. On the chain a tiny charm was attached—a rough-edged heart.

"Oh, my." Charlotte looked up into his eyes, and she could barely breathe under the tenderness in his gaze.

He seemed to shake himself then. "It's a real gold nugget that came shaped that way. Some old geezer had it, and I traded him for it. Think of it as a souvenir."

His words held a chill, but she wanted to believe some of his heart came with the tiny gold charm.

Across the room, Philip rose from the floor and stared at them. Gabe turned around, and Philip's eyebrows rose in an unspoken question.

Gabe glanced away. "I'm going to wash up for dinner."

Charlotte slid her necklace into her apron pocket, but she fingered the heart shape a moment before she went back to setting the table.

If someone asked her to define love, she wasn't sure she could. She had loved her father with the devotion of a daughter. It was a love that had always been with her. She had loved Oliver with all the excitement of a young woman who at every step was being pursued by a love-smitten young man.

Oliver had always been attentive. They met in school. He escorted her to every school and church function. He came by her home several nights a week to sit and converse with her and her father. She relished being the center of his world.

When he suddenly announced that he was going to Colorado to seek gold, it nearly froze any feelings of love she had. But when he asked her to marry him, promising to return with riches that would set them up for life, she promised him her undying devotion. She believed him to be investing in their future, so that must mean he would always love her.

The feelings she experienced now were so different. She rarely saw Gabe. He seemed to avoid time alone with her. Yet often she thought she could see past his rough exterior and guess what he might be thinking inside. The briefest of smiles from him could make her heart sing, and just having him sit across the table from her made her feel like everything fit into its place.

"Dinner is ready," she called. Sliding into her seat directly across the table from Gabe, she looked into his eyes alone and asked, "May we bless this meal with prayer?"

"I will," Gabe said.

Chapter 5

Gabe surprised himself with the offer to pray. He had been giving God a lot of thought lately. He knew his parents and Aileen's parents claimed to be Christians. He also knew he couldn't judge who God was from a handful of people, not when he saw God's goodness in everything Charlotte did and said.

She lived a genuine faith. He rarely saw a hint of question from her about her status in the household and how her future would work out. She trusted the brothers. . .but more so, she trusted God.

Gabe prayed, asking special blessing on the food and the hands that had prepared it.

When he looked up, Charlotte's gaze met his with a hint of tears on her lashes. He shifted in his seat. He hadn't meant to make her cry.

Philip shoved a pot of mashed potatoes at him, and he tried to give his full attention to Charlotte's good cooking.

He didn't understand his brother. Charlotte was a wonderful

person. She clearly loved Sarah and gave her wonderful care. What more could Philip need to see before marrying her? Philip needed her, and she needed him.

Gabe had heard about the incident in the store, and it frustrated him that Philip's stalling would bring such reproach upon Charlotte. Something had to be done. Maybe Philip just needed a push.

Gabe looked across the table. Charlotte smiled at him. His meat stuck in his throat, and his heart did a funny little dance. He looked away and grabbed his mug of coffee.

Yes, something needed to change. These tight living arrangements were getting to him.

❧

Alaska's long night of darkness and a fresh layer of snow cloaked the town, yet every building seemed to dance with the usual nighttime revelry of drinking, gaming, and carousing. Gabe stood on the back stoop of the store and couldn't think of sleeping or bringing this holiday to an end.

A flash of light streaked above a distant mountain range. Gabe watched as it came again and flickered like a flame taking hold of a wick. The light spread out, displaying fingers of blue, green, and pink.

Why would God go to the trouble of painting the night sky like that?

Gabe felt the answer deep inside him. *For me.*

"Charlotte should see this." Gabe opened the door and stepped back inside.

Charlotte sat alone in the room with a book. "Philip is in

the loft, putting Sarah to bed," she said. "She was getting very cranky."

"Well, good. Come outside. I have something you should see."

She gave him one of her electrifying smiles. She took the blanket on the back of the rocking chair and wrapped it around her shoulders like a shawl. He held the door for her, and they stepped out onto the top step together.

She looked up at him expectantly. Her eyes sparkled in the light from the barely closed door. She sucked her lower lip in as she waited. . .waited for him. He nearly forgot why they were there. He turned to the night sky.

"What do you think of that?"

"Oh. . ." Her breath sang past her full lips. "I've never seen anything like it. What is it?"

"It's unique to the North Country. They are called the northern lights."

His gaze returned to her. She stood with her hands clasped at her breast, holding the blanket yet appearing to be in worship. Her face seemed to take on the colors from the sky, radiating with childlike wonder.

"Gabe, do you ever wonder why God went to all the trouble of making even the smallest thing in nature beautiful?"

He smiled. "Sure. I guess He pays attention to details."

"He even counts the hairs on our head." She touched his sleeve. "Gabe, God wants to share every detail of life with us—all our joys and all our pains. Do you know you can talk to Him about anything?"

Her touch was poignant, even through his coat. His thoughts

slowed. He wanted to believe like she did. He wanted to trust God like that.

Yet he also wanted to touch her cheek and see if it felt as soft as it looked. He wanted to pull her close and draw strength from her faith.

No, he couldn't. He had to get away.

"Why are you letting the cold in?" Philip asked from the doorway. "Oh, excuse me. . . ."

"No." Charlotte suddenly seemed terribly nervous. "I was just going in. Take a look at the lights for yourself." She rushed past Philip, her blanket slapping at them both.

Gabe admired her rigid stride, then turned to his brother. Frustration that had been simmering in him erupted. "When are you going to marry that woman?"

Philip laughed. "I should be asking you that."

Gabe glared at him. "I brought her here for you. She's been waiting weeks for you to get used to the idea of marrying her. She has been nothing but patient with you and loving toward your daughter. What more do you need?"

"I care for Charlotte. . .like a sister, and I wouldn't think of marrying her."

The word nearly exploded from Gabe. "Why?"

"I couldn't marry any woman my brother looked at in that way." Philip raised his chin as if he enjoyed holding something over his older brother. "What kind of *brother* gives a woman a golden heart necklace? Of course, you are in love with her."

"What. . . ?" A disturbing emotion clawed for Gabe's

attention. "No, you are mistaken. You don't know anything. You *have* to marry her."

"No." Philip stood with his feet planted firmly apart, and he looked at Gabe like their father did when he waited for his son to confess to a mistake.

"Yes. Yes you must." Gabe felt a panic rise in his chest. "I can't!"

❧

Charlotte strode across the room before she realized the door still stood ajar, and she could hear everything the brothers said. She didn't want to draw attention to herself by moving to close the door. She turned to the ladder that went to the loft.

The men's conversation became distinct, and she froze with one foot raised to the first rung.

Philip refusing to marry her lifted a feeling of dread that she had been carrying from the boat, even before she knew him to be a kind and decent man.

When Philip challenged Gabe's attraction to her, Charlotte's heart soared. She was right. Gabe didn't look at her as a sister and friend. His heart spoke in those tender looks.

"I can't!" Gabe's voice thundered in the room.

Charlotte slumped against the ladder.

Philip grated a response. "Give it up, Man. Can't you see—"

"No. You don't see. There's Aileen."

"She's gone, Gabe. Married."

"But. . .our father. . ."

"When are you going to stop looking at him through that situation?" Philip asked. "Aileen's father ended your engagement, not our father. And if Aileen had loved you enough, she would have found a way to change her father's mind. Don't let Aileen and her father put this wall between you and your father. Stop fighting. The battle is over, and the girl is gone."

Gabe tromped down the steps. Charlotte could hear him grumbling, then his voice became more distinct.

"Don't tell me what to do, Little Brother. We're talking about your future, not mine. Go ahead and marry Charlotte. It's for everyone's best."

A tear trickled down the side of her nose, but she didn't move. She couldn't even breathe.

Gabe continued, "Next week I'm starting up the trail, and you won't have to worry about how I look at Charlotte."

Philip made a noise.

"I'm gone," Gabe seemed to add for clarity.

Charlotte caught a sob behind her hand. She clawed her way up the ladder as tears clouded her eyes. Not giving thought to her best dress, she flung herself onto the mattress beside the sleeping child and curled into a ball.

Not even at the deaths of her father and Oliver had she felt such searing pain. Rejection. It must be worse than death.

Why is this happening, Lord? Did I do something wrong? Should I have kept my heart locked up tight and ignored this love for Gabe?

Just when a new and special kind of love had blossomed and she felt hope to carry into the years to come, it had been cut off—severed as completely and painfully as if she had lost a limb.

What am I to do, Lord? Where can I go?

Sobs shook her body long into the night. Relief would not come in answers, only in exhaustion.

❧

Before anyone else stirred the next morning, Gabe left the store with a pocketful of money. He had worked more than a year for two of his father's business competitors to finance this trip into the Yukon. The first order of business would be to buy a tent. He would make his purchases in other stores in Dyea and Skagway. He wouldn't ask his younger brother any favors. Besides, he needed to stay away from the store.

Hopefully, if he stayed away, the time alone would help Philip, Charlotte, and Sarah to form a family bond. He'd only go to the store to sleep once in awhile. He'd need to start getting acclimated to the cold. He'd be sleeping in a tent for the next six months to a year.

He headed to the Yukon Outfitters building, hoping to meet up with the three men who just a month ago had agreed to team up with him for the trip up the Chilkoot Trail. His steps were slow. He tried to concentrate on his goals, but they seemed hazy. Getting down to the business of preparations would surely clear his mind.

But before he entered the large warehouse building, he found himself talking to God. *I know if I get a ton of that gold, it isn't going to bring Aileen back. Maybe I don't care for her anymore.*

And I know that no amount of gold is going to fix what my father has done. I don't think I could impress him with gold I dug with my own bare hands.

Sometimes I don't even know why I'm still going to Dawson.

I just know I can't take Charlotte. The Yukon is no place for a woman like her.

Philip is stubborn. He needs Charlotte. She'll be good for him.

God, can't You just make it all work out?

Trust.

Yes, I've trusted them to Thy care, God.

Trust.

But have I trusted myself to Thy care, as well?

Gabe stood with his hand on the knob of the door until someone asked him to move. He stepped inside and was promptly greeted by two of his trail partners.

Chapter 6

January 20

Charlotte moved this and dusted that in the confined kitchen while Philip and Gabe talked at the back door. Sarah hopped in front of her uncle, begging to be picked up. She hadn't seen him for a month and demanded his attention now. Gabe swung her up into his arms as if she weighed no more than a feather.

"We've finished stashing our outfits at Finnegan's Point. We'll camp there now and pack up trail. There should be no reason for me to return to Dyea, so I'll say good-bye now." He squeezed Sarah. "Take care of this little one. I trust you to do right by our girls, Brother."

Charlotte looked up. Gabe kissed Sarah's ear, causing the child to laugh, but if he glanced at Charlotte through lowered lashes, he gave no indication. Her heart tugged her toward the door, but she kept her feet firmly planted by the stove.

Gabe handed Sarah to her father. With a quick pat to

Philip's back and the briefest of nods to Charlotte, Gabe turned and walked down the alleyway between buildings.

She had been dreading this day ever since Gabe had announced his leave at Christmas. She had held onto some hope that he might say something to her—anything that might tell her he loved her and couldn't let her go.

It seemed now that leaving came easy to him, and his gold fever—coupled with fever for retribution—was greater than any affection he might hold for her.

Philip returned to the store, Sarah pulled her doll cradle into the middle of the floor, and Charlotte surveyed her home. She lived here, but this wasn't *her* home. She didn't belong here. She didn't want to be here if she couldn't be with Gabe.

She slapped at the table with her rag. She felt trapped.

It was Gabe's fault that she was here. He charmed the Chileses, and he charmed her too with his good looks, good manners, and tenderness to boot. Why couldn't she see this dead-end road before she took it?

Gabe wanted things his way, but she and Philip weren't his puppets. They would lead their own lives.

A week later she had an announcement for Philip at the dinner table.

"I've been composing some letters. I haven't sent them yet, but I'm hopeful that someone in Reverend Chiles's church or in one of my father's last two congregations will help me find a worthy position. I just may have to ask to borrow money for my passage. I—I will repay you."

Philip leaned back, studying her. "What's all this? I owe

you more than I can ever give you. If you must return to California, of course I'll pay your way. But wait until the weather is more amicable for travel."

Charlotte relaxed.

Philip pulled a sheet of paper from his pocket. "Perhaps you would be interested in this." He spread it out on the table. "I've been drawing up plans for a house. I hope you like them."

Charlotte felt her guard rise again. Could he be thinking marriage *now?* It was much too late for even the most congenial arrangement between friends or business partners.

"Philip, I. . ." She reached behind her neck and unclasped the oval locket she still wore. "It's not right for me to wear this. I release you from any promises Gabe made on your behalf. He shouldn't be telling either of us what to do."

She laid the locket on the sheet of paper.

Philip said nothing, just looked at her.

Charlotte clasped the other chain still around her neck and unconsciously fingered the heart-shaped nugget.

"Dear Charlotte, if I could have ordered a sister from Sears and Roebuck, she would have been just like you. You are a remarkable woman." He smiled at her. "Hold onto that nugget like a promise. I know your heart belongs to Gabe. . .and his heart belongs to you. He just hasn't admitted it yet."

Charlotte gasped.

"I want you to stay and make this your home for as long as you wish. He'll eventually come back."

She tried to choke back a sob. "Gabe has been such a dolt, but. . .I miss him so."

Philip reached out and awkwardly rubbed her shoulder. Sarah looked up from her plate of barely touched food. "I eat, Lottie. Don't cry, Dear."

Philip tried to hold back a laugh. Charlotte giggled even as tears trickled down her cheeks. Sarah rolled her shoulders toward her chest and grinned.

When Charlotte had dried her tears, Philip said, "I got something in the mail yesterday and haven't known what to make of it." He pulled another paper from his pocket.

"This is a letter from my wife's aunt. May I read it to you?" Charlotte nodded.

Dottie,

Please excuse my lack of communication. Life does have a way of rushing by. My dear Henry had been sick so long and I was so consumed with taking care of him that I lost touch with you and your brothers. I was appalled—yet strangely thrilled—to hear you had taken up residence in Alaska. Your father would be proud of your adventuresome spirit.

Henry passed on this fall, and I find myself looking for a diversion from the emptiness of this big old house. I fear I could go insane with nothing to do.

Please write back and let me know if there is space enough in your home to have me visit. I would so like to see you and the child you named after your mother.

Yours truly,
Bessie Aldredge
Portland, Oregon

Philip looked up. "What would you tell the woman? Dottie spoke fondly of this aunt. She reportedly is quite a lively one. How do I tell her of. . .of Dottie? Should I let her come?"

Charlotte felt sorry for Philip. What a place to be in to have to tell a person of her loved one's death—especially when the pain was still so fresh for himself.

"She will have to know, and I can help you compose the letter."

"But should I let her come? Would she still come?" Philip stared at his daughter. "I could use someone like her. And. . ." He looked at Charlotte. "You could feel comfortable staying with another woman around."

Charlotte laughed. "What would you do with two women and a child underfoot? I'd still be in the way."

She reached across the table and patted his hand. "Write her, Philip, and see what she says. Maybe she'll be able to come and take my place once I've found a position."

Philip nodded slowly. After a moment, she tentatively added, "If she doesn't come, I could take Sarah back to California with me. To your parents or to your wife's parents—"

Philip's fist hit the table. "No!"

His anger stunned Charlotte.

"I–I'm sorry. My parents can't handle a toddler. D–Dottie's folks are gone." Philip buried his face in his hands. "There is no other way. Sarah and I stay together."

Charlotte swallowed the lump in her throat that responded to his visible pain.

No easy answers—and certainly not a new wife—would fix

Philip's grief and bitterness.

❦

Gabe plodded uphill. He shifted his heavy pack and bent into the wind. Snow whipped at his cheeks, and the cold burned his nostrils. The weather was getting worse. He could barely see where to place his next step, and some spots along this part of the trail could be tricky.

He let out a moan. No one would hear him over the wind. Wilderness surrounded him, and he didn't even know why he insisted on putting himself through this torture. Did he want to anymore? Where had all that driving purpose gone?

He tripped against a rock, but he kept moving. The goal for the moment was to reach the cache and unburden himself of this load.

Awhile later with the goods stashed, he and his partners headed back down the trail, sliding and sometimes almost running when the trail smoothed out. They would only pack one load this day.

Gabe shivered as he all but hugged his camp stove. The snowstorm raged for a second day, blinding and confining them. They could only cut wood and sit in the tents.

His companions became irritable when no progress up trail could be made. They griped at each other and argued over the fall of their card hands. Gabe stayed away from the games. He'd had little card experience; besides, he could hardly sit still long enough for one round.

Twice before when they had encountered downpours that made the uphill climb treacherous, Gabe had gone back down the trail into Dyea on errands for mail, newspapers, and supplies. He didn't stop in Monroe's store, but he found ways to learn that his family faired well—and that Charlotte still lived at the back of the store. . .unmarried.

He craved diversion. The nearly six weeks of twice-a-day trips up and down the trail kept him too busy and too tired to think. They each packed fifty- to one hundred-pound loads on their backs and could transport even more if a sled could be used. The trail wound sharply around boulders, and often ice hung down from ledges above, requiring one to duck under it. More often strong headwinds barreled through the Dyea River Valley, drifting snow over the trail.

They would pack their outfit sometimes only a mile up trail, then they would move their camp to the new cache and start packing again. Stacks of supplies lined the trail, and even without sufficient law enforcement, everyone knew that to steal from someone else's cache meant to risk death.

Gabe stretched out on top of his sleeping bag, which lay on top of a row of crates and sacks of supplies. He estimated it to be nearly noon, yet the sun barely reached him through the snow and trees.

Gabe dug through his clothing bag and found a small Bible. Though not often read, it had been with him since childhood. He would read a psalm. He opened to the Twenty-Second Psalm and heard David cry out to God in his agony. Pursued and scorned by enemies, David always seemed plagued by trouble. Even animals circled him, tearing at him. No strength was left in him, and he pleaded to be saved.

Closing the book after skimming the end of the psalm, Gabe wondered about the things that followed him. He felt pressured, shadowed, hunted by unseen aggressors.

Oh, God. . . He knew that only God would listen to him, befriend him. His trail partners didn't know the real Gabe Monroe. He only let them see the surface. No one made an effort to dig deeper. He was a fair and hardworking partner, which satisfied them.

He stared at the Bible, trying to shake off the weight on his soul. What did he fear?

He couldn't seem to keep thoughts of Charlotte away. Her brown hair, blue eyes, and comely figure were admirable; but he especially appreciated her quiet grace and strong faith. He could never be worthy of such a woman. His brother was much more settled as a respected businessman and father. Eventually Philip would see it too.

Did he fear that Philip wouldn't get around to marrying her? Could he be worrying about Charlotte's security? Or. . . was she more dangerous to Gabe if she remained unattached?

He stood up, shivering. The shaking hurt his muscles, and he couldn't control it. He moved around the small space, flapping his arms and stamping his feet to generate warmth.

But the motion couldn't drive away his nagging fears. *Okay, Lord, what if my plans fall apart? What if none of the things I've been reaching for mean anything?*

But I have to repay what my father took from Aileen's family.

Though it is not my debt.

Who am I trying to impress? Who is left?

Would giving up the gold hunt be more painful than this present agony?

But what is my purpose, and what is there to go back to?

Charlotte.

Gabe shook his head as he leaned over the stove.

But I don't know that she cares for me. She should despise me for taking her to this country where she can be the target of gossip and improper advances from some of the men because she doesn't have the protection of being a married woman.

He picked up the Bible again. He desired to read about a godly woman. He considered the stories of Mary, Ruth, and Esther, then decided on Ruth. She lived in a foreign country and relied on God to provide her needs. God did so through a man named Boaz.

Philip was Charlotte's Boaz, wasn't he?

Chapter 7

Sarah sat on the floor by the heating stove in the rear of the store methodically removing small items from a box, then putting them back in. Philip and Charlotte shared cups of coffee at the table while they watched her. The furniture was much nicer than what they used in their living quarters, and she had long wondered why Philip didn't use the table and chairs in his kitchen.

Traffic through the store had virtually halted. Most stampeders who wintered in town were now up on the trail making a push for the pass before the spring thaw.

Philip suddenly cleared his throat. "Michael has told me that he had a couple businessmen mention seeing Gabe in town once, a week or so ago."

Charlotte's heart suddenly dipped. "Why didn't he stop in?"

"Isn't it obvious?" Philip stared at his coffee mug. "He loves you, and the pain of not being with you is eating at him. Still he is too stubborn to admit to not getting his way. He found out he couldn't manipulate things. He couldn't control his heart."

She felt heat pulsing in her cheeks.

"Sooner or later he's going to realize that he has to give up trying to change the past and grab onto the future."

Charlotte looked at Philip with his head still bowed. He could also be talking about himself.

They sat in silence, each lost in their own thoughts. Philip sipped at his coffee, but Charlotte ignored the now cold brew in her cup.

"I finally received a letter from Aunt Bessie," Philip said.

Charlotte sighed. She herself had received a couple letters in response to her job search. Though polite, kind, and sympathetic, no one could offer her work while times were still financially precarious. What could she do?

"She'll come within a week or two, assuming the ships are running, and she sounded positively thrilled by the invitation. Though, I'm afraid she may try to play mother hen." Philip slumped in his chair like a youth.

Charlotte laughed in spite of her circumstances. "I have a feeling that the woman will be just what you and Sarah need."

"And you," Philip offered.

She waved away the comment. "It's time I think of moving on."

Philip scowled at her. "And where do you think you're going?"

"I–I could. . ." Her thoughts spun, and she almost spoke the first silly notion that came to mind.

He continued to study her, even though Sarah tried to hand her father a block of wood that she had been playing with.

"See Uncle Gabe?" the toddler asked.

"Maybe so," Philip replied as Charlotte turned away from

his scrutiny. "Maybe so. From what I can gather, Gabe and his group should have reached the Scales about now where their outfits will be weighed and redistributed before the climb up the pass."

"He's been gone two months. That's only around seventeen miles," Charlotte said. "Are you sure that's all the farther he's gone?"

"No, not positive, but they're each packing at least a thousand pounds without horses and without hiring any packers. And then there are the storms we've been having," Philip said, beginning to smile.

Charlotte shifted in her chair and spilled some of her coffee. "That's all very interesting."

"And you want to go," Philip stated. "You want to go after him, but you'll need to do it before he crosses the summit."

It seemed as if Philip had plucked the crazy idea out of her own mind. She coughed. They had to be crazy to even mention it.

"You can't get past the summit's customs check without the required supplies," Philip continued enthusiastically. "So you need to go as soon as possible. The store is slow, and Michael's free now. He's been up that trail many times with a cargo company that hauls loads for a penny a pound. He knows it well, and I fully trust him to get you through. You could be there in two—maybe three—days."

Charlotte shook her head even as she let herself imagine what she might have to endure on a trek up that trail.

"Leave now before Aunt Bessie arrives, or she might try to talk some sense into us romantics."

Charlotte burst out with laughter. "But. . .but how are you going to manage everything—the store, the cooking, Sarah? She's become more energetic these days. The walls can barely contain her."

Philip contemplated his little girl. "Guess I can't tie her to my back like a papoose, but we'll survive until Bessie comes."

Sarah leaned against Philip's leg and smiled up at Charlotte with her dimples flashing.

Charlotte couldn't believe this crazy idea suddenly looked doable. Was Philip right? Did Gabe really care for her? Could a little push make him admit those feelings?

This would take some prayer, but finally she said, "Let me cook up some extra food for you."

Philip smiled. "That would be appreciated."

The last day of March didn't give any promise of spring's arrival. The cold morning air bit at Charlotte's face, and she adjusted her scarf to better cover her nose and cheeks. She carried a light pack of clothing on her back, while Michael walked beside her with a heavy load of food supplies and sleeping bags. They had been hiking at least an hour, even though darkness still cloaked the valley.

Charlotte's body ached this second day on the trail. Her routine at the store didn't require a lot of exertion, and last night's hotel accommodations did nothing to live up to its grand name. A large tent displayed the sign for the Palace Hotel and Restaurant. It had a dining area and a sleeping area. Charlotte had to lie fully clothed on a cot in an open room with other cots and endure the snores of a dozen men. At least the meal had been hot and filling.

Her boots slid in the snow, and again she was grateful for the skirt she had shortened for the hike. It rained the day they started out, but not far up the trail, they encountered snow.

Trying to conserve her energy and focus on the snow-covered trail, Charlotte rarely spoke to Michael. He seemed to understand her need for silence and left her to her thoughts. And they were many.

Where would they find Gabe? How would he receive her? What if he rejected her? Was this love she felt worth the risk?

She pictured Gabe on the day they met, tomato covering his boots. She recalled how she'd admired his light blue eyes— the kind of blue that peeked out of a snow pack.

He appeared strong and determined, yet boyish, when he had stood on the steamer's deck with wind whipping his dark hair. Was it then she began to love him?

He showed kindness toward her when they shared about their lost loves. Their many chats aboard ship had sealed their friendship.

Even though she was intended to be Philip's wife, it was Gabe's tenderness toward Sarah that tugged at her heartstrings.

The way she felt for Gabe couldn't be controlled, and it scared her. She didn't know what to do with such emotions when he seemed so unattainable. She tried desperately to ignore things he did and said that seemed to show his heart, but no one could ignore the gift of the heart-shaped nugget.

Now she was free to offer her love to Gabe, but would he be ready to accept and return that love?

After a late lunch of cold fried bacon, corn bread, and ice

water, Michael said, "We'll stop at Sheep Camp tonight. I feel a storm brewing."

By morning—after another night in humble conditions—Charlotte heard the snowstorm howling and knew they would make no progress on the trail that day.

❧

Gabe and his partners had managed to haul about half of their goods to the summit by March 31. Then two days of very foul weather set in, paralyzing their progress again.

Moving at a snail's pace, it had taken more than two months on the trail just to reach the summit. Then they had a boat to build and miles of lakes and rivers to navigate before they'd ever reach Dawson and stake a mining claim. With all the people on the trail—sometimes one right after the other climbing the "Golden Stairs" to the Chilkoot Summit—he wondered if there still could be any gold left in the Yukon.

Gabe drifted through the camp town, seeking someone who could make a better pot of coffee than he could master. Most of the thousands who called this their temporary home chose to keep inside due to the foul weather.

He made for a tent that served as a mercantile and postal exchange. He'd been checking for mail nearly daily with no results.

The shopkeeper sorted mail beside the stove as Gabe asked if there was anything for him.

"Monroe? Seems like I did see that name." The bald man dug into a large canvas bag. "Ah, yes, I was just about to send this on to Lindemann. It's been here awhile."

"But I check mail regularly."

The older man just shrugged.

"Never mind," Gabe grumbled, then added a thank-you as he took a small bulky package from the man.

He stopped just inside the store's door to open it. The return address read Monroe of San Francisco, California, and he hesitated. Pulling the brown paper open revealed a letter and a pocket watch.

Gabe turned it over. This belonged to his father. The golden design was unmistakable.

He slowly unfolded the letter.

Dear Gabe,

I write this to you while flat on my bed. It has taken a wrenched back to make me stop and take notice of what things are most important in life. I've raged at the Lord a lot while staring at the ceiling. Even your mild mother knows to stay away.

Gabe could picture his father's anger at being confined.

I need to tell you that I'm sorry I wasn't totally open with you about my dealings with Miss Aileen Mayer's father. I was trying to protect my family and business. I thought I was involved in legitimate business with Mr. Mayer, but when I learned of illegal trafficking of goods between here and China, I pulled out. I've paid fines to the city and confessed my poor management of this situation to your mother and God, but I need you to understand. Mr. Mayer is shady, and he was, and still is, using his daughter as a business pawn.

Gabe felt his stomach twist. It was true.

Please accept this watch. It was your grandfather Monroe's. The nuggets in the cover are from his gold strike. My father taught me about good business, honesty, and faith. I've not always done well to take the time and care to instill those lessons in you boys. Praise God you turned out fine, thanks to your mother.

If you should see fit, there is a position in the company for you. I would enjoy sharing my father's teachings with you.

Sincerely, [scratched out]
With love,
Your father, B. Monroe

Relief flooded Gabe. His father's forgiving and contrite tone soothed him, and the need to continue fighting the man seemed to disappear.

Gabe stuffed the paper and watch into his coat pocket and started walking. The snow whirled down the mountain in heavy flakes, clouding his vision. Then he bumped into a signpost. "We buy and sell outfits," it read.

Chapter 8

April 3 dawned feeling almost warm despite the altitude. Charlotte was eager to leave camp. Sheep Camp had little to boast but tents and dirt and hordes of people. Even if Gabe had a tent in the town, she felt most confident of meeting him on the trail or at the Scales.

Michael came to her as she fastened her backpack on. "The natives are saying we shouldn't go any farther up the trail due to avalanches," he said.

"Avalanches? But. . .but Gabe is up there."

"He'll take care of himself, but I'm not taking you anywhere today." He turned and left, striding between tents.

Charlotte parked her belongings back in the canvas hotel, then she strolled through the camp town. Melting snow crunched under her feet, and she was grateful for the warm sun.

Two women sat on crates of provisions just outside a small, privately owned tent. Charlotte stopped to chat with them about where they were from and where they were going. She unwound her scarf under the bright morning sun.

A muffled boom, followed by a roar, barreled down the trail from the summit. The camp came instantly alert. Some men scrambled down the trail away from the noise while others started climbing toward it.

Charlotte's heart pounded. Avalanche.

She left the other women and wove through rows of tents, looking for Michael.

Before noon another, louder roar filled the valley. She caught a sob in her throat as she thought of Gabe possibly trapped by a wall of snow.

Tripping on a tent stake, she rounded a corner and came upon Michael talking to a group of men.

"Miss Charlotte, now don't fret." Michael put his hands on her shoulders and looked in her eyes. "Don't lose hope."

Charlotte looked up at the kind man through her tears.

"I'm heading up the trail with a group to. . .help," he said, then pointed to one of the men. "This man has a wife in camp, and we'll take you to her."

In a tiny tent that seemed to lean against the mountainside, Charlotte met a petite woman and her equally small daughter of about ten years. The woman looked peaked. They huddled by their camp stove and seemed to have no energy for chitchat. Charlotte had enough to think about without making conversation. The waiting tore at her nerves, and she soon left the tent.

The camp swarmed with people. Many came down trail from the Scales. Charlotte started asking men if they knew Gabe Monroe. She made her way through camp, working toward the trail's incline. Just past the horse bridge, she met a group of men pulling a sled. Two bodies lay on the sled, twisted and frozen.

She turned back to camp. She couldn't see any more of this. She lost what remained in her stomach beside a large tent. She looked up only to see men hauling avalanche victims inside that very tent.

Hurrying away, she sought refuge in her mind as she repeated the Twenty-Third Psalm. "Yea, though I walk through the valley of the shadow of death. . ." Shadows couldn't hurt her, but the dread they brought with them stifled her hope.

She stumbled into the hotel. The smell of hot coffee wafted from the stove, and though the proprietor didn't seem to be around, Charlotte helped herself. She sat down at one of the plank tables, resting her head in her hand.

Sometime later, Michael came through the main tent opening, dragging two backpacks. A man who looked vaguely familiar followed him. Michael set the packs down before he noticed her.

"Dear Miss Charlotte, I didn't expect to find you here," he said. "This is Mr. Jarvis, who is with Gabe's party."

Charlotte nodded at the men but didn't voice any of the questions that most pressed her.

Michael moved around the table to her side and cleared his throat. "Mr. Jarvis believes Gabe left camp before dawn to pack a load to the summit before light. A Ken Davies of their party also went packing." Michael pointed to the pile of backpacks. "Some of this has been confirmed as belonging to Davies."

Charlotte felt numb from the tips of her fingers to the core of her heart. How could this be? Why would Gabe have taken that climb under such conditions?

She pushed past the tingle of tears in her throat and said, "When can we leave? I don't want to be here when they haul his body into that tent."

Michael pulled back. "We. . . .we don't know Gabe will be among them. This town is full of men who came back from the Scales ahead of the last slide." He seemed to silently seek Mr. Jarvis's opinion. "Besides, I feel obligated to Philip to find out for sure."

Charlotte couldn't speak. She just nodded as the men excused themselves and returned to their duty.

What now? What was there for her to do?

She should pray, but the pain was so intense, she couldn't form legible words. So she laid her head in her arms and wept.

When she finally raised her head, the hotel proprietor quietly worked beside his stove, putting together food for the dinner hour. Looking up, he offered her some beef broth and potatoes.

After nibbling at the fare, Charlotte headed outside, steering clear of the morgue tent. She aimed for a sign that had caught her attention the day before.

With each footfall, she became more determined that Gabe could not be dead. She pressed her chest where the golden heart nugget rested between her blouse and coat. He must be at the top of that summit.

She stepped inside a small tent where a man sat at a desk

made of two crates labeled as provisions. He raised his brow in question when he saw her.

"You sell outfits for the Yukon?" she asked.

"Certainly. That's what the sign says," he replied.

"I. . .how much?"

He frowned at her, then named an outrageous price.

She withered. If she had that kind of money, she would have returned to California by now.

Turning, she pulled back the tent flap to leave as a man stepped in. Tall and broad, he had a beard covering his face.

"Excuse me," Charlotte mumbled.

"Ma'am."

She glanced up into arctic blue eyes. Though the skin around them appeared chapped and leathery and the bones looked more pronounced, she recognized him.

"Gabe!" She flung her arms around his waist and squeezed with all her might.

"Well. . .I. . .Charlotte." He stared at her as he pulled her away from him. "You're the last person I expected to see here."

Charlotte sobered as she gazed at him. Trail life had aged him, yet he looked so good in his rough garb.

"How did you get here?" he asked. "What was Philip thinking, letting you leave Dyea?"

"He blessed my trip and sent Michael with me."

Gabe shook his head. "What for?"

"To find you."

"But. . .why?" Gabe gazed at her beautiful face, tinged red by the wind. Her eyes nearly danced as she looked up at him.

She had never looked more loveable, and a fierce need to protect her swelled within him.

"You can't stay here. This trail is much too dangerous for—"

She placed both of her hands on his chest and pushed. He back-stepped out of the tent and away from the shopkeeper's eyes. A determined looked settled on her face.

"Gabe Monroe, you brought me to Alaska, and you will see me out. I'm not going anywhere without you."

He felt a grin twitch at his mouth even before his brain could register his thoughts. Her feisty attitude surprised him, but he knew he just loved her all the more.

He crossed his arms in front of his chest. "What will I do with you?"

She shrugged and glanced away, giving the first indication that she might not be so sure of herself.

He reached out just to touch her cheek, but he couldn't stop from pulling her into his arms.

"My dear Lottie." He cradled her head against his chest, and she wrapped her arms around him. "So much has happened to me in the two months on this trail. I discovered all that is really important is that I surrender my stubborn will to God. . . ."

She squeezed him.

"And that I can love again."

She pulled back and gazed up at him. "Truly?"

"For real this time," he whispered as he leaned down to touch her lips with his own.

The touch stirred the embers of his lonely soul to a flame. He clutched her tightly to him. If God put this woman in his life—as only God could—then he would never let her go.

❧

They walked hand in hand through the camp town. Though still bustling with thousands of stampeders, a solemn attitude permeated the atmosphere. The highest risk-taking had just been played out in front of them all.

Charlotte leaned into Gabe's arm. "Your partner said you made that climb this morning. Why?"

"Well, I went up before dawn to mark my cache and was at the summit when the avalanche let go. I hiked down the long way." Gabe glanced at her. "You see, I had already decided to sell my outfit. I was labeling it for the buyer, and. . .I was going back to Dyea. . .for you."

She looked up at him through her tears. "I couldn't wait long enough. I had to find you." Heat touched her cheeks.

Gabe threw back his head and laughed. "I love you, Charlotte Vance."

Her heart did a giddy dance, and a smile pushed back her cheeks.

"What's your middle name?" he suddenly asked.

"Uh. . .Ruth."

His laughter rang again through the valley, and people turned to stare.

"Well, Miss Charlotte Ruth." He stopped walking and pulled her around to face him. "I will be your Boaz, if you will be my Ruth."

He had never seemed so happy to her. Seeing him so did more to thrill her soul than the proposal she had for so long pined.

"Gabe, you. . ." How could she be at a loss for words now? "I. . .you are a wonderful man, and I love you so."

She rose on her toes and boldly planted a kiss of promise on his smiling lips. His arms engulfed her as he picked her off her feet and swung her around until they both turned giddy with dizziness.

He set her back on her feet. "What now, my dear?"

"Now?" She reached up to feel his short beard. "Well, my love, I've been wondering what the other side of that mountain looks like. In fact, I was in that store to price outfits. . .just in case I had to pursue you all the way to Dawson—seeing as how I couldn't accept the idea that you could be dead."

Chuckling, Gabe linked arms with her and started them down a grade. "I would have packed you up and taken you with me when I started this trip if I had thought gold country was any place for a lady. Now—though I'd love to see if all the grand tales are true—the real reasons for going don't exist anymore."

He pulled a watch from his pocket, and Charlotte admired the old design.

"It belonged to my father. He sent it to me with a letter that I just got yesterday."

Gabe stared down the valley, and Charlotte waited for him to finish his thoughts.

Finally, he said, "We can head back to Philip's store. Maybe I can help him out for awhile, until. . .until I'm sure I'm ready to go home—back to California and the family business."

Charlotte patted his arm. "I'll go anywhere with you, Gabe. . . even to gold country." This hike up the Chilkoot Trail had flared a sense of adventure in her she'd never known she possessed.

"It's not necessary. . . ."

"I heard your grandfather was a gold miner. Don't you want to see what drove him?"

"Sure, that's what started this whole adventure. . .until I mixed in some of my lesser motives."

"Then let's go," she said, having made up her mind.

He looked down into her eyes. "But Philip will likely make more money in his store than I can dredge out of any creek bed."

She shrugged. "Let's just do it for the adventure," she stated, then stopped. "But I don't have an outfit."

Gabe thought awhile, then said, "Davies died in the slide. He didn't have a wife or anything. We'll use his supplies and mail his folks a fair price."

He put his arm around her shoulders and pulled her tight. "I'm not forgetting the risk we would be taking by continuing the trail. And it's a shame that kid had to die when his dreams were so strong."

"We can't know why things happen the way they do, but I'm so thankful God spared you."

They strolled along for awhile, then Gabe said, "Now about the marriage business. Don't you think you've waited long enough to become a Monroe?"

Charlotte laughed. "Long enough to be sure I marry the right man."

He gazed lovingly down at her. "Think there might be a reverend in this unusual town?"

"We'll find one." Charlotte smiled broadly.

❧

Four days later, on April 7, 1898, Gabriel Black Monroe married Charlotte Ruth Vance on the summit of the Chilkoot Trail. The wind whipped at the little customs shack where a small party huddled together for the occasion. At first word of the upcoming wedding, Michael had returned to Dyea so Philip could make a quick trip up the trail to stand as his brother's witness.

As Gabe made his vows to her, Charlotte knew she had never felt so cool on the outside while so warm and content on the inside. She relaxed against the arm of the man she looked forward to being with for the rest of her life—a life full of promise.

REBECCA GERMANY

Rebecca considers herself an old-fashioned kind of girl who loves old-fashioned kinds of romance. She was hooked from a young age, and it was a natural progression when she chose to devote her life's work to books and writing. **Heartsong Presents** inspirational romance series and book club started in October 1992. Rebecca joined the **Heartsong** team exactly one year later and was named managing editor in 1995 and senior fiction editor in 2002. She has written several things, and her first work of fiction was a novella published in a collection from Barbour Publishing. She now has five novellas in print along with a few compiled gift books. Single, but contentedly enjoying life on the old family farm, "Becky" has several hobbies (like reading, singing, gardening, crafts, quilting, and so on) to keep her very busy.

Love's Far Country

by Colleen Coble

Chapter 1

Houghton, Michigan—August 1898

Alexandria Peters clasped her gloved hands together in her lap. Her right leg wanted to jitter nervously, and it was all she could do to appear calm and composed. The huge leather chair she sat in nearly swallowed her up as completely as she feared her uncle would do. She sucked in a shaky breath. She'd faced worse than this and survived it.

Her uncle had always terrified her. To her childish ears as she grew up, his gruff voice sounded as though a lion spoke, and from his dealings with her father, she knew he could be just as heartless as a lion on the prowl for his next meal. She didn't intend that meal to be her or her brother, Will. They'd been through too much, she and Will.

After Father died, her brother had been lost, rudderless. Now that he seemed to know what he wanted, she would move the world to make sure he had what he needed. He was all she had left now, as she was all he had. Father would expect nothing less than for her to be strong and brave.

She glanced around the library as she waited for Uncle Reginald to arrive. Walnut bookcases filled with leather-bound books encased the room like fortress walls. Her uncle prided himself on being well read, and the library was a testament to his obsession with knowledge. He'd never seen how his knowledge was of no eternal value when his dealings with people were so ruthless.

The door behind her opened, and she stiffened her shoulders for the coming battle. Uncle Reginald's pale blue eyes flickered over her face, and he nodded. "You're looking particularly fine today, Niece."

His smooth ways put her on her guard. He was at his most charming when he worked on some nefarious scheme. Well, he wouldn't get the best of her. She knew what he was capable of. She'd seen the men he used and discarded along the way like the empty tins of snuff he collected.

Tilting her chin, she nodded. "Good morning, Uncle Reginald."

He settled his slight frame behind the huge polished desk and flipped open a ledger. "I've been going over your father's books, Alexandria. His death has left you and Will in precarious circumstances."

Her stomach tightened at the mention of her father's death. Suicide. The reality still smacked her in the face. She never would have thought her father would be so cowardly as to kill himself. *Sorry,* the note on his desk had said. As if sorry would change the reality of leaving her and Will on their own to face an uncertain future. Sorry wasn't good enough in Alex's opinion. Over the past month she'd wished he was still here so she could tell him so to his face.

"Your father's investments were wiped out in the Panic. If he'd only listened to me. I tried to tell him not to invest in the Philadelphia and Reading Railroad, but Lane always thought his judgment was second to none." Uncle Reginald pursed his thin lips and shook his head. "Even the house is fully mortgaged."

Alex's stomach churned, and she fought a rapidly rising nausea. She'd not thought it as bad as that. She would have to let the house go. This was worse than anything she'd imagined. "What about the summer house on the Keweenaw Peninsula?" she asked desperately.

"Gone. He sold it last summer."

A slight smile played around Uncle Reginald's lips, and Alex wanted to scream or cry, anything to wipe that supercilious attitude from his face. Didn't he care at all that they were desperate? A wave of dizziness passed over her. No wonder her father had been "too busy" for their annual jaunt to the cottage.

"Is there anything left at all?" she whispered. What would she and Will do? They couldn't stay with Uncle Reginald. Within a month they would be ready to follow their father to the grave just to get away from him. Gentle, sensitive Will would never survive the experience.

"Not much." Uncle Reginald's eyes sparkled as though he was enjoying her shock and dismay. "About two thousand dollars."

That wouldn't last long. Alex's thoughts whirled, and her

fingers gripped the arms of the chair for support. "What about Will's school fees?"

"Luckily, they've been paid through the end of next year. But there will be no money for college."

"Nothing else left at all?" she asked through tight lips. Her thoughts raced. There had to be some way to get the money for Will's college. She couldn't let her father's cowardice destroy her brother too.

"Well, there's a steamboat out in Alaska." Her uncle laughed. "The *Dawson Belle*. Some man by the name of Philip Monroe uses it to haul goods from Seattle to his store in Dyea to outfit the miners flooding the area. He leased it for a pittance before the gold strike. The lease runs out next month though. Maybe you could negotiate a more attractive return from this Monroe. Things in the Klondike are booming, so he should be willing to give you a little larger cut."

Alaska. She'd seen the papers proclaiming it the richest gold strike in history. "Would it be enough to live on?"

"A flat lease wouldn't be. But if you could convince Monroe to give you a percentage of the profits, it might suffice. I would be happy to negotiate it for you." His eyes narrowed as he obviously contemplated the coming confrontation with anticipation.

The last thing she wanted was to have Uncle Reginald involved in her affairs. There was only one way. She took a deep breath. "That won't be necessary. I'm going out there myself." Alex stood and smoothed her skirt.

"You can't do any such thing!" Her uncle jumped to his feet and glowered at her. "Alaska has swallowed up more men than you can count. A woman alone has no business out there. Cold, snow, hardship. I forbid it, Alexandria!"

Once the thought had taken hold, it refused to let go. She could make this Monroe a proposition and take an active role in the business of bringing supplies in for the miners. "The weather can hardly be much worse than here on Lake Superior, Uncle. And this is nearly a new century. Women are just as competent as men. Father always said I had a head for business. If there's money to be made in Alaska, then that's where I'll go. I have Will to think of. He has his heart set on studying medicine, and I have to find a way to make that happen."

"That boy always had his head in the clouds," her uncle grumbled. "Leave him with me, and I'll knock some sense into him. If he'd go into the copper mining business like me, he could make enough money that he'd never be in the predicament your father was in."

Mining was the last career Alex would want for her idealist brother. She'd do whatever she had to in order to prevent such a fate from befalling Will. Her uncle's philosophy was to put a young man in as a miner to learn the business that way. He'd done it with his own three sons, and Marcus, the youngest, had died as a result.

She wasn't about to risk Will that way. "Thanks for your offer, Uncle, but Will loves his school. He shall stay there while I journey to Alaska to make our fortune." Her heart beat fast at the thought. She was about to have adventure in her life.

Adventure. There had been times she nearly screamed with the boredom of her life in Michigan's Upper Peninsula. So far from bright city lights and the things she'd only read about in the papers, she'd longed to step out of the life she knew and see something of the world. Father had always talked about taking her to the Pacific Northwest someday, and she'd read all she could get her hands on about Washington and Oregon. Now she would journey to Seattle and then on to Alaska.

Alaska. Just the thought of that far-off country made her shiver. Alaska, where blue whales frolicked in the water and majestic mountains reached for an expansive sky. It was a thought both terrifying and exhilarating.

Over the next two weeks, she packed her personal belongings and prepared the house for sale. Everything had to go. The only thing Alex managed to keep was her mother's prized collection of blue-and-white china. Clara, their housekeeper of nearly twenty years, promised to hold onto it for her.

Her uncle tried several times to talk her out of her decision, but she knew he didn't want her to go because she was escaping his authority. Reginald Peters hated loss of power above all things. Will wasn't happy about it either. She'd written him posthaste at his boarding school in Chicago, and he had answered immediately with a plea to be allowed to go. She'd reassured him of her safety, and now she stood on the threshold of a new life.

Her best friend, Elizabeth, followed her around the house as she made her final inspection. "I'm so jealous," Elizabeth pouted. "I shall be stuck here in Marquette while you travel the world."

"I'll write often and describe everything I see," Alex

promised. "I must be going. The train leaves in an hour."

Elizabeth trailed her disconsolately to the buggy. "I begged Father to allow me to accompany you, but he refused," she said.

"As would any father," Alex said. "My own would have forbidden this journey, even if he could have accompanied me. Pray for me, Elizabeth. I face many dangers and struggles yet ahead." She hugged her friend, then lifted her skirt and clambered into the buggy. She turned to look at the home she was raised in. When next she came this way, it would belong to some other family.

In her mind's eye, she could see her mother in her brightly colored silks playing croquet on the lawn and her father sitting in a lawn chair with a tall glass of lemonade as he watched his wife and daughter. Those times were gone forever. Mama had died giving birth to Will two days before Alex's tenth birthday, and now Father was gone too. Their home had faced other tragedies and survived, but this one had dealt it a death blow. The stone and mortar culled from mines in the area made up a dwelling, no longer a real home for the Peters family.

Waving good-bye to Elizabeth, Alex turned her face forward and prepared to face a future without the security of the wealth she'd always known. She could only hope she was up to the task ahead.

❧

Philip Monroe stood on the deck of the *Dawson Belle* and directed the stevedores as they unloaded the supplies from Seattle. Sometimes he woke up with the aurora borealis shimmering through his window and still couldn't believe he was really here. The first years had been hard, especially with Dottie's death. But he and Gabe had made it through together. Now that Gabe was a married man and off seeking gold with his new bride, Philip had to fight off feelings of loneliness.

He sighed and flipped open the cover of the pocket watch. Glancing at the watch's hands, he grimaced. If Alex Peters didn't show up soon, he'd have to order the captain to shove off, and that might put the man's nose out of joint. He'd probably come out for a personal inspection to assure himself the boat had been well taken care of. But the weather waited for no man, and he had more supplies to buy before winter set in; so the man had better be along at once, or Philip would have no choice but to send the steamer on its way. A part of him hoped that was the case. The last thing he wanted to deal with today was negotiations.

It was ridiculous the man was coming out here to negotiate a simple lease. Philip was a fair man, and he'd realized the boat could command a higher lease with the gold rush going on. Maybe the man was on his way to the gold field as well. It was possible. Men from all walks of life had tossed away their livelihood in search of the precious metal that seemed to turn their brains to mush and their common sense to an addlepated pursuit of wealth.

That life of uncertainty was not for Philip. The life of a merchant was much more stable and sure. No matter who they were, miners needed supplies, and he provided a needed service. But not without a boat, so he hoped he could get as fair a price from this man as he had from his father.

"Looks like the boat is about ready to shove off." Michael Stanton, the manager of the store here in Dyea, pushed his hat to the back of his head. About fifty, Michael's calm, take-charge attitude never failed to calm Philip's agitation.

"Just about. Mr. Peters is going to be too late to inspect it."

"Alex Peters just arrived and is waiting for you in your office at the store." A smile tugged at Michael's mouth.

"Why didn't you bring him here?" Another delay, just what he didn't want. Too impatient to wait for an answer, Philip brushed past Michael and hurried down the long dock to shore.

Monroe's had been the first miner's supply store to open in Dyea, a fact Philip was proud of. Since its first day of business in a tent, it had grown to encompass nearly a block along the water. He strode through the door, intent on dealing with Alex Peters and getting back to his business. The crowd of miners purchasing supplies for the long trek into Dawson parted to make way for him.

His office was behind the counter, back in the living quarters he and Gabe had used when they first came here. At the thought of his brother, he reminded himself to make sure the letter he'd just written got sent off with a miner heading to the Yukon.

Philip opened the door to his office and looked around, but it was empty. Where had the man gotten to now? He didn't have time for this today, and he clenched his teeth in frustration. Then he heard a light cough and saw a dark head move in the wingback chair. Mr. Peters must be rather short.

Pasting a smile to his face, Philip walked around to the front of the chair with his hand outstretched, then froze. A young woman sat in the chair. She was so small, she appeared to be a child sitting in an adult's chair. Her dark hair, nearly blue-black, was pulled back and swept up into a coronet of curls that peeked from beneath her stylish bonnet, while a feather coyly drooped over one eye.

Those dark blue, almost violet, eyes were regarding him with some disfavor, and he realized how he must look to her. Dressed in his work clothes, she must think him an employee. Was she Mr. Peters's daughter or wife?

He held out a hand to her. "I'm so sorry. I was expecting Alex Peters. I'm Philip Monroe. Will Mr. Peters be back soon?"

"I'm Alex Peters," the vision in lavender silk said with a warm smile that revealed perfect white teeth and a dimple deep enough to drown in.

Philip caught his breath. There had been few times in his life when he'd lost the power to talk, but this shock rendered him speechless. He blinked, but she refused to vanish from his chair. What was a lovely young woman doing here on her own? There had to be some mistake.

Alex Peters rose and extended a hand clad up to the elbow in white silk. "I'm sorry. I didn't realize you were expecting a man. My full name is Alexandria, but no one calls me that." Her violet eyes caught his in a direct gaze. There seemed to be grit and determination in her stare that seemed out of character with her fashionable attire.

In a daze, Philip took the hand she offered. "Pl—pleased to meet you, Miss Peters."

"Call me Alex," she said. She clasped his hand briefly, then released it and settled back into her chair. "Shall we get down to business?"

Still stunned, Philip went to the chair behind his desk and dropped into it. He didn't know what to think. "I need to be getting on my way. The snows won't be long now, and I have barely enough time for two or three more trips to Seattle." Alex's eyes widened, and Philip couldn't help but notice her thick lashes and the strong statement of her winged eyebrows.

"Surely you can take time to discuss business?" she asked.

"Send your man to see me next week, and we'll discuss it," he said. "I'm sure you have more important things to do."

"I have no man, as you put it," she said. "I handle my own business." She opened her beaded purse and took out a paper. "I propose to split the profits with you, sixty-forty. Sixty for you, and forty for me. I believe that's more than fair."

It took a few moments for what she was saying to sink in. He stood to his feet. "That's outrageous! I can't agree to such a ridiculous demand. I was planning a simple, flat lease. I'd up the amount I'm paying, of course. That's only fair, but your proposal is ludicrous."

"I already have a better offer," she said quietly. "Wilson Players offered me a fifty-fifty split. For my father's sake, I wanted you to have the first chance of continuing to use the boat."

Wilson Players would do anything to bankrupt Monroe's, but Philip wasn't about to reveal something so personal to this woman. In spite of her fastidious appearance, it was obvious an astute brain lurked behind those gorgeous eyes.

In desperation, Philip contemplated his options. She had him over a barrel. The steamboat crew was already aboard and ready to go. The business owners in Dyea would be lining up to accept her offer. Steamboats of the caliber and size of the *Dawson Belle* were as scarce as women like Miss Peters here.

"You leave me no choice, Miss Peters," he said.

She inclined her head, and he was struck by the graceful line of her neck and shoulders. Averting his eyes, he tugged at the collar of his shirt. The sooner they concluded their business and Alex Peters was gone, the happier he'd be. He was aware of her like no woman he'd ever met. Even his attraction to Dottie had taken weeks not minutes to develop.

Alex pushed the paper she'd taken from her purse across the surface of the desk. "I have the papers ready for your signature," she said.

Without looking up, Philip read through the one-year agreement. "Wait a minute! This says you will be consulted about shipments and types of goods sold."

"I intend to remain in Alaska, Mr. Monroe. The *Dawson Belle* is my only chance to provide a living for me and my brother. There is money to be made in trade here, and I assure you you'll find me a congenial partner."

"Partner! I've always had a free hand in my own business."

"And you'll continue to do so. I wouldn't dream of interfering in Monroe's. But the *Dawson Belle* is all my father left to me, and I must maximize that single asset. Surely you can understand that."

Her tone was that of an adult trying to explain something

to a child, and it raised Philip's ire. He understood it, but that didn't mean he had to like it. Still, what choice did he have? Pressing his lips together, he signed the paper in a bold script and shoved it across the desk to her.

Folding it up and placing it back in her purse, she rose with a rustle of her silk skirts, a sound he found both maddening and tantalizing. He'd forgotten what a lovely creature a refined woman was. His thoughts drifted to Dottie. Strangely, he found his heart not so sore at the memory of his dead wife. The realization pained him.

"Are there accommodations to be found in Dyea, Mr. Monroe?" Alex asked.

Philip laughed. "Not much, and certainly not anything fit for a lady." Maybe she'd take a hint and get back on the boat that brought her, though looking at her determined chin, he doubted it.

"I shall have to see what I can find." Her gentle voice was unperturbed.

Hating himself for his softness, he knew he couldn't let her go roaming the streets alone. It would be like tossing his daughter, Sarah, to the killer whales. "I maintain a guest room for business associates. You are welcome to use it." At her raised eyebrows, he hastened to reassure her. "My wife's aunt Bessie recently arrived. She lives with me and cares for my three-year-old daughter. I'm rarely home this time of year, so you needn't worry about appearances."

"You're married?"

"I'm a widower," he said shortly.

"Oh, I'm sorry."

From her sorrowful eyes, he knew she meant it. "Thank you," he said gruffly.

"I shall accept your most gracious offer," Alex said. "Could we go there straightaway? I find myself longing to freshen up. Then I would like to see the *Dawson Belle*."

With a sinking heart, Philip realized there was no way the boat was going to weigh anchor that morning.

Chapter 2

D yea was a cesspool, an open sore on the face of the pristine wilderness that had so enchanted Alex on the trip to Alaska. However did the people bear living in such a stinking pit? Holding a handkerchief to her nose, she followed Philip Monroe's broad back across the muddy street, though she wasn't at all sure she should call this quagmire that sucked at her boots like a ravenous beast a street.

Her first sight of the town had been enough to make her want to turn tail and run back to the safety of Michigan, but Alex couldn't afford the luxury of waiting for some prince to rescue her from her predicament. Will was depending on her, and she refused to let him down. Shacks and tents dotted the landscape right up to the majestic mountains that crowded closely to the harbor. Noisome and rank, the stench of humanity was nearly overpowering.

Men leered at her as Philip assisted her across the raucous town, and she was glad of his protection. She passed men playing cards, several fights with crowds yelling encouragement, and drunken men lying in the mud. On the Seattle-bound train, she had never imagined a place as wild and untamed as this. The man striding confidently through the streets as he cleared the way for her was nearly as untamed as the landscape. When she'd come face to face with him in his office, it had been all Alex could do to keep from staring.

Philip Monroe's face looked as though it had been chiseled from the mountains that surrounded Dyea. Eyes the color of Lake Superior on a stormy day looked out at the world with a worn cynicism that made Alex want to know what had put that pain and weariness there. A firm chin told her he was not a man to give in to adversity, and she was astounded she'd forced him to agree to her terms.

Now she wondered what she'd gotten herself into. Her father always told her she could do anything she set her mind to, that the world was changing and there was room for a clever woman to stand shoulder to shoulder with men, that she was the equal of anyone. Seeing the depravity in these streets, she only knew she would stand no chance without Philip Monroe's protection.

Poor man, to be left alone so young and with a daughter to raise. What had happened to his wife? There would be time to find out over the coming months. Alex intended to take an active role in maximizing her profits. There was little time to waste in order to have what she needed to send Will to school.

They reached the end of the street, and Philip stopped in front of a building. "Here we are."

Unpainted but sturdy, the house perched right on the edge

of the muddy street. Only the front door had been painted. Philip pushed it open and called out, "I'm home."

Moments later the sound of small feet running down the hall caused Alex to turn. A little girl who looked like a miniature version of Philip with dark curls and gray eyes came running to meet them. She flung herself against Philip's legs, and he swung her into his arms.

"This is Sarah," Philip said. "Sarah, this is Miss Peters. She's going to stay with us for awhile."

Alex was astounded at the way his rugged face softened with his daughter's arrival. He looked almost approachable. She blinked back her surprise and smiled at the child. "Hello, Sarah."

The little girl regarded Alex solemnly. "You're pretty," she said. She reached out and touched the silk of Alex's gown. Her eyes widened at the feel of the fabric.

Philip set his daughter on the floor. "Run and tell Aunt Bessie we have a guest."

The child scampered off, and Alex gazed around the entry hall. Through one doorway she could see into a comfortable parlor with green upholstered furniture and a real Persian rug. Through the door to the left, a walnut dining-room table with ten chairs sat on another brightly patterned rug. Philip had obviously made sure he possessed an adequate home for his daughter.

A few moments later, she heard a thumping sound come down the hall. Leaning heavily on her cane, an older woman dressed in black bombazine came toward her. A smile creased her plump face, and her cheeks were pink with excitement.

"I couldn't believe it when Sarah said a beautiful lady was here." Stopping in front of Alex, she took Alex's hand and pressed it firmly. "Welcome, Child. Call me Aunt Bessie; everyone does."

Somewhat overwhelmed by the warm welcome, Alex smiled. "Call me Alex."

"Oh ho, you're Alex Peters. Not quite the businessman you were expecting, eh, Philip?" Aunt Bessie cast a sly grin at her nephew.

To Alex's astonishment, Philip's cheeks turned red, and he looked almost angry again. Maybe she should have explained she was a woman in her telegram, but she'd been afraid he would refuse to meet with her. She'd found it best to forge ahead with her plans and give him no choice.

"Miss Peters will be staying with us for a few days," Philip said. "I must get back to the boat, so if you'll help her get settled, I'll run along."

"I would like to see the boat," Alex said quickly. She needed to make it clear to him that she was staying more than a few days. If his hospitality didn't extend until she had the money to set up her own household, then she needed to know now.

Philip's lips tightened. "Very well. Aunt Bessie will show you to your room, and I'll come back in about an hour to escort you." He then turned and went out the door.

"That man works too much," Aunt Bessie said sorrowfully. "He hasn't figured out yet that work is no cure for grief."

Alex's curiosity was further piqued by the woman's remarks,

and she wondered how long Philip's wife had been dead. She told herself it was none of her business, but she couldn't deny that the man intrigued her. She was normally wary of men since her engagement had been broken, but Philip had already gotten past her defenses with the pain she saw lurking in his eyes.

"Well, it's welcome you are, Miss, though you'll find Dyea the devil's own playground. I've told Philip it's no fit place to raise a child, but he's assured me he will make sure we stay safe. Come along, and I'll show you to your room. Then I'll fix us some tea."

Aunt Bessie continued to babble as she tapped her cane along the floor and up the stairs. Clutching her valise, Alex followed the older woman. Glancing around, she saw a photograph in the upstairs hall of a beautiful young woman.

"Who is that?" she asked, stopping in front of it.

Aunt Bessie looked over her shoulder. "Sarah's poor mother."

"She's lovely," Alex said. Stepping closer, she gazed into the smiling eyes of the young woman.

"That she was. Philip loved her madly. After she died, he refused to eat, and it was only little Sarah's sobs that finally roused him back to life."

"So she died in childbirth?"

Aunt Bessie shook her head and dabbed a tear with her handkerchief. "Cholera struck Dottie when Sarah was a year old. Philip blames God, though I've told him the Almighty always has His reasons. No one has been able to get through to him, not his brother nor me. I fear he'll turn into a bitter old man if he doesn't release his pain somehow."

"He has a brother? Where is he?"

Aunt Bessie smiled. "I've not met him, but I hear his high spirits tend to get him into trouble. You see, he brought a wife back from San Francisco for Philip." Her smile deepened.

Alex's stomach tightened. She couldn't deny the disappointment that rippled through her. "I thought Philip wasn't married."

"He's not. Gabe got more than he bargained for, and *he* married the girl. They're off looking for gold. Once I came out, Philip didn't need Charlotte—that's Gabe's wife—to look after Sarah. But it's left Philip even more alone."

That explained the sadness in his eyes. Alex resolved to try to help him. She knew all about the pain of loss and how it sometimes can twist your confidence into doubt and worry. But her faith was the only thing that got her through her fiancé's perfidy and then her father's death. Pity welled in her heart for Philip. He must feel as lost as a crab boat in the Bering Sea.

The older woman left Alex to freshen up in a comfortable but sparsely furnished bedroom. Bare plank floors were softened with a rag rug, and a washstand held two rough towels and a sliver of soap. Removing her hat, Alex slipped out of her soiled dress and poured water from the pitcher into the bowl.

Once she'd washed and put on a clean dress, she felt almost human again. She brushed out her hair and coiled it on the back of her head, then opened the door and made her way back downstairs.

She and Aunt Bessie had just finished their tea when Philip

arrived looking windblown and cross.

"Are you ready?" he asked abruptly.

"Certainly." Alex rose and settled her shawl around her shoulders.

"Come along then. The boat should have been out of sight of land by now." He offered her his arm, but it was clear he'd rather touch a Kodiak bear than her.

Was he always so prickly around women or was it just her? Alex wanted to refuse his aid, but she knew she'd land in the mud if she attempted to walk unassisted. Stiffly, she placed her hand on his arm. In the street she cringed from the same appraising stares she'd endured on the way to the Monroe residence. Her stomach roiled again at the stench, and she wondered why Philip chose to stay here.

"Why haven't the churches done something about cleaning up this place?" she asked.

"There are no churches here," Philip said shortly. "Not here nor in Skagway."

No churches? No wonder sin seemed rampant on every hand. Her misgivings increased. Maybe she should just take a look at the operation, then leave the rest to Philip. He might be angry at her insistence on a share of the profits, but she thought him a fair man. He would see she was paid what she was owed. She could go back to Michigan.

But what was left for her there? Her home belonged to someone else by now. She would rather face a pack of wolves than live with her uncle. Squaring her shoulders, she resolved to hold on and work through this. It was unpleasant, but so was being poor. Having a hand in the business would ensure a future for her and Will.

They reached the long pier, a rough affair that testified to its hasty construction by many gaps in the walkway.

"Careful you don't fall through," Philip said.

Alex was conscious of the flexing of his muscles through the fabric of his shirt and the sheer masculinity of his presence. Her fiancé, Morgan, had never affected her like this, and she wondered if maybe she was just too exhausted to erect her usual barriers. After a good night's sleep, she would be able to distance herself better.

The *Dawson Belle's* hull rode high in the water with her hold now empty. Deck hands with their mouths open stared at Alex as she stepped aboard and gazed around.

"If you'll take a quick look around, I'll get you home so the captain can shove off. We're already two hours behind schedule," Philip said.

Though he didn't say it, Alex knew he blamed her for the delay, and she felt a niggle of guilt. She bit her lip and resolved not to let him intimidate her. She had a right to inspect this boat. It belonged to her, not to Philip. She lifted her chin and strolled slowly along the deck.

Philip took her into the hold and pointed out the stalls for transporting livestock and the compartments for supplies, then pointed out the crew's quarters. The longer she looked around, the more she wondered if she could make a difference in turning better profits. Philip seemed to know his business very well.

Back on deck, Philip practically vibrated with impatience.

"Now if you're satisfied, let's get you back to the house, and the captain can weigh anchor."

Feeling like a naughty child, Alex followed him toward the rickety pier. Impatience rolled off Philip in waves as big as the breakers crashing on the shore. She felt like bursting into tears, but she stiffened her back and lifted her chin.

"You might think my input worthless, Mr. Monroe. You'd like nothing better than for me to board my steamer and go back to Seattle. But I think eventually I might surprise you. Shall we go?" She stepped to the gangplank. Lifting her skirts, she made her way onto the pier without mishap. Trying to keep her skirts out of the mud, she marched toward the muddy streets without waiting for him. What an insufferable man! His wife was better off in heaven without having to deal with such a disagreeable husband.

Moments later the mud was sucking at her boots, and she nearly toppled. Strong fingers gripped her elbow, and she managed to right herself. "Thank you," she said without looking at him.

"There's no way I can talk you out of this, can I?" he said softly.

"No, there is not," she said. "My brother is depending on me, Mr. Monroe, and I am determined not to let him down. Just as you must provide for Sarah, I must provide for Will. I can promise you I will do everything in my power to be an asset to you and not a liability."

"That's a powerful promise," he said.

Alex could hear the amusement in his voice. Pressing her

lips together, she glanced up into his gray eyes. Taken aback at the compassion in his gaze, the angry words died on her tongue.

"I didn't realize you had the responsibility for your brother," he said softly. "Your father left you no provision?"

"Only the *Dawson Belle* was left to us," she said, fighting the sting of tears. It was easier to fight with him than to accept his sympathy.

"Then we must do what we can to make it pay its way," he said. "Shall we call a truce, Miss Peters...er...Alex?" He thrust out his hand.

"Very well," she said, taking his hand. The warm press of his fingers shot a thrill of something she couldn't name straight to her stomach, and she had to wonder if maybe she was coming down with something. She felt almost feverish as she pulled her hand away.

They reached the house, and Philip opened the door for her. "I'll be back once the boat leaves, and maybe we can discuss more fully what role you intend to play in the shipping business."

Excitement stirred in her stomach. Was he really succumbing so readily to her determination? Her eager smile died when she saw the wariness in his face. He was merely humoring her. She doubted he would let her have any real say in the shipping business without a fight, but that was all right. No doubt he'd never had to deal with a woman in business before. The proof was in the pudding, as her grandmother used to say. She would show him.

She went to her room and took off her hat. Sitting by the

window, she looked out at the majestic peaks that cradled the town like a giant clenched hand with knuckles thrusting into the blue sky. If she could focus on the beauty of God's creation in this place, maybe she could overlook the lawlessness and the filth in the streets. If ever a place needed God's grace, it was this town. Maybe He had sent her here to make a difference. If so, she just prayed she was up to the task.

Resting her elbow on the windowsill, she propped her chin on her hand and wondered where to go from here. She had some idea of the types of things she wanted to have brought to Dyea for the miners. Things like cookstoves, rugs, cooking utensils, other items that a man might not think of. There seemed to be plenty of wives with the miners, and they would be quick to demand some of the things they'd left behind in civilization as well, such as gingham, sewing necessities, and ribbon. A man like Philip would call them luxuries, but the women would call them necessities. At least that was her hope.

She could only pray God would give her the grace to see this thing through. What would she do if this venture failed? Not only would Will be unable to attend school, but she herself would have nowhere to go. All her bridges were burned behind her, and the future was the only path that held any promise. She had to earn enough to get a start somewhere, a place for her and Will to call home.

He'd wanted to come with her, and she'd considered it, but gazing into the muddy streets and the rowdy activity below her window, she was glad Will was safely ensconced in boarding school. A place like this could turn a boy's head to dreams of striking it rich. The Bible said that he who wanted to be rich fell into a snare. Alex had no desire for wealth, only for enough money to see to their needs. And God had promised He would take care of those. She just had to trust Him.

Chapter 3

Alex spent the next day settling into her room and getting to know her hosts. She knew she couldn't stay at the Monroe home forever and determined to find some other place to live, and though Philip assured her he was looking for a room, there were none to be found. Though some miners had moved onto green pastures, the empty buildings she'd seen weren't fit for habitation. And it would take money and time to make something suitable. She would have to watch for something worth buying or renting.

Two days after she arrived, she donned a serviceable cotton skirt and blouse, put on her old boots, and prepared to begin to know what the miners' wives needed. She went down the stairs and paused at the door to the parlor. Sarah was on the floor in front of Aunt Bessie. Tears rolled down the child's cheeks as the older woman worked a comb through the little girl's thick curls.

"Sit still, Child," Aunt Bessie said. "I can't get these tangles out with you squirming like a worm after a rain."

"It hurts," Sarah sobbed.

"You're a big girl. It's about time you quit crying over getting your hair combed."

Alex flinched. Her own head was tender, and her heart stirred with compassion. "Let me try," she said, setting her purse on the hall table and moving into the room.

Aunt Bessie handed the comb to her. "I declare, this child hates to have her hair combed worse than anyone I've ever seen."

Alex patted Sarah's cheek. "I'll try not to hurt you," she whispered as she sat on the sofa and pulled Sarah to her. "I know what it feels like." Starting at the tips of the lustrous dark curls, she gently worked the tangles out of Sarah's hair. The little girl's sobs diminished, and Alex felt the child relaxing back against her knees. Within minutes Sarah's hair was neatly combed and pulled back on top with a bow.

"Come see me tonight before you go to bed," Alex told her. "I always braid my hair at night, and it keeps it from tangling."

Sarah crawled up into Alex's lap and threw her arms around her. "It didn't hurt!"

Alex cuddled the little girl close. "I'm glad."

Sarah scampered down and ran to get her doll from the floor by the window. "Now Mary's hair! She doesn't like to have her hair combed either."

Alex took the doll and began to smooth its hair. Aunt Bessie took the teapot from the table beside her. "The tea is still hot, Child. Would you care for some?"

"Thank you, that sounds wonderful."

Aunt Bessie handed her a cup of tea, and Alex gave the doll

to Sarah before taking the tea. She took a sip. "Philip has spared no expense to see that you have nice things," she said. "This teacup is Royal Doulton."

"The tea set belonged to my grandmother," Aunt Bessie said. "Philip has no patience for what he calls fripperies. I brought the furniture and the rugs when I came. You should have seen the way he was living when I arrived. Chairs made from scrap wood, pallets on the floor for beds. Disgraceful, I told him. If he intended to keep my great-niece in this wilderness, he would have to do better than that by her. He has since admitted things are much more comfortable now."

At least he'd listened to Aunt Bessie, which showed he didn't discount a woman's opinion totally. "Good," Alex said. "I'm going out now to speak with miners and their wives and see what they're missing from home."

"Be careful, my dear," Aunt Bessie cautioned. "You really shouldn't go alone. It's not safe."

"I'll be fine." Alex wasn't about to stay cooped up in the house. The sunshine lit the mountains with gold and rose lights, and she wanted to feel the breeze on her face.

"Did you sprinkle your handkerchief with cologne?" Aunt Bessie asked. "The odor is quite oppressive."

That was no news to Alex. The stench promised to be the worst part of living here. She nodded and rose from the sofa. "Thanks for the tea."

"Oh dear," Aunt Bessie tittered. "I really wish you'd wait for Philip to escort you." Her face brightened. "I know, you must go to the store. You can chat with the miners and their wives there. Philip has a table in one corner for socializing. Commandeer it and invite the ladies to stop and chat."

It was a really good idea, and Alex had to admit she'd been dreading going out to face the leers of the men. "I think I'll do that," she said slowly.

Aunt Bessie lurched to her feet and took her cane. "I have a basket of freshly baked cookies you can take with you. That will lure the ladies. I never met a woman who didn't have a sweet tooth, and such treats are few and far between out here. Come along, Dear."

Alex followed her to the kitchen and took the cookies with gratitude, then set off for the store. At least she knew the way. Men jostled her, and several fell into step beside her, trying to strike up a conversation. Pressing her perfumed handkerchief to her nose to block out the stench of the open sewage trenches running beside the street, she ignored them all and hurried to the store.

Monroe's was packed with men and women, and she saw no sign of Philip. The men crowding the store looked eager, but the eyes of most of the women held more than a trace of trepidation. Alex didn't blame them. Her own excitement for her new business venture had ebbed like the tide when she saw Dyea.

She pushed through the crowd and found the table Aunt Bessie had mentioned. A woman already sat in one of the chairs. About twenty-five, she wore her blond hair loose on her shoulders, and her blue eyes held a trace of weary cynicism.

"May I join you?" Alex asked.

"Suit yourself," the woman said.

Alex slipped into the chair next to the woman and pulled the gingham napkin back from the basket. "Cookie?"

The woman's eyes brightened. "Real cookies?" She leaned forward and sniffed, then took one. Taking a bite, she closed her eyes and moaned. "Oh, that's heavenly." She opened her eyes and stared at Alex. "What are you after that you're giving away cookies?"

"A friend and maybe some information," Alex said.

"What kind of information?" The woman narrowed her eyes.

Alex wondered what had caused the woman to be so suspicious. "I'm partners with Philip Monroe, and we want to make sure we're seeing to the needs of the miners and their wives. What things do you particularly miss from home?"

The woman's eyes grew misty. "Afternoon tea with scones, a real stove instead of cooking over an open fire, milk and butter, eggs, fresh vegetables. I could go on and on. This place is a no-man's land."

"What's your name? I'm Alex Peters."

"Camille." A ghost of a smile touched her face. "It means innocent, so it's not really appropriate anymore." She reached over and took another cookie. "If you knew what I was, a proper lady like you would be out of here so fast, you'd leave your shoes behind." The cynicism in her eyes returned, and her mouth had a hard line to it as though she were steeling herself for contempt.

Alex's eyes widened as the meaning of Camille's words sank in. A prostitute, that's what Camille meant. She stared into the young woman's eyes and saw the loneliness and self-contempt there, and her thoughts drifted to her mother. She'd often told

Alex that when she'd met Alex's father, she'd been on the streets and hungry enough to consider such a life. Only God's grace had saved her from such a fate.

This woman had not been so fortunate. Pity made Alex reach across the table and take the young woman's hand. "I'd like to be a friend, Camille." Jesus hadn't been afraid to reach out to the castaways. If she wanted to follow Him, she needed to help this young woman.

Camille's mouth dropped open, then she recovered her composure and jerked her hand away. "Don't be stupid, Miss Peters. Respectable women don't mingle with ones like me. Don't get me wrong—I'm not complaining. I got a good life, enough food, a place to stay. I live better than I did when I was digging through the garbage in Seattle."

"How did you end up here, Camille?" Alex softened her voice.

The other woman looked away as though she couldn't bear to see into Alex's eyes. "My husband left me when our baby died. The doctor said I rolled on him in my sleep, but I know I didn't. I don't know why he died." A tear slipped down her cheek, and she swiped at it angrily. "My husband said I wasn't fit to bear any more of his children. We'd just moved to Seattle, and I didn't know anyone. The landlord threw me out; I had no money, no friends, no family. When Estelle offered me this job, I told her no. But hunger has a way of changing a person's mind."

"I'm sorry," Alex said softly.

Camille stared at her curiously. "I think you might really

care," she marveled. "If you're a Christian crusader, you might as well save your breath though. God turned His back on me long ago."

"God never turns His back on His children," Alex said. "He's still waiting for you to turn to Him."

Camille laughed bitterly. "He'll be waiting a long time then." Her gaze flickered past Alex's left shoulder. "Here comes your rescuer all ready to snatch you from my tainted presence."

Alex turned to see Philip hurrying toward them. She smiled and lifted a hand in greeting.

Philip stopped beside her. "You shouldn't be out without an escort. I heard this morning that some women were attacked out by the pier last night." He nodded to Camille, then turned his attention back to Alex.

"I heard about that," Camille said. "Two women from the house next to ours. Some men would say they deserved it."

Philip nodded. "Unfortunately, you're probably right. You both had better be careful." He turned his gaze back to Alex. "When you're ready to go home, I'll escort you. And you too, Ma'am," he added with a glance at Camille.

Alex couldn't explain the thrill she felt at Philip's matter-of-fact manner with Camille. He wasn't rushing her from Camille's presence, nor was he acting like the other woman was a pariah to be ignored. Her respect for the man went up a notch. Instead of arguing with him, she nodded. "Thank you, Philip."

Philip nodded at Camille. "In fact, it might be best if you went home now," he said. "I'll escort you."

Alex's charitable feelings toward him vanished. Was he throwing Camille out? "She's not ready to go yet. We're having a nice talk."

"I can see that. But I don't want men to get the wrong idea about you and why you're here."

Alex clenched her fists in her lap. "That's ridiculous!"

"It's all right," Camille said softly. "He's right. You're respectable, Miss Peters. Until you lose your respectability, you have no idea how valuable it is. I'll be going now. Don't bother to walk me home," she told Philip. Moving stiffly, she made her way to the door.

Shaking with anger, Alex watched her go. "You had no right to do that," she said through clenched teeth. "I'm a grown woman and can choose who my friends will be. You have no idea what she's been through."

"I pity the women forced into that kind of existence," Philip said. "But I have to think of your welfare."

"My welfare or your reputation?"

A muscle in Philip's jaw twitched. "Both. I have a daughter and aunt to consider as well, and I would hate for people to think you're staying at my house for some other reason."

Alex gasped. "No one would think that unless you insinuated it! Your aunt is a perfectly good chaperone."

"In our eyes, but this isn't the civilized place you're used to, Alex. People talk, especially men who are lonely for women. If you want to be safe moving about, you'll avoid contact with women like Camille."

Alex fished in her purse and brought out a small pistol.

"I assure you I can take care of myself. And I don't have to compromise my Christian duty to do it."

Philip laughed. "That little pea-shooter? You would likely be attacked before you even thought to grab it. Mind what I said now. Dyea is a hard town, and I don't want you to get cut on its edges."

"You let me worry about my own safety," Alex said. "And I'll thank you not to meddle again in the friendships I choose to make. I want to help Camille. Do you know in which house she works?"

A flush stained Philip's cheeks. "What kind of man do you think I am, Alex?" he asked jerkily. "I don't patronize those kinds of houses."

Alex hadn't thought of how her question would sound. "I'm sorry," she said hastily. "I didn't mean to suggest you went there. I thought you might have seen her around." She didn't know Philip well yet, but she knew integrity when she saw it.

He nodded to her. "I'll send over some miners' wives for you to talk to. The cookies are certain to be a draw." He left her and went back to the counter.

Within moments, women were crowding around the table and talking to Alex. As she discussed all the things they missed about home, she found herself watching for Philip's dark head in the crowd of men buying supplies.

She told herself she was being foolish. It was obvious what he thought of her. Something in her heart stirred when he was around, something she had never felt before. Her thoughts drifted to Morgan. When he'd asked her to marry him, she'd thought herself the luckiest girl alive. His family owned the land bordering theirs, and it seemed the natural progression of things to join the two families.

It hadn't taken long for the stardust to fall from her eyes though. Morgan would have been the first man off the boat lining up to visit the house where Camille worked. He'd probably have picked Camille out of the group too. She was his type with her blond hair and blue eyes.

Her stomach roiled as she remembered finding him with Susan. Susan was supposed to be her good friend, but that hadn't kept her from going after the man Alex loved. She blinked and shoved the memories away. Susan had gotten what she wanted, and Alex was thankful now. Morgan was no more faithful to Susan than he'd been to Alex.

But that was all behind her now. Philip was nothing like Morgan. His devotion to his dead wife was proof enough of his fidelity. Her gaze wandered back to his face as he waited on a grizzled miner. A customer wouldn't have to worry about Philip cheating him. Honesty, integrity, and caring radiated from his face. But whenever God was mentioned, he clammed up and withdrew. That reality saddened Alex. Especially in a place like this, the Savior's presence was vital. She would not have been able to face the debauchery without the Lord.

The cookies were gone, but the ladies still lingered, eager to hear of news from home. They wanted to hear the latest reports about the Spanish-American War, and Alex recounted tales of the Rough Riders that had been hitting the papers. The ladies exclaimed and discussed it all until her head ached and she longed to rest. But watching Philip's unflagging attention to his duties spurred her on. She had to carry her end of the bargain, or Philip would think she was a useless partner.

Of course, he likely thought that already. That realization stung, and Alex was shocked to discover she wanted his admiration. The way things were going, that was one desire that would likely never come to pass. Philip was as likely to notice her womanly qualities as a stallion would be likely to notice a turtle moving under his feet.

Chapter 4

The warm aroma of baking bread wafted up his nose as Philip opened the door to his home. From the parlor, he could hear Sarah's squeals of delight, and he grinned as he waited for her to come rushing to greet him. Several moments passed, then she giggled again, and he realized she didn't know he was home. Moving to the door of the parlor, he peeked inside and found his daughter seated on the floor beside Alex. They were playing tiddledywinks, and Sarah's rapt attention on Alex stirred a feeling Philip was horrified to recognize as jealousy.

He wanted Sarah to look only at him with that kind of glow in her young face. Though Alex had been here just a week, his daughter had quickly fallen under her spell, as had Aunt Bessie. Philip had to admit she had a charismatic way about her that drew people like bees to a flower petal.

Dressed in a soft yellow gown that brought out the lights in her dark hair, Alex looked like a flower this evening. With her hair so close to the color of Sarah's, she could almost have been his daughter's mother. The thought made him tug at his collar. The sooner she left Dyea, the better.

He cleared his throat, and Sarah looked up and saw him. "Daddy," she cried, jumping to her feet and running to him.

He picked her up, and she wrapped her skinny legs about him and cupped his face in her hands. "Have you been a good girl today for Aunt Bessie?" he asked.

Out of the corner of his eye, he saw Alex stand and smooth her rumpled skirt before gliding to the sofa. Why did she have people call her Alex? She was much too feminine and beautiful for such a masculine nickname. Why not Lexi or even her full name of Alexandria? She fascinated him, and though he tried to tell himself it was only because he was lonely for a woman's touch, he knew better. There was something about Alex herself that was mesmerizing.

"Daddy, you're not looking at me," Sarah said reproachfully.

She tugged at his nose, and he crossed his eyes and screwed up his mouth to make her giggle. Sarah kissed him noisily on his cheek, and he set her down. "Run along and tell Aunt Bessie I'm home and ready for supper. I'm starved."

Sarah scampered off, and he found himself staring into Alex's violet eyes. He didn't like the feeling that rushed over him when he was in her presence—like he was a small boy again in English class searching for the right spelling of a word.

"You didn't come to the store today," he said. The overstuffed chair by the window seemed to be at a safe distance, so he sat in it and leaned back as though he were entirely at ease when in fact his palms were sweating like they always seemed to do when he was in her presence.

"I was preparing a list to talk to you about," she said, leaning forward.

The earnestness of her gaze made him blink. "A list? What kind of list?"

"I've been talking to the ladies, and there are so many other items we need to bring over. I have it right here." She stood and brought him a paper.

"Sit down; I don't like someone standing over me," Philip said. He winced inwardly at the crossness in his tone. She always seemed to bring out the worst in him, and he knew it was because he didn't want her to sense the attraction he felt toward her. Scowling, he began to read.

"Kitchen stoves take up too much space. And what's this?" He waved the paper in the air. "Ribbons, chocolate, bed linens, pillows." He frowned. *Corsets?* What nonsense is this? This isn't Boston; this is the gateway to the Yukon. The miners have no need of these fripperies."

Alex seemed to take no mind of his dismay. She leaned forward. "You know how much time I've spent talking with the miners' wives, Philip. These are things they wish they could buy. The necessities are all very well and good, but if they're to carve out a home, even a temporary one, women like to have some of the luxuries. I know we could sell these things at a handsome profit if we had them."

Philip found it hard to think with her pleading gaze on him. He cleared his throat and looked back at the paper. "There is only a certain amount of space on the boat. We've been turning a nice profit with the necessities."

"I know, and I don't want it to appear I'm criticizing your choices. In the beginning, the necessities were desperately wanted. But there are other boats bringing those in. At any one of the supply tents, miners can buy blankets, coffee, tin utensils, that sort of thing. Why can't we sell some of the other things, the items people will pay generous sums to get?"

"We're doing fine, Alex." Why couldn't she let him worry about it? She'd talked with the miners and their wives for one week and thought she knew what they needed. It was ludicrous.

"But we could be doing better." Frustration shone from her eyes. "I have Will to think of. Right now we're competing with every other supply store. The miners have money to spend, and they'll spend it in Monroe's only if we have some unique products they really want."

Philip rubbed his chin. "I don't know, Alex. It would mean taking up space I could fill with items I *know* will sell. I'm not a gambling man."

She drew a deep breath. "Let's try one load where you bring in a few of the items on my list. We'll see how they sell before we commit to a whole shipload. That's fair, isn't it?"

"I suppose so," he admitted. "What do you want to bring first?" He glanced down at the list again.

"Two cookstoves for sure and small amounts of the rest of the things on my list."

Reluctantly, he nodded. "All right. But I'll have to see it to believe it."

Alex clapped her hands together, and he found himself

smiling at her childlike enthusiasm. He averted his gaze from her lovely face. She was much too enticing for his peace of mind. He never wanted to go through the pain of losing someone he loved the way he lost Dottie. The thought of losing his daughter was enough to wake him in a cold sweat at night, and he didn't need someone else to worry about.

"Thank you, Philip," she said softly. "Some of these things will really make life easier for the miners and their wives. I know the cookstoves will be a godsend. This past week I've put myself in their shoes and asked what I would miss the most if I were out prospecting for gold. This isn't all about money, you know. I want to help them. Their lot is a hard one, and if there's anything we can do to make it easier, I want to do it."

For some reason, he believed her. He'd seen the way she befriended everyone who came in the door of his store. It was getting so that miners and their wives alike looked for her seated at the corner table before they asked for any supplies. At least he wasn't the only one who reacted to her charisma.

"Time to eat," Aunt Bessie called from the dining room.

He stood and offered his arm. "May I escort you to the table?"

She gave him a smile that warmed him from head to toe. "I'd be delighted."

Her fingers rested lightly on his arm, but he felt her presence so strongly it was as if he could feel her touch through his every pore. He almost flinched from the weight of it. What was this power she seemed to have over him and everyone else who came into contact with her?

He led her to the table and seated her beside Sarah. Settling Aunt Bessie in her chair, he then went to the head of the table and sat down. A bowl heaped with mashed potatoes was in front of him, and he picked it up.

"Daddy, can we say grace first?"

Sarah's voice stopped him as he prepared to ladle the potatoes onto his plate. He stared at her, aghast at what she was asking. "What nonsense is this?" he asked gruffly.

"Alex says we should thank God for giving us all things like our food and clothes."

"God also robbed you of a mother," Philip said through gritted teeth. He regretted his words when his daughter burst into tears. He got up and went to her. "I'm sorry, Darling," he soothed.

"God is my friend," she sobbed. "Alex told me so, and I asked Jesus in my heart today."

Rage filled him. He narrowed his eyes and looked into Alex's glowing face. She didn't look a bit penitent or cowed. "May I speak with you in the parlor?" he asked icily.

For a moment her eyes filled with uncertainty, then she nodded and rose from her chair. "Eat your dinner," he told Sarah and Aunt Bessie. "We'll be right back." As he followed Alex's straight back into the parlor, he heard Aunt Bessie soothe his daughter with a gentle prayer for the food.

He shut the door behind them. "I'll thank you to leave my daughter's religious instruction to me," he told her.

Alex's face whitened, but she faced him squarely. "You didn't seem to be doing any spiritual training," she said. "I've heard you blame God for your wife's death, and I'm sorry for that, Philip. When hard times like that come, all we can do is cling to His promise that He'll go with us through the valley. You've shut Him out, and you have that right, but don't take Sarah down with you."

He clenched his hands at his sides. "Sarah is my daughter, not yours," he choked out in a hoarse whisper. It was either that or shout at her.

The color leached from her cheeks, and he realized she was more upset than she first appeared.

"I love Sarah already," she said in a voice so soft he had to strain to hear it. "God loves her even more, Philip. And He loves you too."

"He has a mighty strange way of showing it." He made no effort to hide his bitterness. "Cholera is a horrible way to die, and my wife—" He broke off as his voice faltered.

Compassion filled her face, and she reached out and gripped his right fist. "Let go of your bitterness. It will only destroy you and Sarah. I've heard what a strong Christian your wife was, and Dottie is in God's presence now. She's not in pain anymore. Try to think of her there instead of how she died. Death is but a step into joy, Philip, it's not something to fear. God will forgive you, if you but ask."

"Forgive *me?* What did I do to Him? He's the one who should be asking my forgiveness."

Shock radiated over her face at his words, but he didn't care. The hurt and pain came rushing out of him in a torrent as black as a spring mudslide. "We were happy, the three of us.

Then in spite of my prayers for our safety, in spite of Dottie's devotion to Him, He took her and left me without a wife and Sarah without the mother who loved her so."

"Oh, Philip." Alex put her other hand on his fist as well, cupping it in both her hands. "I feel your pain, but so does God. Let go of it and let God heal it." Tears slid down her cheeks.

He jerked his hand away. "No! He betrayed me." Shocked to discover tears in his eyes, he turned and rushed out of the room before she could see his weakness. But the greater shock was how much he wanted to do just what she said—to let go of his pain and bitterness and turn to God for healing. To recover that relationship he'd once had. Nothing could heal him though. He knew that too well to try.

ॐ

Alex felt the weight of his pain, and her eyes welled with tears. Her shoulders slumped, and her legs trembled as she made her way to the sofa. He must have loved his wife very much to have taken her death so hard. All she was trying to do was to teach Sarah about God. Rubbing the back of her hand over her eyes, she sighed.

Sometimes she wondered what she was doing here. She still felt the weight of the stares when she ventured out into the streets. An unmarried respectable woman seemed to attract a lot of attention, unwanted attention as far as Alex was concerned. She was beginning to realize the only man's attention she might welcome was that of Philip, but after seeing his bitterness toward God, she knew a relationship with him would be impossible.

For as long as she could remember, God had been a presence in her life as real as her own father's. She dimly remembered asking Jesus into her heart when she was about Sarah's age, and she had tried to walk every day in the path He wanted. To be united with a man who didn't share her devotion was unthinkable. Yet the thought persisted that God had put her here for a purpose, though she didn't see how she could make any headway with Philip's hostility.

She sighed and rose from the sofa. Her stomach rumbled as she walked back to the dining room. Aunt Bessie was clearing the food away.

"I'll just have a bite before you take it, Aunt Bessie," she told her.

"Of course, my dear. I was saving your plate." She indicated a plate of food covered with a cloth before carrying the dirty dishes from the room. Alex bowed her head and gave God thanks for the food. Though she was hungry, the first morsel she put in her mouth tasted like straw. How was she to get through to Philip? She so wanted to see him without that weight of bitterness on his shoulders. Forcing herself to chew, she managed to get down the rest of her dinner.

Her spirits drooped as she finished her dinner and got up to go to her room. Stepping into the hall, she flinched at a dark shadow near the staircase. Philip loomed from the shadows cast by the kerosene lamps.

"I wanted to apologize," he said. "I never meant to make you cry." His voice was low.

The pulse in her neck throbbed, and her stomach clenched

at his nearness. "I forgive you," she said. "I wish you could forgive yourself."

He took a step back. "What do you mean?"

"You blame yourself for your wife's death, don't you? And because you can't live with what you feel is your own fault in the matter, you are even more vengeful against God." Alex was almost as shocked as Philip by her words. Until they had bubbled out of her mouth, she hadn't realized what his real problem was, but once she spoke the words, their truth resonated in her heart.

Philip's mouth dropped open, then he swallowed hard. "How did you know?" he whispered.

"I–I think it was God," she said.

He gave a sound of inarticulate distress, then ran his hand through his hair. "She didn't want to come. I forced her to leave behind her family and everything she loved. We'd been here only three weeks when she took sick. She was gone in two days." The sigh that issued from his lips sounded as mournful as the wind outside the house. "I've asked myself over and over why God didn't take me since I was the one who wanted to come. It isn't fair!"

Alex reached out to touch him, then let her hand drop back to her side. It wouldn't be seemly to offer him the solace a close friend might give, though she longed to. "God never said life would be fair, Philip. We are to serve Him even when we can't see through the veil that covers our eyes."

The anguish faded from his eyes, and he gave a twisted smile. "How did you get so wise?"

Alex laughed. It was either that or cry. "I'm not wise. I'm just telling you what God says in His Word. Trust His love, Philip. Trust that He knows what's best for you."

Philip reached out and touched her cheek. "You're so beautiful," he said. "And even lovelier inside. You make me wish I could forget the past and go on."

Alex's heart began to thump against her ribs as though it longed to jump right into Philip's arms. She didn't know what to say, so she said nothing. The touch of his hand on her cheek was like nothing she'd ever felt before. What would he do if she turned her head so her lips could touch his palm and kissed it? The brazen thought brought heat to her cheeks.

He drew her to him and his lips touched hers. The rush of blood to her head made her feel faint, and she wanted the kiss to go on forever. Then the reality of her situation came flooding back. She couldn't let herself feel anything more for him than friendship. She pulled away hastily and stepped back.

The tenderness vanished from his face, and he dropped his hand from her cheek. "You'd better go to bed," he said.

Alex didn't need any more encouragement. The Bible said to flee temptation, so she turned and raced past him up the stairs as if a polar bear were on her heels. A bear couldn't be any more fearful than the feelings Philip's touch had stirred.

The next morning there was a new awareness between her and Philip. It was almost an agony to be in his presence. Alex found herself watching his every move, noticing the way his hair fell across his forehead, the way he pursed his lips when he was thinking, the tenderness he showed his daughter and aunt.

He would be a wonderful husband.

Shocked at herself, she wondered where that thought had come from. Philip was not the man for her. She wanted a husband who loved God as much as she did. So what did she do with these feelings she had for him? They grew stronger the more she was around him. Maybe it was time to think about going back to Seattle. But the thought brought so much pain, she put it out of her head. One thing was sure: She was falling in love with this man, in spite of her best intentions.

Chapter 5

The next two weeks were agony for Alex. She was afraid to experience again the strong attraction she felt toward Philip. He couldn't be God's choice for her, not with bitterness eating away at him. Several times she felt his gaze linger on her face, then jump away as though he too feared to think about her too much. It was just as well. She found it too difficult to ignore him when he set out to charm her.

As she went down the steps to the kitchen, she resolved to try to put it all behind her and keep her focus on things she could do something about. Aunt Bessie wouldn't like what Alex planned today, but she was determined to make a difference in this town.

The older woman smiled when Alex entered the kitchen. "There you are, my dear. Did you sleep well?"

"Very well, thank you. I wondered if you might have a large basket I could borrow?"

"Of course, there are several in the pantry. Let me get you one." Aunt Bessie began to brace herself against the edge of the kitchen table as if to rise.

"No, no, I'll get it," Alex insisted, and Aunt Bessie settled into her seat once more.

"My you made a lot of cookies yesterday. And pies! I wonder if you thought to feed an army?"

Alex emerged from the pantry with a large wicker basket slung over her arm. "I'm taking them to some people in town," she said. "Thanksgiving is a good time to show the Lord's love to others."

"Oh? To the miners, perhaps? That's a fine way to garner good will toward the store."

She might as well get it over with. Aunt Bessie would find out sooner or later. "Actually, I'm taking them to the girls at Estelle's."

If the older woman's distress hadn't been so real, the way her jowls sank and her eyes widened would have been funny. She shook her head violently. "Oh you must not, my dear. What will people think if they see you going in there?"

"If they know me at all, they will know I wish only to share God's love with the women," Alex said firmly. "Jesus was reviled for associating with harlots and sinners. Can we as His ambassadors do any less? Thanksgiving is in two days, and I want Camille and the others to think about God and His love for them."

Aunt Bessie clasped her hands in her lap and gave a slight moan. "Whatever will Philip say?" she muttered.

Alex wondered the same thing, but she resolved to let nothing stand in the way of doing what she felt led to do. She packed the basket with goodies, adding jars of jam, tinned meat, and other delicacies she'd purchased from Monroe's.

"I'll be back in a bit," she told Aunt Bessie. In spite of her brave words, she wondered how the women would receive her. Her stomach clenched as she walked across the street. The cold Arctic wind blew through her hooded cloak, but at least with the heavy frost last night, the mud didn't suck her boots nearly off her feet.

As she approached Estelle's, her legs trembled, and she nearly turned and hurried away. She'd never been in such a place and feared the things she might see inside. Her determination was the only thing that made her press forward.

She thought she might throw up as she stepped to the door and raised her hand. Her hand fell against the door almost of its own power. *Please let Camille answer the door, Lord.* Her heart thumped against her ribs. An interminable time seemed to tick by as she waited for someone to answer.

Then the door swung open a crack and she heard a voice say, "What do you want?"

"Co—could I see Camille, please?" Alex's voice wavered, and she sucked in her breath. The door opened wider, and she realized the voice belonged to Camille.

"You're the lady from Monroe's!" Still uncombed, Camille's hair hung to her waist, and she wore a wraparound dressing gown. "You shouldn't be here." Her gaze darted past Alex as though she wanted to make sure no one was watching.

"May. . .may I come in?" Alex peered past Camille into the dim recesses of the rough frame house.

"Maybe that would be best. At least people won't see you associating with me." Camille stepped aside and allowed Alex to enter.

Alex moved forward on legs that felt as though they were made of seaweed. The inner room reeked of smoke and booze. Dirty shot glasses and overflowing ashtrays littered the side tables.

"You want to come up to my room?" Camille's tone was doubtful.

"No, no that's fine." Alex pulled the basket from her side and set it on the coffee table. "I brought you and the other girls a few treats." She lifted away the napkin on top and began to pull out the contents of the basket.

Camille's eyes widened as the pile of foodstuffs grew. "Oh my," she said. "My mouth is watering just looking at them. Girls!" she called.

Two other young women poked their heads over the banister from the upstairs landing. One had red hair too bright to be anything but artificial and the other had frizzy dark hair. They both wore identical expressions of boredom and listlessness.

"My friend has brought us cookies and pies and all kinds of other things." Camille took a cookie and bit into it. Closing her eyes, she gave a sigh of satisfaction. "They're wonderful."

The other girls needed no further invitation. They hurried down the stairs and were soon sampling the treats.

"Won't you sit down?" Camille said, hastily swiping the ashes from the sofa.

Alex smiled and gingerly perched on the edge of the sofa.

The knot in her stomach began to ease. At least they hadn't thrown her out.

"Does Mr. Monroe know you're here?" Camille asked.

Alex's smile faltered. "No," she said.

"He's going to be mad," Camille predicted. "Hey, Nola, how about fixing us all some tea? We'll act like real ladies for awhile, sipping tea and eating cookies. I guess I should introduce you. Nola is the one with the red hair, and Renée is the brunette."

The other girls merely nodded, though their eyes were friendly. Nola went to make tea.

The other girl, Renée, picked up a cookie. "You reckon we should invite Estelle to join us?"

"She didn't get to bed until an hour ago," Camille said. "We'll save her some cookies."

Renée nodded. "I think I'll help Nola with the tea." Taking another cookie, she went to find her friend.

Glad for the opportunity to talk to Camille alone, Alex clasped her hands together in her lap. "I haven't seen you around, Camille. I was hoping to run into you in the store again."

Camille smiled, but there was more than a trace of irony in her face. "I thought after Mr. Monroe's reaction that he might not appreciate me showing up to taint your reputation."

"Mr. Monroe has no say over what I do or what friends I associate with," Alex said. "I like you, Camille."

Color came into Camille's face, then her eyes grew luminous with tears. "I'm not worth your time, Miss Peters."

"God thinks you're worth everything to Him, and I think so

too," Alex said softly. "He hasn't given up on you, Camille, and I'm not going to either. Thanksgiving is coming, and I wanted you to know God loves you. If I can help you, please let me."

The tears escaped Camille's eyes and rolled down her cheeks. She sniffled, then swiped her arm across her eyes. "I'll remember that, Miss Peters. But there's nowhere else for me to go, no other work I'm fit to do."

"We'll think of something, Camille," Alex promised. Maybe she could talk Philip into hiring her to help out in the store. She would be good with customers. But Alex didn't dare say anything to Camille about her idea until she talked to Philip. She had a sinking feeling she knew it would be an uphill battle to get him to agree to such a plan.

She knew but for the grace of God, she could be in Camille's shoes. When her father died, what if she had no other resources at all? What if she faced starvation the way Camille had done? All the good things in her life were but a gift from her heavenly Father.

She drank her tea with the women, then picked up her empty basket and took her leave, promising to call again soon. Somehow she felt as though she'd made a difference. Now was the time to talk to Philip while she was still encouraged by her reception from Camille.

The store was practically empty when she went inside, which was an unusual occurrence. The newest crop of stampeders, the fledgling miners bound for the Yukon, must have come and gone with their supplies. Philip and Michael Stanton, the store manager, stood behind the counter sorting nails into bins. When the bell on the door tinkled, Philip turned, and his gaze caught hers. For a moment she thought she glimpsed a yearning that made her heart pound.

She swallowed hard. "Hello, Philip."

He came around the counter with a wide smile. "You're a genius!"

"What are you talking about?" She hadn't expected such a warm reception.

"The shipment of luxury items came in this morning, and nearly all of it is sold already. The two cookstoves were gone before we got them unloaded. Everything went at premium prices too. We've made a hefty profit. I think you'll be pleased with your share. You should have no trouble paying Will's tuition next year."

He reached her then, spanned her waist with his hands, and lifted her into the air. Her thoughts whirled as fast as her body as he spun around the floor with her. "We have time for one more shipment before the snow arrives and the shipments slow because of weather. I'll have the whole boat loaded with luxuries this next trip." Setting her on the floor, he kept his hands on her waist and stared into her eyes.

Her mouth went dry, and she knew she should move away, but his gaze held her captive. Dark gray with white flecks, there was a tenderness in his eyes she'd never seen before.

"I think you've bewitched us all," he said softly. "I—" He broke off.

Alex was afraid to ask what he'd been about to say. "I'm glad the shipment did well," she said. "Are you willing to listen to another idea?" She had to get them back on a business relationship somehow, though everything in her innermost being longed to stay in his arms.

She shifted and his hands fell away from her waist.

"What's your new idea?" The euphoria faded from his voice, and he stepped back. Though his expression was still friendly, the other expression, the one that she longed to see, was replaced by politeness.

"Do you have time to sit down a minute?" She gestured to the table in the corner.

He glanced back toward the counter. "Michael, I'm taking a break. If you need me, I'll be at the table."

"No problem," Michael said, continuing with his work of sorting.

Alex knew Philip would never agree, but she owed it to Camille to try. "You mentioned the other day you could use some help here in the store. I have someone in mind for the job."

One eyebrow lifted. "You're hired. I think I could get used to having you around," he said, a smile lifting the corners of his mouth. That look of tenderness flickered in his eyes again before disappearing behind the mask of geniality.

"No, not me," she said. "Camille."

"Camille?" He frowned. "Who is that? Do I know her?"

Her heart surged at the disappointment in his voice. "You met her the first time I came to speak with your customers." Her stomach clenched as his expression changed.

"The prostitute? You want me to hire a prostitute to work with customers? That's one way to bring them in." He gave a short bark of a laugh. "You're joking, right?"

"I'm totally serious," she said. "She was forced into that life, Philip." She told him about Camille's baby dying and her husband's reaction. His expression grew more thunderous, and her heart sank.

"He doesn't sound like much of a man," he said. "But surely you see how inappropriate it would be for me to hire her?"

"I see nothing of the sort," she said. "It's not like Dyea is Boston, Philip. It's wild and lawless. No one would question your right to hire whom you wish."

"Maybe not, but that wild and lawless aspect is exactly what would bring the trouble. What if the men think she is still working in that way? I'd be constantly breaking up fights and having to defend her from questionable advances."

"Maybe at first," she admitted. "But the town would soon know she had decided to make a change in her life. Surely they would see how admirable that is."

He smiled sardonically. "You're such an innocent, Alex. Most men would take that as a challenge and an invitation to prove it couldn't be done, that her nature was still the same."

"Please, Philip, you said I was a genius. Help me help Camille. What if Sarah found herself in such a situation?"

His brows drew together. "You don't know what you're saying."

"I know I could have been in Camille's shoes. If the *Dawson Belle* hadn't been still in my ownership, I might have been starving like she was. God will bless you for your mercy, Philip."

He blinked and instead of flying into a rage at the mention

of God, he nodded slowly. "I've been thinking maybe you were right about what you had to say about God, Alex," he said. "I'm going to try to let go of the bitterness."

Joy rose like the morning tide in her throat. "Oh, Philip, that's wonderful!" She clapped her hands together, then reached out and grasped his hand. His strong fingers closed over hers.

"But I don't know about this Camille thing," he said.

"Have some trust, Philip," she whispered. "If God calls us to do something, He will work out the details."

"I haven't trusted Him for a long time. I'm not sure I know how anymore." He squeezed her fingers. "Would you have dinner with me tonight, Alex?"

She gave a nervous laugh at his change of subject. "We have dinner together every night."

"No, I mean just you and me. We can talk about Camille some more. Clancy's tent has the best steaks in Dyea," he coaxed.

Alex chewed on her lip. Maybe God was opening a door for her. She wished it were so. Maybe talking with Philip at length would help her see if he was sincere and if he'd really turned back to the Lord. "All right," she said.

He squeezed her fingers again, then released them. "About six?"

"I'll be ready." But she wasn't sure if her heart was prepared to face the onslaught of Philip's charm and charisma. Her defenses were falling like a milled forest of trees.

Chapter 6

Philip felt almost euphoric as he watched Alex's tiny figure walk away from the store. Part of his elation was the decision to turn his back on the bitterness at last and part was the thought of beginning a relationship with Alex. He loved her; he knew that now. And he suspected she might feel the same. The feelings overwhelmed him.

"I'm going out for awhile," he called to Michael. Grabbing his coat, he strode toward the water. A williwaw wind shooting down the mountains whipped the water out in the Gulf of Alaska into big waves topped by white caps. The wind brought a spray of seawater over his face, and he wiped it reflectively. The power of the sea brought back the way he'd felt when Dottie died, like a tiny cork bobbing in waters beyond his control.

For the first time since his wife died, he realized that though he might be tossed by the waves of life, he was like a ship in a bottle and that bottle was the protection of the Lord. Though he might see the waves through the glass, God held his life in His hands. Nothing could touch him if he trusted

God. Alex had been right. It was his own guilt and shame that plagued him the most.

If he'd even asked God and been assured the move to Alaska met with the Lord's approval, he would have someone to blame, someone bigger than himself. But he'd moved knowing in his heart it was what *he* wanted. Knowing Dottie wasn't cut out for life on the frontier, he'd done it anyway. Knowing he had a small daughter who shouldn't be exposed to such hardship as the trip out here, he'd done it anyway. It was his own willfulness that had brought about the loss of his wife. His fault, not God's.

Along the storm-tossed sea, he knelt in the sand, its cold wetness seeping through his pants, and turned his heart back toward God. It was nearly a half an hour later when he finally rose and walked back toward town. The burden was gone, and he felt clean and new. He thanked God for bringing Alex along to show him how wrong he'd been.

He thought of the locket in the chest in his room. Handed down from his grandparents, he had thought to give it to Sarah, but how lovely it would look around Alex's neck. He didn't deserve her; he knew that. But Lord willing, she could overlook his shortcomings and love him as much as he loved her. He intended to spend the next weeks showing her what a difference she'd made in his life.

As he neared town, he heard screams and shouts. The choking smell of smoke was carried on the wind, and he broke into a run. Fire! He knew it had been sheer luck that had kept the town from being burned out before. It seemed their good fortune had run out.

His heart in his mouth, he ran toward his home. Flames flared high into the stormy sky from its roof, and black billows of smoke poured from the door and the windows. Several other buildings were similarly engulfed. He fought his way through the crowd, the acrid heat burning his lungs and throat. Coughing, he managed to get to the door of his house. It could burn to the ground, though it was only six months old, as long as his family and Alex were safe.

"Whoa, Man, don't go in there!" Michael grabbed him and held him back as he prepared to plunge into the raging inferno.

Philip fought against him, struggling to free himself. "I have to save them!"

"They're out. Your daughter and Aunt Bessie are at the store," Michael assured him.

"And Alex?"

"Last I saw her, she was heading to Estelle's. I tried to get her to fix some coffee and stay put, but you know how she is. She insisted on going out to see if she could help."

Philip nodded. "Keeping her corralled is like trying to keep the sea in a box."

Michael's teeth shone in his blackened face as he grinned. "I have a feeling she's going to keep you hopping."

Philip's face burned. Were his feelings so obvious?

"Daddy!"

He turned as Sarah came hurtling toward him. "You're supposed to be in the store," he scolded. "How did you get away from Aunt Bessie?"

"I want Alex," the child sobbed. "I'm scared, and she makes it all better."

"I'll find her," he told Sarah, handing her to Michael. "You go with Michael back to the store, and I'll find her." He had to find her. He couldn't lose her, not when he'd just realized how much he loved her.

He kissed his daughter, then ran toward Estelle's. The town was in a state of pandemonium. Men and women shouted, and screams and cries of distress and sorrow reverberated on the air. He prayed for Alex's safety as he pressed through the throng. The frigid November air increased the suffering as men carried buckets of water to combat the fire.

Reaching Estelle's, Philip was shocked to discover the building totally engulfed in flames. The heat forced him back, then he grabbed a bucket of water from a passing stampeder and doused himself with it. It froze on his clothes almost as soon as it touched him. Rushing through the heat, he made it to the doorway of the house.

"Alex!" he shouted above the fire's ravenous roars. He strained to hear through the crackles and crashes as the fire devoured the dry building. There was no answer. A tug on his sleeve distracted him as he prepared to enter the house.

"Mr. Monroe, don't go in there. It's no use." Covered in ashes, Camille's mouth twisted, and tears left rivulets of white in her soot-stained face. "She's gone, little Alex is gone. She's dead, and all she wanted to do was help me." Wailing, she covered her face with her hands.

In detachment, Philip noticed the burns on her hands and

clothing. "You're wrong," he said slowly. "I just saw her this afternoon."

"I'm sorry, Mr. Monroe," Camille sobbed. "The ceiling collapsed. I heard her scream." Her sobs increased, and her words became incoherent.

Philip's gut twisted, and he thought he might be sick. Heaving, he bent over, gasping to keep the contents of his stomach from coming up. It couldn't be true. Hadn't he just turned his life over to God again? Surely God wouldn't be so cruel as to rip her away now that he'd finally opened himself to life and love again.

Staggering like a drunk, he reeled away from the fire still consuming the town. It could all burn as far as he was concerned. His eyes felt dry and gritty, though he longed for the release of tears. This couldn't be happening again. The strength left him, and he sank to his knees in the sand. Shuddering, he imagined his tiny Alex falling beneath a burning ceiling, then cried out in agony.

The tears came then, and he fell face forward into the sand. Alex had brought life and love back to him, and the thought of the years ahead of him without her seemed a desert of time.

"Why, Lord?" he whispered. He realized in that moment he had two choices. He could blame God again and nurse his bitterness the rest of his life, or he could choose to rest in God's care. The wrong decision when Dottie died had left his life empty and sour as vinegar. This time he would choose God. Though he didn't understand how life could twist so cruelly in his hands, he would trust God.

❧

When the kitchen ceiling collapsed, Alex knew it was all over for her. She would die in this heat and choking smoke. Coughing as the raging fire raced to catch her, she turned her face away. She couldn't look. A hole in the floor gaped in front of her, and hope was resurrected. Crawling along the hot floorboards, she managed to get to the hole and slide down into the blessed coolness of the root cellar.

She knew the fire could reach here, the ceiling and roof were likely to come raining down on her like a Sodom and Gomorrah. It was too dark to see clearly, so she crawled along the dank earthen floor, feeling her way. No light shone in here, no obvious avenue of escape. She likely had only moments before the fire would come to find her like a child playing hide and seek.

She came to an opening in the wall. Coolness rolled from it in waves. Eagerly she followed it back to where it ended. Not sure exactly what it was, she nestled against the wall, too exhausted to go on. At least she was in a small cavelike place where earth covered her head. The debris might bury her, but the fire would likely pass her over.

The roar of the flames increased, and with an ear-splitting sound, the floor above her collapsed. The stench of burning wood rushed over her, and the bright flicks of fire lit the cellar with an unearthly glow. Several beams lay across the exit from the hidey-hole she'd found.

She coughed as the fire sucked the oxygen out of the air. Gasping for breath, she squeezed back as tightly against the earthen wall as she could get, pressing her face and breathing in the dank scent of the dirt. At least it was better than the choking smoke.

Please, Lord, don't let my death turn Philip's heart from Thee again. Remind him that Thou art in charge. And let my death be quick and merciful. The air felt as thick as flour dust, and she found it harder and harder to breathe. Sucking in the searing air, she felt herself losing consciousness and turned toward the blessed oblivion with relief.

✍

When she awoke, Alex wondered where she was. Dim light radiated in front of her. Was this heaven? Blinking, she tried to assess her circumstances. She was no longer burning up, but she wasn't cold either. The air she pulled into her lungs still seemed tinged with smoke, but at least she could breathe. Coughing, she tried to sit up but found herself too weak and fell back against the hard ground at her back.

Well, she was alive—at least she'd established that much. She should be dead, but evidently God could still use her here. The skin on her face felt tight and parched, and her mouth was dry. Licking her lips, she prayed for strength, then tried to scoot along the floor. The wood that had fallen into the cellar was still hot, though much of it was consumed. Managing to get to her knees, she held the wall for support and lurched to her feet. The earthen roof above her head was only four feet from the floor, so she had to crouch as she tried to shuffle to the opening of her little cave.

The dim light from the hot coals revealed a half-consumed

floor joist blocking her exit. Immodest though it was, she lifted her skirt and wrapped it around her waist to keep it from grazing any sparks that might set it aflame, then stepped gingerly over the joist. Hot debris littered the floor, and she was soon gasping from the heat again and longing to scurry back to the relative coolness of her small cave.

Craning her neck, she looked up through the gaping hole above the cellar into the night sky. She could hear distant shouts. Clearing her throat, she tried to call for help.

"Help." The sound that came from her throat was little more than a gasp. Swallowing dryly, she tried again. "Help me!" Her cry was a little louder, so she sucked all the saliva she could find from her mouth into her throat and shouted again. "Help!"

No head popped over the edge above her, so she looked around to see if there was a way to crawl out by herself. Everything was too hot to touch, and she felt helpless tears welling up. "Help me, Lord," she whispered.

As if in answer to her prayer, she heard a noise above her.

"I thought I heard something over here!"

It sounded like Philip's voice. Hope surged in her chest, and she tried to shout again. "Here, I'm here!"

It was only a croak, but it was enough. Philip's face came into view in the moonlight and the glow from the dying embers.

"Alex?" His voice was incredulous. "Stay there. Don't move."

As if she were able to go anywhere. She stifled a giggle. His head disappeared, then reappeared a few moments later.

"I'm going to let a rope down to you. See if you can tie it around your waist, and I'll hoist you up."

She nodded; then aware he might not be able to see her head move, she raised her voice. "I'll try."

"Good girl."

A rope slithered toward her, and she reached out and grabbed hold of it. With stiff fingers, she looped it around her waist and realized her skirt was still attached there. Her face grew hot at the thought that he might have seen her like that, and she quickly let the skirt drop to her ankles, then tied the rope around her waist, praying he could lift her before her skirts caught fire.

"I'm ready," she called.

The rope jerked, and she was lifted off her feet. Grasping the rough hemp in her raw hands, she closed her eyes. Moments later she felt Philip's hands grasp her by the arms and lift her free. She opened her eyes and stared into his face.

"Alex, I thought you were dead," he whispered. His face was streaked with soot, but his eyes blazed with passion.

He clasped her to his chest, and she burrowed against him. Safe, she was safe. "I thought I was too," she said, finally pulling away.

He ran his hands over her face and arms. "Are you all right? Are you burned?"

"Nothing serious. What about Sarah and Aunt Bessie?"

"They're fine. Worried about you, of course. Before I could bring myself to tell them, I had to know for sure, so I came here to look. Camille said she saw the ceiling collapse on you." His voice choked with emotion.

He lifted her into his arms and carried her through the

smouldering debris. She clung to him, relishing his strength, glad to be able to relinquish her cares to his broad shoulders. Miners and their wives exclaimed in delight and amazement as he strode through the crowd with her in his arms.

Camille rushed to her, kissing her hand. "Alex, you're alive! I prayed to God He would save you."

Almost too exhausted to respond, Alex pressed her hand. "Thank you, Camille. God answered your prayer."

Her eyes drooped heavily, and she moved toward the blackness of oblivion again. This time when she awoke, she was in the living quarters at the back of the store where Philip and Sarah had lived when they first came to Dyea. Clean sheets covered her, and there was only a lingering trace of smoke odor.

"Want a drink of water?"

She turned her head and stared up into Philip's face. Tenderness radiated from his gaze. Holding a glass of water, he slipped an arm under her and propped her enough for her to sip at the cool refreshment.

"Thanks." She studied his face. The lines around his mouth were balanced by the glow of love in his eyes.

He knelt beside the bed and leaned his face close to hers, then ran his finger over her cheek in a loving caress. "I couldn't have borne it if you'd died," he whispered. "But you'll be so proud. Even when I thought He'd taken you, I decided to trust God."

Joy exploded over her. They had both clung to God in their trials instead of turning away.

"And I learned something else tonight," he continued. "I've

learned some things are more important than money. Things like hope, love, commitment. I love you, Alex. When I thought you'd died, I wanted to die too. I love you so much." His eyes burned with the intensity of his emotions.

"Oh, Philip," she whispered. "I love you too. I didn't want to love you. I wanted to just be your friend, but I couldn't help myself."

"And to think I wanted to ship you right back to Seattle," he said tenderly. "Will you marry me, Alex? Our life here might be hard, but I'll care for you the best I know how."

"I love you, Philip," she whispered. "If I say yes, will you hire Camille to work in the store?"

He laughed, and the joy of it filled the room. "You drive a hard bargain, Alex. I'll say yes if you will."

"Yes," she said as his lips met hers. It was an affirmation of all she believed in, all that she wanted to do for the Lord. Was there any greater destiny than this?

Epilogue

T he Ice Queen held Dyea in her cold grip. For days, snow and wind pummeled the mountaintops and valleys all along the Alaskan Gulf. Alex hadn't dared to venture outside the small snug house Philip had purchased as blizzard after blizzard blew through. The last two days had finally brought blue skies in the short, few hours of daylight they had.

She had spent the days teaching Sarah her letters and making a few things for Christmas as well as putting the final touches on her wedding dress. Her wedding. Just whispering the words brought a smile to her face and a song to her heart. The weeks since the fire had flitted by, and the day grew near.

Her only sorrow was that Will wouldn't be here to participate in her happy day, but Chicago was a long way from Alaska, and the weather would not be conducive to travel in either location. Philip's family was her family now too, and she would have to be content with that. His family should be arriving any time for the ceremony tomorrow.

Alex put the last stitch in the lace on her wedding gown and laid it aside. Stretching the kinks out of her back, she yawned, then stood and hung the dress over a dressmaker's mannequin Philip had brought in for her from Seattle.

A smile played about her lips. Philip would be a wonderful husband, thoughtful and kind. She still couldn't believe she had found a man like him in this wilderness.

A familiar tapping came down the hall as Aunt Bessie moved along the floor with her cane. The tapping paused at the doorway, then the older woman poked her head in the door. "I thought I'd find you here," she said. "We have visitors."

"Visitors? Who would come out in this weather?"

"Someone who wants to see you wed," Aunt Bessie said, her faded blue eyes twinkling.

Alex's stomach clenched. It was probably Philip's brother, Gabe, and his wife, Charlotte. Would they like her? Though she'd longed to meet them, her nerves jangled as she followed Aunt Bessie down the stairs to the parlor.

The room seemed filled with people. Her confused gaze took in a man beside Philip with the same sturdy build and dark hair. Beside him stood a short, attractive young woman. Several other men stood by the window, then her stare settled on a slender young man with merry blue eyes.

"Wi–Will?" she stuttered. "Oh, Will!" She ran straight into her brother's arms and hugged him tightly. Her hands clutched his forearms. He'd filled out since she'd last seen him and now seemed more adult, almost a man.

"You didn't think I'd let you get married without me being

here, did you?" he said softly. "And I brought Mama's blue-and-white china to you. You can't set up house without it. Philip unpacked the crates in the kitchen."

He squeezed her tightly, and Alex burst into tears. "Oh, Will, I've missed you so. However did you get here?"

Philip stepped close and put his arm around her. "I sent him a ticket, though I must admit I was concerned he wouldn't make it in time with the way the weather has been. But I knew the day wouldn't be as special for you without him here."

Alex gave him a loving smile and released her brother. "You spoil me," she whispered.

"And I intend to do just that the rest of our lives together," he murmured. "Come, meet my brother, our father, and my sister-in-law." He tucked her hand into the crook of his elbow and led her to the others and made the introductions.

After receiving all their well wishes, Alex excused herself to make tea. She could tell she and Charlotte would be great friends. The other young woman had a pleasant, open look about her that drew Alex. There would be many days and years ahead of them to bond the two families together.

The low sound of voices carried to where she stood in the kitchen and mingled with the clink of china as she prepared the tea in the familiar blue china. Both of the homey, happy sounds made her feel as though this place were truly home now that all their loved ones were here.

An arm slipped around her waist from behind. "You look lovely today," Philip whispered. "I still find it hard to believe that tomorrow you'll be my wife."

She turned in his arms and clasped her hands behind his neck. "God has truly blessed us," she said.

He kissed her, a lingering caress that she felt to her toes. "I have something for you, but I wanted to give it to you now in private." He stepped back a pace and slipped his hand into his pocket. "My grandfather gave this to my grandmother fifty years ago. I want you to have it. Our children will carry your fire and spirit, your bravery and love for others." He placed a small box wrapped in tissue paper in her hand.

A lump formed in Alex's throat. Was that how he truly saw her? A wave of love passed through her, and she shivered with the force of it. Her fingers stiff, she took the box and began to tear the tissue paper away from it. Opening the lid, she saw a gleaming golden locket.

"It's beautiful," she whispered.

"You deserve pearls and diamonds, but this locket is the most precious thing I own," he said in a choked voice. "That is, it was until I met you." He took the locket from the box and fastened it around her neck. "You hold in your hand all my love," he whispered.

Tears burned in her eyes, and her throat tightened with the effort not to cry. "As you hold mine," she said. She closed her fingers around the locket. The metal quickly warmed.

He took her in his arms again and held her tightly against his chest. "The journey has been long for me to find you. I never imagined the world held a woman as fine as you."

"I traveled far to find you." Alex cupped his face in the palms of her hands. "But the distance was nothing with you at the end of my journey." Love's journey had been far indeed, and it might take them to even farther, more remote places, but she didn't care as long as she and Philip were together. Together they would build a home no matter how austere the landscape. No journey was too far when love went with them.

COLLEEN COBLE

Colleen and her husband, David, make their home in Wabash, Indiana, where they are restoring a Victorian home. They have two grown kids, David Jr. and Kara. Though Colleen is still waiting for grandchildren, she makes do with spoiling her "grandpup" Harley and her "grandcats" Spooky, Damien, and Alex.

She is active at New Life Baptist Church where she sings and helps her husband with a young adult Sunday school class. A voracious reader herself, Colleen began pursuing her lifelong dream when a younger brother, Randy Rhoads, was killed by lightning when she was thirty-eight. She now has numerous fiction titles in print. Colleen's books have appeared on the CBA bestseller list, and they also make frequent appearances on the **Heartsong Presents** Reader favorites annual poll. Visit her Web site at www.colleencoble.com.

A Letter to Our Readers

Dear Readers:

In order that we might better contribute to your reading enjoyment, we would appreciate your taking a few minutes to respond to the following questions. When completed, please return to the following: Fiction Editor, Barbour Publishing, Inc., P.O. Box 719, Uhrichsville, OH 44683.

1. Did you enjoy reading *Gold Rush Christmas?*
   - ❏ Very much—I would like to see more books like this.
   - ❏ Moderately—I would have enjoyed it more if _____
   _____
   _____

2. What influenced your decision to purchase this book?
   (Check those that apply.)
   | ❏ Cover | ❏ Back cover copy | ❏ Title | ❏ Price |
   | ❏ Friends | ❏ Publicity | ❏ Other | |

3. Which story was your favorite?
   - ❏ *With this Ring*
   - ❏ *Band of Angel's*
   - ❏ *A Token of Promise*
   - ❏ *Love's Far Country*

4. Please check your age range:
   | ❏ Under 18 | ❏ 18–24 | ❏ 25–34 |
   | ❏ 35–45 | ❏ 46–55 | ❏ Over 55 |

5. How many hours per week do you read? _____

Name _____

Occupation _____

Address _____

City _____ State _____ Zip _____

E-mail _____

$\mathcal{H}$EARTSONG ❤ PRESENTS

Love Stories Are Rated G!

That's for godly, gratifying, and of course, great! If you love a thrilling love story but don't appreciate the sordidness of some popular paperback romances, **Heartsong Presents** is for you. In fact, **Heartsong Presents** is the premiere inspirational romance book club featuring love stories where Christian faith is the primary ingredient in a marriage relationship.

Sign up today to receive your first set of four, never-before-published Christian romances. Send no money now; you will receive a bill with the first shipment. You may cancel at any time without obligation, and if you aren't completely satisfied with any selection, you may return the books for an immediate refund!

Imagine. . .four new romances every four weeks—two historical, two contemporary—with men and women like you who long to meet the one God has chosen as the love of their lives. . .all for the low price of $10.99 postpaid.

To join, simply complete the coupon below and mail to the address provided. **Heartsong Presents** romances are rated G for another reason: They'll arrive Godspeed!